A RIGHT COZY HISTORICAL CRIME

A RIGHT COZY CRIME

WENDY H. JONES   LEXIE CONYNGHAM   OLGA WOJTAS

SHEILA DENE' LAWRENCE   MARTI M. MCNAIR

LISABETH EARLY   GARETH WILLIAMS   DIANNA SINOVIC

SHEENA MACLEOD   MEG WOODWARD

BARBARA STEVENSON   LORETTA MULHOLLAND

LISA HARKRADER   PENNY HUTSON

Scott and Lawson Publishing

To my Sisters in Crime Worldwide who support and encourage each other, day by day. You've got this.

CONTENTS

INTRODUCTION

I am going to be bold here and say humans have long been fascinated by history. The past intrigues us and we find ourselves drawn towards knowing what life was like in previous centuries. Love it or hate it, the past determines where we are now and often shapes the future. Literary historical fiction, such as books by Phillipa Gregory and others, open up new worlds and allow us to explore the past in an accessible manner. However, being literary they can often be more in depth and may be offputting to some readers. Fascinating? Yes. Interesting? Yes. Truly accessible. Yes and no depending on your reading tastes.

Another genre which is becoming increasingly popular is Cozy Mystery. Here, the reader finds themselves investigating crimes, in the company of amateur sleuths who seem to muddle along and get themselves into all sorts of scrapes; yet, somehow, they always seem to catch the guy or gal.

In our time-starved, modern day world, short stories are also becoming increasingly popular. Therefore, contemporary readers are often searching for books which can be read on the commute or in the lunch hour.

A Right Cozy Historical Crime combines all three, with stories from rural Scotland to American Cities and from the pens of some truly great authors. My wish is that you enjoy your visit to the past and find yourself engrossed in the words and worlds within it.

Wendy

Wendy H. Jones

Author and Publisher

Chapter One

A MONSTER IN THE VILLAGE

Lexie Conyngham

Something very odd is happening in Mrs. Michie's cottage – her tenant is not at all suitable for the delightful Scottish village of Ballater. It falls to Hippolyta Napier, wife of the local doctor, to investigate. Could a happy ending be possible, even for a monster?

THE FIRST HIPPOLYTA Napier knew about the matter was when Mrs. Michie, a woman nature had never designed for running, came pelting towards her across the village green.

'Mrs. Napier. Oh, Mrs. Napier. Is the doctor in? I need the doctor – or the minister – or the constable, or someone.' Mrs. Michie flapped at the evening air with the tails of her shawl, as if she could disperse the problem like smoke from a blocked-up chimney. She was a most alarming colour. Hippolyta put a hand out to steady her.

'Mrs. Michie, whatever's the matter? Come inside, please. Dr. Napier will be back any minute.'

'I can't go in, I must go back. Oh, Mrs. Napier. My poor cottage.'

'Your cottage? Which one?' Even as she asked it, Hippolyta thought it sounded a silly question. But Mrs. Michie, a youngish widow, owned several cottages in the village, which she let out to visitors. They were always clean and well-kept, though small for a family, so the venture did not make Mrs. Michie particularly prosperous and she did most of the work herself.

'The one in the lane over there,' said Mrs. Michie, catching her breath, though her face was still flushed. Her bonnet was crooked, and her boots, Hippolyta noted, were scraped about the toes. 'Bedroom and maid's room, parlour and kitchen, and a drying green. It has been empty for a week but I have a woman coming to take it tomorrow, and I went to dust and sweep and clean the windows and set the fire and – and so on.'

'Of course.' Mrs. Michie was taking refuge in domestic details, and Hippolyta began to wonder what all the fuss was about.

'And I've got none of it done, Mrs. Napier, for there's a monster in the house.'

'A what?'

'A monster. Oh, a monster.' She waved her hands wildly. 'Or maybe the Devil. There was a funny smell – maybe it was sulphur. I should fetch the minister – ministers know about the

Devil, don't they? But what if it's not the Devil? What if it's some kind of wild beast? Who is it who deals with wild beasts? Should I find a gamekeeper? But it's no a fox, not at all. No, no – a monster.'

'I'm sorry, Mrs. Michie, I don't think I understand. What kind of a monster?'

Mrs. Michie shook herself, and her bonnet tilted further. She jammed it down on her head, then started an untidy enumeration on her fingers, as if counting might bring it under control.

'Its hair is wild and its eyes are staring and it has a strange smell, and it roared at me. It seized me by the waist and spun me round, and then dragged me to the door and flung me out in the lane. From my own cottage,' she squeaked, as though such behaviour would have been perfectly acceptable in a strange house.

That, at any rate, explained the boots and the bonnet. A monster, here in Ballater? And a violent one? What was to be done? Such a situation had not arisen in her time in the village – and, she assumed, for some considerable time before that. When she had left her parents' home in elegant Edinburgh to marry Patrick Napier and move to this spa town in the Highlands, her friends had warned her against wolves and bears, but this did not sound like either of those. Wolves would not grab you about the waist, and bears would be more likely to drag you into their den than to throw you out of it. No bear would want to turn down a tasty snack, even one in a bonnet and boots.

'Let me fetch my servant, and then I'll go back with you and look.'

She stepped back to her front door and called for Wullie. The boy came at once. Small and scrawny, he was unlikely to appeal to a bear, but he had a fine turn of speed.

'Wullie, we are to look for a monster in Mrs. Michie's cottage,' she told him. 'If it should emerge and eat one of us, you are to run for Dr. Napier straightaway. Dr. Napier will know what to do.'

Thus reassuring herself, but baffling the wide-eyed boy, Hippolyta Napier led the way across the green and down the lane to Mrs. Michie's cottage.

'That one, there,' Mrs. Michie whispered from behind her.

'There are no lights on,' Hippolyta murmured.

'Why would a monster need lights?' asked Mrs. Michie reasonably. 'He can see by the light of his own glowing eyes.'

'Maybe he's gone out,' Hippolyta suggested. 'How long has he been there? What could he have been eating?'

'People,' quavered Mrs. Michie.

'I haven't heard of anyone going missing,' said Hippolyta. 'Nor anything. Not even a hen.'

'It'll be starving,' said Wullie, 'whatever it is, ma'am. I couldna do a week without food.'

Wullie could not, in Hippolyta's experience, do much more than five minutes without food, but she made no comment.

'It might not have been there so long. Whatever it is.' She drew a deep breath, braced her shaking shoulders, marched over to the door and knocked.

The echo drifted through the house, as if something inside had frozen, listening. She nearly jumped out of her skin when her knock was answered by three heavy blows on the other side of the door. Mrs. Michie screamed. Hippolyta leapt backwards so fast she nearly fell over, and scuttled ignominiously back to Mrs. Michie and Wullie. Mrs. Michie clutched Wullie's shoulders hard.

'Will I go for the doctor, ma'am?' said Wullie, braced to run.

'Yes, Wullie. Quick as you can,' said Hippolyta, before considering that really, they could all have gone for the doctor and put some sensible distance between themselves and the cottage. But Wullie was away already, bare feet pounding the ground. Mrs. Michie had pressed herself hard against the wall of the cottage opposite hers. A few doors had opened after Mrs. Michie's scream, and a few women, not averse to being interrupted in the making of supper, had emerged to see what was going on. They formed a huddle almost opposite the mystery cottage, watching.

'A monster?' asked one, scratching her head. 'I thought that cottage was empty this week, Mrs. Michie?'

'So did I,' said Mrs. Michie, then added, testily, 'I wouldn't have let it out to a monster.'

'Aye, I thought there was someone in there,' said another woman, nodding comfortably. 'There was a light on last night.'

'No, no,' Mrs. Michie hurried to correct her. 'That's his glowing eyes, ken?'

'Did you see it, then?' asked the woman, and Mrs. Michie was delighted to give her account again, showing the damage to her boots and encouraging gasps and groans from her neighbours. Hippolyta stood to one side and watched the end of the lane. In a moment or two – sooner even than she had hoped – she saw the familiar, handsome shape of her husband, Patrick Napier, and, to her extra delight, the outline of their friend Durris. Mr. Durris was the sheriff's officer: between them, he and Patrick could deal with almost anything. Almost anything – and Hippolyta could usually help if they got stuck.

'What's going on?' Patrick called. 'Wullie was making no sense – he claims there's a monster in a cottage.'

'Oh, Dr. Napier. He's right,' gasped Mrs. Michie, abandoning her neighbours for a new and grander audience. 'There's a monster in my cottage. It threw me out.'

And she told her story again, with no embellishments this time. Dr. Napier was known as a sensible man, unimpressed by any patient's wild stories.

'Have you seen this creature?' Patrick asked Hippolyta.

'No – but when I knocked at the door it knocked back, much harder.'

'Hm,' said Durris. 'Some wild beast, perhaps?' But he looked far from convinced, and turned back to Mrs. Michie. 'Did you see it clearly? What did it look like?'

'A wild thing,' cried Mrs. Michie. 'As tall as a man, but with a great shaggy head, and claws, and fierce eyes. And a funny smell. And roaring. Roaring.'

'Hm,' said Durris again, and exchanged looks with Patrick. 'Tell me, Mrs. Michie, was it wearing clothes?'

'I – ah – ah –' Mrs. Michie flapped her hands suddenly, and blushed to the band of her bonnet. 'Aye, it was.'

'Maybe it had stolen them,' suggested one of the neighbours, and a couple of others nodded.

'It's no a bear, then,' said one neighbour sensibly. 'It must be a monster.'

'I think we should make a closer examination,' said Durris firmly, and led the way over to the cottage. The windows were shuttered on the inside, and no light was visible. Durris knocked briskly on the door – much more confident than Hippolyta had been – and the crowd held their breath. Hippolyta felt her heart beating, waiting for the knock in reply. But nothing came. Durris looked back at Patrick, nodded, and turned the door handle. The door opened into darkness, and Durris and Patrick went inside.

The cottage was not a large one, and there would have been little to explore before they encountered whatever was in there. Seconds passed like infinity. Then there was an enormous crash, a cry of alarm, and some very peculiar growling. Hippolyta squeaked, and ran for the door.

'Patrick.' she cried. But Patrick did not reply. Instead, a figure appeared in the doorway, catching its sleeve on the latch and tugging it free. Hippolyta blinked.

They had only a moment to take it in. Wild hair, wild eyes, grunting and panting, and then it was away, along the lane at a terrific pace, and into the dusk.

'Monster. Monster,' cried the neighbours, pointing after it, but not one of them had the nerve to follow it. Hippolyta was more concerned about her husband.

'Bring a light, someone,' she cried, and plunged into the dark of the cottage.

The source of the crash was obvious. The cottage's front room had been furnished with a dresser, holding dishes and plates, all of which were now on the floor under the tumbled dresser, along with Patrick and Mr. Durris. In the lamplight, Hippolyta could see that they were both awake and alert, and in a moment both had been dragged out and dusted down.

'Cuts and bruises,' said Patrick lightly, with a smile at Hippolyta. She knew he did not wish to worry her, and smiled back, though she would assess the accuracy of his statement later. Durris looked in much the same state, and rubbed his head where the top of the dresser had caught it.

'He escaped, then?' he said.

'He did. Who wants to run after a monster?' asked Hippolyta. Mrs. Michie, surveying her ruined cottage, nodded.

'You see now what I meant?' she asked. 'Terrible, it was. And that growling.' She shivered violently. 'That's no human, is it?'

But only Hippolyta had been close enough, when the creature had tugged its sleeve free from the door latch, to hear it pause in its growls and mutter,

'Oh, bother.'

Durris was promised to them for supper, and so Hippolyta was able to carry on to the social engagement she had been going to when Mrs. Michie had interrupted her. She would hear all Durris' thoughts later. But he did stop her before she left.

'Mrs. Napier, I daresay the whole story is around the village already, but I should like not to spread it further than necessary. Just say that a man is on the run, and I shall start up a search party in the morning. There is no sense now, at dusk. And I have a feeling such a creature will not be hard to catch.'

'Of course,' said Hippolyta dutifully. 'But I think it is not a creature, or not the way Mrs. Michie means.'

He raised his eyebrows, warm brown eyes questioning.

'Monsters don't take snuff, you mean?' he asked. 'Did you smell it?'

She smiled. Mrs. Michie must not have smelled much snuff before.

'That, and speaking the King's English,' she said, 'if only briefly.'

'We'll find him,' said Patrick, touching her arm. 'Now we'll go and tidy up and make a start, and we'll see you later. No gossiping, remember?'

Hippolyta made a face at him. She was bound to take tea at the Strongs', and their maid, Margaret, was a remarkably efficient gossip. There would be no need for Hippolyta to add to her store.

The Misses Strong lived at the top of the green, in the house of their late brother, the village's lawyer. Thanks to his profession, they had a wide acquaintance even as far as Edinburgh, and often visitors to the village, there for the spa or the fresh Deeside air, called on the sisters. On this occasion, Hippolyta, daughter of a lawyer herself, had been invited to meet a father and daughter who were to be given tea – not dinner, nor supper, Hippolyta had noted with interest. Perhaps the pair were pressed with social engagements and could only squeeze in a fly cup, or perhaps, if they were visiting the spa, their diets were difficult and tea was all they could manage in polite company. Hippolyta, for whom curiosity was as breathing, was eager to find out.

'Here she is,' said Miss Ada Strong, when Margaret showed Hippolyta into the parlour. 'We thought you might have been eaten by the monster.'

For Heaven's sake, thought Hippolyta, smiling all the same.

'Monster? Oh. Mr. Durris said that there is a man on the run, that is all,' she said as smoothly as she could.

'I told Margaret it couldn't possibly be a real monster,' said

Miss Strong, the elder sister, sensibly. 'Ada, you must not spread rumours.' Not that Miss Ada would pay any attention. Miss Strong turned to the guests standing politely by the parlour table. 'Mrs. Napier, may I present our guests, Mr. Arthur from Dundee, and his daughter Lucinda.'

Miss Lucinda Arthur was much more noticeable than her father. Dressed in the height of fashion, she was almost as slim as Hippolyta and only a little younger, with elaborately curled fair hair and blue eyes busy with calculation. She took advantage of her curtsey to survey Hippolyta from boots to bonnet, and smiled politely. Mr. Arthur sagged a bow. Hippolyta wondered if Miss Arthur took after her mother: apart from their pale, sharp faces, there was little resemblance between them. He looked exhausted, but the spa up at Pannanich was very bracing for those worn out by professional life, or so Patrick often told her.

'Is – is there really a monster in the vicinity?' Mr. Arthur asked, as they all took their seats. His voice was scrapy and uncertain, and he glanced at his daughter for guidance. Certainly he looked like a man on the edge of a collapse in his health. Hippolyta wondered if she should fetch Patrick forthwith. 'I have been told,' he went on apologetically, 'that there may well still be wolves, up here in the wild country.'

Before Hippolyta could open her mouth to offer reassurance, Miss Ada pursed her lips and said,

'Aye, well, there's strange things out there, that's for certain. And who knows if it might be wolves? Or worse?'

'Ada,' snapped Miss Strong. 'Be sensible.'

'Where are you staying, Miss Arthur?' Hippolyta asked, keen to leave thoughts of wolves and monsters. She still felt unsettled, even though she was sure it was not a real monster. But then what form did monsters take? There were a few she knew about who had looked very much like humans.

'We are staying at the inn, for now, Mrs. Napier,' said Miss Arthur, her lips pursed. 'It seems a respectable enough establishment, I suppose.' She touched a yellow silk flower formed of a twist of ribbon, adorning the elaborate cuffs of her dress, indicating that she herself was above that class.

'It is, indeed, a most respectable establishment,' Hippolyta assured her. She was wearing her best day dress, but it was much less decorative than Miss Arthur's and she felt a sorry lack of yellow silk flowers.

'Though not, perhaps, one you'd want to stay in for long,' added Miss Ada. 'Not for a week, or anything like that.'

'No,' agreed Miss Strong. Hippolyta blinked. Miss Strong had always had a good opinion of the inn.

'Oh, I doubt we'll be staying as long as a week,' said Miss Arthur, dismissively. 'But tell me, Miss Strong, where do the better class of people stay?' She smiled, a sideways little smirk. 'We are looking for a friend of ours who has gone ahead of us.'

'Without telling you where they were staying?' asked Miss Ada.

'We think a letter went astray,' said Mr. Arthur, with a look at his daughter. She gave a little nod, and he relaxed slightly.

'That's right,' she said. 'But we believe he came here.'

'The hotel up at the spa is the best accommodation,' said Hippolyta, not sure what game the Misses Strong were playing. 'The inn is probably the second best. But there are private houses for renting, of course, and some of them come with servants and everything organised if your friend is not travelling with his whole household.'

'And certainly the spa is patronised by the gentry and the nobility,' added Miss Strong.

'If that's what you're looking for,' added Miss Ada, as if it wouldn't be the kind of thing she would go for herself.

'That sounds like the place our friend would stay,' said Miss Arthur with certainty. 'Don't you think, Father?'

'I suppose,' said the man wearily.

'In any case, you can visit the wells without staying at the hotel,' said Hippolyta, anxious that he should benefit from the water, before he collapsed.

'No time ...' he murmured, watching his daughter. 'No time.'

'I hope there is nothing the matter?' asked Miss Strong. 'A concern over your friend's health?'

'No, he is perfectly healthy,' said Miss Arthur. 'Or was when we last met. We only fear missing him again, should he decide to move on ... could he move on?' she asked, suddenly worried. 'If someone had come this far – all this way – is there anywhere further they might go, or would they have to turn back?'

'Aye, there's miles to go yet,' said Miss Ada, nodding. 'Miles and miles, each path wilder. If there are monsters down here, just think to yourself what it might be like further into the mountains?'

'Hush, Ada,' said Miss Strong. 'My sister is being foolish, Miss Arthur. Of course it is perfectly safe, and there is a road of some decency all the way to Braemar these days.'

'If you can find anybody there speaks the King's English,' added Miss Ada, then looked at her sister and for once subsided. 'No, I'm jesting – anybody you meet will speak English well enough.'

The King's English, thought Hippolyta – just like the monster. Miss Ada was right, for most of the folk in Braemar still spoke Gaelic, and the Arthurs might indeed struggle to make themselves understood. But Miss Strong seemed very keen not to deter them, all the same. Yet the kind thing would be to let Mr. Arthur stop and rest and take the waters. Assuming Mr. Arthur wanted to – and assuming his daughter would let him.

When the Arthurs had departed, to walk back down to the inn, Hippolyta lingered, hoping that Miss Ada's noted lack of discretion would show itself. She was rewarded.

'Fit a pair. Maybe the monster'll eat them,' muttered Miss Ada, and returned to her chair to swing her short legs briskly over the edge. And again, for once her sister agreed.

'We've never liked them,' she explained to Hippolyta. 'Well, he was all right, in his youth, but not a bone in his body to stand up to anyone. His wife was a bully, and his daughter's the same – well, Mrs. Arthur's dead now, of course,' she added thoughtfully.

'No loss,' said Miss Ada, and Miss Strong did not pass comment.

'Who is this friend they're pursuing?' asked Hippolyta.

'No notion,' Miss Ada shrugged. 'I hope for his sake they dinna find him. If he owes her money she'll have him flayed for the siller in his pooch.'

'English, Ada,' said Miss Strong absently.

'Aye,' said Ada, with a half-hearted scowl. 'So tell us about this monster, then, eh?'

'Not a monster, I'm fairly sure,' said Mr. Durris at the supper table. 'Setting aside the smell of snuff – and even a bear might roll in that, I suppose, if we had bears – there was what you heard, Mrs. Napier, and also the fact that several neighbours noticed lamplight about the place over the last week.'

'And a well-cut suit of clothes,' added Patrick.

'Certainly a monster of some distinction,' said Hippolyta. 'But what could he have been doing in Mrs. Michie's cottage for a week?'

'We shall ask him when we find him,' said Durris. 'And we shall find him. The search parties are organised, and a full description has been collected. We know he headed off towards Braemar, for the gardener at Dinnet House was back late and saw him passing the end of the drive, and a farmhand at Glengairn told the constable about meeting a stranger last night. I've a feeling the monster is indeed a stranger to the country and will stick to the roads – we'll find him at first light, or not much after.'

Hippolyta was not, of course, expected to assist with the search, though as a good housewife and the wife of the local physician she did spend a little time before breakfast ensuring that her store of bandages and salves was ready. But once the men were away, she took herself down to the inn and had the stable lad set up her pony and trap that were kept there. The pony could do with some exercise.

The stable lad at the inn was well-paid for his attention to the pony, for the beast had a reputation and the stable lad was prepared to be brave. Hippolyta liked the boy, and was haunted by guilt at leaving him to the pony's mercies. For the lad at the stables at Pannanich, however, she had no compunction: the boy, Sandy by name, was slimy towards wealthier guests, and disrespectful of lesser ones, particularly the invalids, but worst of all he treated the horses and dogs in his care badly when he thought no one of influence was watching. Hippolyta had seen him on several occasions and was gathering evidence to give to the hotel keeper. Today, however, she hoped the boy would serve a more useful purpose than usual, and the horses and dogs might have some satisfaction.

She crossed the Dee by way of the wooden bridge, the pony's little hooves hollow on the planks. On the south bank, amidst pale birch trees, she turned and headed up the hill towards the spa, the Dee spreading below to her left. It was a steep drive: she knew the pony would be even more irritable by the time they reached the top.

Hippolyta stopped the trap in the stable yard, going to the pony's head and looking about for the lad Sandy. After a long moment, Sandy peeped around the door of a stall, eyed her up and down, and emerged reluctantly to stand just at the door, out of the pony's reach.

'Ah, Sandy,' said Hippolyta, bringing the pony forward slightly. 'Are you busy just now?'

'I'm always busy, missus,' replied Sandy, though if he was he hid it well.

'I mean the hotel. Plenty of guests?'

'Aye, I suppose. Plenty of horses.'

Hippolyta took another step forward, and Sandy eyed the pony thoughtfully. They had met before.

'Any empty rooms?'

'I wouldna ken, missus.'

'Oh, I'm sure you know all the gossip. Any guests, perhaps, who arrived and then left more quickly than expected? Perhaps leaving their horse behind?'

'I couldna say, missus.' Not the same as 'I wouldna ken', she noted. Sandy's gaze had lighted on her reticule, and a glint of hope appeared. Sandy liked cash donations. Hippolyta thought self-righteously that she had no intention of rewarding his indis-cretions – where her own morals were in encouraging the same indiscretions she chose not to think. She eased the pony another step forward, and noted Sandy's hand feeling for the doorpost. The pony watched him, too, no doubt remembering their previous meetings.

'Let me help you,' she said, in a friendly fashion. 'A gentleman in a well-cut suit, perhaps from Dundee?' Sandy blinked. 'He would have left unexpectedly, perhaps five or six days ago.'

'Six days, missus,' said Sandy, then blinked. 'I mean, six sounds more likely than five,' he added, unconvincingly. Hippolyta and the pony took another step. They had not been far away to begin with: now the boy was almost within reach of the pony's notorious teeth.

'Goodness, how I wish I could find him.' Hippolyta exclaimed suddenly, and let go of the pony's bridle. The pony lunged forward, ignoring the trap, and seized Sandy's right arm in its yellow teeth. Sandy squawked in alarm and pain. He looked at Hippolyta with complete understanding.

'His name's Melrose. Henry Melrose.' he gasped. 'He's from Dundee an' all. The master was saying he didna ken how long to keep his room, or if he should tell the sheriff's man Mr. Melrose was away – he's left all his stuff and everything. Oh, missus, take the pony away. Please.'

'Come now,' said Hippolyta, laying a hand again on the pony's bridle. The pony, amenable only to Hippolyta – and then only sometimes – gave a little nod of satisfaction at its revenge on behalf of horses everywhere, and turned aside.

'Henry Melrose,' Hippolyta repeated. 'Very kind of you, Sandy. I'd go and run that arm under some cold water, though. It could be a bad bruise.'

She returned to the village and took the pony back to its usual stable, but as she emerged to walk home she noticed a new buzz about the place. People stood in twos and threes, talking in low voices, and pointing, she noted with some dismay, towards her own house on the green. She hurried there, and opened the front door cautiously. Patrick met her in the hall.

'We have the monster.' he said, waving at the parlour door. Hippolyta started. A monster in the parlour? But Patrick did not look overly concerned, and led Hippolyta in to see.

The shutters were closed and the lamps lit. Mr. Durris stood as Hippolyta came in, and bowed. But for once he had little power to attract her attention.

The monster lay on the sopha, feet up on cushions. A pair of excellent boots, one of them now sadly cut about, stood on the floor beside him. His suit of clothes, which had been fine, was muddy and torn, and there was a smell of dank water about him. His hair was indeed wild, and he had a good growth of beard, but otherwise the monster was a rather ordinary, chubby young man with a pained look of bewilderment on his pink face.

'Good day to you, madam,' he said in a hoarse voice. 'Please forgive me for not standing: they tell me I have broken my ankle, and I can well believe it.'

'He must have hit his head,' said Patrick. 'He's a little dazed – though a night in a ditch will not help with that, either.'

'You don't remember your name, do you?' asked Durris, a note of cynicism in his voice.

'I believe I can help there,' said Hippolyta. 'Mr. Henry Melrose, is it not? From Dundee?'

The man jumped, then grunted with pain.

'Damn it,' he said, then cast a quick apologetic glance at Hippolyta. 'I believed that in heading north I was escaping all this civilisation – that I could flee into the safety of the wilds. Not that I was very good at it when it came to managing in the wilds,' he added. 'I should perhaps have done better to sit and await my fate somewhere more comfortable.'

'Your fate being Miss Lucinda Arthur?' asked Hippolyta.

'Good heavens,' said Henry Melrose, 'Are there still witches here, too?' Then he frowned. 'Or have you met her?'

'I have,' said Hippolyta, taking a seat in an armchair to face him. 'She seems a determined young woman.'

'Oh, she's that.' sighed Melrose. 'She'll have me before a minister before the year is out – especially now I cannot run.'

'A breach of promise case?' asked Durris, not without sympathy.

'A trap,' Melrose corrected. 'And her father does anything she tells him to, so when a respected local man of law says you have proposed marriage to his daughter, and you deny it, who do people believe?'

'Forgive me for asking,' said Hippolyta, 'but why does she want you? I mean,' she added hurriedly, 'why specifically you?'

'I inherited my father's business,' said Melrose, 'a very successful jam manufactory. Not that Miss Lucinda has much interest in jam, but she is very interested in the money that flows from it. I would almost give it all up to escape her,' he added bitterly. 'At least, after I have paid for the damage to that little cottage that gave me sanctuary. I'm afraid I left quite a mess. I'm very sorry.'

Hippolyta looked up at Patrick, then over at Durris. Patrick cleared his throat.

'Well, hot water and shaving things,' he said, 'and then something to eat.'

'Oh, thank the Lord,' cried Melrose. By his figure, he was a young man who enjoyed his food, and he could have had little of it in Mrs. Michie's cottage.

'And we shall leave you in peace for a little,' Patrick went on. 'Come, my dear.'

With the arrangements made, Patrick led his wife and Durris into his study. The three made themselves comfortable, and both men looked expectantly at Hippolyta.

'Well,' she said, and told them first about her meeting with Mr. and Miss Arthur, then about her visit to Pannanich. 'It all seemed to join together,' she finished.

'Undoubtedly,' said Patrick, smiling at her with some pride. 'And the Strongs did not like them?'

'Not at all, and they had clearly known them for years.'

'The Strongs are good judges of character,' Patrick acknowledged. 'But what now?'

'He has not given out his name in public,' said Durris, with care, 'not since we brought him in. And as we carried him down the road he seemed very confused. Anyone who saw him would have said so.'

'An act?' asked Hippolyta.

'No matter,' said Durris, 'if he can keep it up.'

They looked about at each other. Patrick's lips twisted.

'You think she would not wish to marry a man who was out of his wits? However rich?'

'He would require quite a bit of nursing,' said Durris, straight-faced. 'Expensive nursing.'

'And there's the appearance of it in society,' added Hippolyta. 'I mean, he could grow worse. He might end up in an asylum.'

'And there's the question of whether or not any minister would allow him to marry, if he were out of his wits,' said Durris.

'On the whole, I should think she would be better off without him,' said Hippolyta. 'And, should the subject come up, I should advise her of that.'

'And will the subject come up?' Durris asked.

'I can go and speak to her at the inn now,' said Hippolyta. 'Take her the bad news – the friend she has been seeking has met with an accident, and the prospects are not good for his full recovery.'

Mr. Arthur was seen to escort his daughter on to the mail coach that afternoon, knocking the dust of Ballater from their heels. Hippolyta, who was watching from the stable where she was attending to the pony, saw Miss Arthur cast a swift glance around as she paused on the carriage steps, as if making sure that no madman – or monster – was likely to catch her.

Henry Melrose stayed at the Napiers' until he was fit to be moved back to Pannanich. Washed, shaved and fed he revealed himself as a paunchy, kindly-faced young man with a fine tenor voice, happy to sing while Patrick played his violin, and concerned about the welfare of the horse he had left up at the spa stables. He could not have fitted in better. At his request Mrs. Michie came timidly to visit him, and was more than recompensed for her fright and her trouble. She warmed to him considerably, and when Melrose realised his prospects of a comfortable return to life in Dundee were limited by Miss Arthur's continuing presence, it seemed a very reasonable solution to marry Mrs. Michie, and stay in Ballater, enhancing her property empire.

But no monsters were ever seen again, in any of the properties.

Author Bio:

Lexie Conyngham is a historian living in North-East Scotland. Her historical crime novels are born of a life amidst Scotland's old cities, ancient universities and hidden-away aristocratic estates, but she has written since the day she found out that people were allowed to do such a thing. Beyond teaching and research, her days are spent with wool, wild allotments and a wee bit of whisky.

Chapter Two

THE MARRIAGE GIFT

Olga Wojtas

A young girl in Renaissance Italy is forced to bow to the wishes of her father the Duke and marry a neighbouring nobleman, a man who frightens and repulses her. But a dramatic turn of events on the day of the wedding leaves both men dead. Is the girl as innocent as she seems?

The Wedding Day: 1

The Duke's palace was always a place of luxury and splendour, but the day of the marriage ceremony surpassed anything we had ever seen. Its vast high-ceilinged hall was adorned with garlands of ivy, laurel and fresh flowers, so many that one could scarcely make out the tapestries hanging on the walls. More garlands were woven along the gold-embroidered linen covering the long banqueting tables, and the air was filled with the scent of roses, orange blossom and incense.

There was sound as well as scent: musicians played lutes, viols and flutes while mountebanks, jugglers and acrobats wandered among the guests, weaving chaos and delight into the rigid elegance of our usual courtly life. The mountebanks improvised farcical skits, and pretended to be learned astrologers, offering guests comic readings of their future, based on the colour of their shoes or the way they sipped wine. The jugglers casually tossed and caught fruit, candlesticks, knives and goblets, while the acrobats balanced on stilts and chairs before somersaulting gracefully to the ground.

Most of the guests were laughing and applauding in delight, but one who didn't was the Archbishop. He sat on a gilded chair, his mitre resting beside him on a silk-covered stool. He had his fingers laced tightly in his lap as though he was trying to stop them shaking. He wasn't an old man, so I reckoned he was in dread of offending the Duke. Of course, he had expected the wedding would be held in the cathedral, a sacred union sanctified in the house of God. But the Duke dismissed that idea with a wave of his hand, saying: 'This wedding shall take place where the people may see the strength of our house - not in the cold shadow of saints.'

I could see it was difficult for the Archbishop as he sat in resigned obedience, having to bless the wedding even though it was nothing to do with a sacrament. He understood why the

Duke wanted the ceremony in his palace: power, spectacle, control. If the Archbishop had tried to challenge the Duke's decision, it would have been political suicide, and probably much worse than that.

There was no altar. Instead, at the end of the hall was a grand elevated dais draped in velvet and brocade. The Duke himself sat in the middle. His shoulders were as broad as ever, and his jaw as strong. He was never a man for laughter, but today his unsmiling face was especially noticeable. His hair usually fell carelessly down his back, but for this occasion it was styled and carefully oiled.

Near him was Lorenzo Canestri, come to claim his bride ten years after the betrothal. I hadn't liked the look of him then, and I liked it even less now. He had a dark, menacing face that put me in mind of a hawk, vicious and predatory. But of course, I had said nothing of the kind to my *colombina*, my little dove. It wasn't my place. Oh, as her nurse I felt as close as a mother, but this wedding was a political arrangement and she had no choice about it. I had to encourage her, reassure her.

But I could scarcely congratulate her as I watched her up on the dais, on the other side of her father. Her face was as white at the linen tablecloths and her eyes looked glassy with fear. She was of perfectly marriageable age, but she looked much younger than her fourteen years. Her wedding dress was a breathtaking thing of crimson velvet embroidered with pomegranates and lilies. Gorgeous as it was, it seemed too heavy for her. Her hair, which had always been kept loose until this day, was twisted into a crown of braids, studded with tiny seed pearls and orange blossom. Her gauze veil was kept in place by a gold circlet.

She glanced towards me, and I smiled to let her know she could go ahead. She turned to her women and one of them handed her the gloves that had been commissioned as a gift for her husband, pale pigskin, exquisitely worked with his initials L and C. Then my little dove walked over to Lorenzo Canestri and deferentially presented them to him.

I saw him grip her hands, possibly to reassure himself that she was wearing the ring he had given her. He gave a curt nod of approval, whether for the gift or for her it was impossible to tell, and tucked the gloves into his belt. He nodded again, this time indicating that she was to sit beside him.

He turned to his retinue and signalled to one of his men, who knelt before the Duke and offered him an intricately carved box. The Duke wrenched the lid open and gave a satisfied grunt when he saw the contents. The gloves my little dove had given Lorenzo Canestri suddenly seemed tawdry. The ones Canestri had commissioned for the Duke were dark red, worked with gold thread and jewels to show not simple initials but the two families' crests.

The Duke tugged them on and sat admiring himself. After a few moments he scowled, shifted in his seat and called for more wine. Suddenly I saw something like disbelief on his face, disbelief that changed to rage as he stared at the gloves and tried to claw them from his hands. He was trying to speak but no words were emerging, and he half-rose, fumbling for the dagger at his belt.

I ran forward, placing myself between him and my little dove, and screamed: 'No.' He blinked, then staggered forward and flung me aside with surprising force for a dying man. He plunged the dagger straight into Lorenzo Canestri's chest and it seemed to me that their souls left their bodies in a single moment.

There was shouting and the clatter of half-drawn swords as the Duke's men and Lorenzo Canestri's retinue confronted one another. But they hesitated, since nobody knew what the quarrel was, and the Archbishop called for calm, rushing forward to pray for the two dead men.

All at once my little dove dropped to the floor. There was no sign that she was still breathing.

One Day Earlier:

The bridegroom's arrival was not quiet. It was a spectacle, designed to show that Lorenzo Canestri was coming to claim his bride not as a supplicant but as an equal. A line of riders swept through the palace gates shortly after midday, their banners fluttering in the summer wind, black and red, the colours of the house of Canestri.

At the centre of the column, surrounded by six armed retainers, rode Lorenzo, sitting straight in the saddle. He wore a doublet of midnight blue velvet and a short mantle fastened at his shoulder with a clasp shaped like a lion's head. He had no sword, since this was diplomacy, not war, but a jewelled dagger hung from his belt.

And behind were gift-bearers, carrying lacquered chests filled with an array of lavish, exotic presents that had everyone gasping and exclaiming in delight. My little dove's serving women excitedly shook out the lengths of oriental silks, delicately tapped the crystal to hear it sing, and marvelled at the beauty of the gold and silver plate.

My little dove had watched his arrival from behind a curtain in an upstairs room, but now it was time for them to meet face to face in the great hall. She hesitated as she reached the doorway, and it was only the soft pressure of my hand on her back that kept her moving forward. When she reached him, she gave a deep, flawless curtsey which she had practised a hundred times, not looking into his face.

He took hold of her chin and tilted it upwards, appraising her as though she was an expensive artwork. Not a flicker of a smile touched his face, although this should surely be the most joyful of occasions, greeting his bride-to-be. Smoothly, he produced a fine ring engraved with his personal emblem and placed it in her palm. He would expect her to wear it on the day of the ceremony as a token of her obedience to him.

'Thank you, my lord,' she whispered.

He paused for a moment, as though waiting for something. Then he said, 'I see you have no gift for me. But soon you will give me the most precious gift of all, yourself.'

The women all chuckled behind their hands and applauded his gallantry, but I saw my little dove flinch.

I nodded to her, to make her speech as her father had instructed.

'I would like to make you another gift,' she said, her voice shaking slightly and her eyes again modestly downcast. 'We have a glove-maker here who my father says is the greatest craftsman north of Rome. I wish him to make gloves for you in finest kidskin.'

Her women twittered approvingly, and Lorenzo Canestri bowed to her in acknowledgement. She was still looking down, but as I stood behind her, I saw his expression, the sudden flicker in his eyes. Not gratitude. Something sharper. Opportunity.

Later that day, I was the one entrusted with visiting the glove-maker, the workshop tucked into a narrow lane, the faded wooden sign reading *Bartolomeo da Lucca, Guantaio al Duca*. I stepped inside the doorway, breathing in the scent of leather, beeswax and lavender oil.

The glove-maker rose instantly to greet me; he knew I was a respected member of the Duke's household.

'For the wedding?' he said with a faint frown. 'Tomorrow?'

'Exactly,' I said.

'I'm afraid we already have urgent and complicated work—'

'That's none of my concern,' I said. 'This is a commission from the bride. The Duke's daughter.'

'But—'

'And since I know you wouldn't want to disappoint either of them, I'm confident you'll get it done in time. I'm sure it's not the first time you've worked through the night,' I said with a smile, and left.

That evening, I helped my little dove get ready for bed, thinking that this might well be almost the last time I did her this service. She hadn't had a chance to ask Lorenzo Canestri whether I could come with her to her new home, and even if she did, there was every likelihood that he would say no.

The bedchamber was lit by beeswax candles, and scented with dried rosemary. I placed the linen night-chemise in front of the hearth to warm.

'Come now, my little dove,' I said. 'It's been a long day, and your eyes are heavy.'

I unlaced her shoes, and undid the garters round her woven silk stockings. I unpinned the veil from the gold wire coif at the back of her head. Then I untied the embroidered sleeves of her gown, unlaced the bodice taking care with the fine brocade, and eased the gown and silk day-chemise over her head before dressing her in her night clothes.

I brushed her hair with long, soothing strokes in the hope that it would relax her, and helped her into bed, tucking the blankets round her. She hadn't asked for either the rosary or the devotional book on the side table, and I decided against saying a prayer. Instead, I started humming a lullaby I had sung to her since she was a baby.

She lay motionless, and when I stopped, she whispered: 'I'm scared.'

I leaned over and kissed her on the forehead. 'Everyone feels scared before their wedding,' I said comfortingly. 'It's natural.'

'Do you remember the betrothal?' she asked.

'Of course I do,' I said, laughing. 'You were so tiny, four years old. When we put that heavy brocade dress on you, I thought you would never manage to stand upright. But bless you, you toddled off to the ceremony as though you were the grandest lady there.'

'I didn't want my father to be angry,' she said. 'You'd helped me to understand that I had let him down because I wasn't a boy, but that he could use me to forge an alliance with the Canestris.'

'And so he did,' I said. 'I'm sure he was very happy with you.'

'But he wasn't,' she burst out. 'You don't remember at all, do you?'

I remembered perfectly. I remembered my sweet little dove suddenly sobbing just as the Archbishop pronounced them man and wife, and the Duke jumping from his chair and roaring: 'Take the mewling brat out of my sight.'

We all had to run to hustle her back to her rooms.

Now, she said: 'The Archbishop told me to take Lorenzo's hand but I was too slow, and Lorenzo grabbed my hand and twisted my fingers. He hurt me.'

And I understood that when she had said she was scared, she was afraid he was going to hurt her again.

'You have to make allowances for him,' I said. 'He was only fourteen.'

'I'm fourteen,' she murmured.

'But boys lack refinement at that age,' I said. 'Now he's a man of twenty-four, who's been well trained by his noble family in how to behave.'

I thought how much I disliked the look of him, and the way he had reacted to her gift of the gloves. But I couldn't say any of this to her. She couldn't escape this marriage, so we would all have to make the best of it.

She was crying softly now. 'I don't want to die.'

'Goodness, child, what a thing to say. You're not going to die.' I felt that was a better response than telling her that although I thought Lorenzo Canestri was a brute, I didn't think he was a murderer.

'My mother died,' she said. 'My mother died when she gave

birth to me. Lorenzo Canestri will want me to give him a child. A son.'

I put my arms round her. 'Not every woman dies when she has a child. Look at me. Here I am, healthy and strong as an ox.'

'But your baby died,' she persisted.

'That was God's will,' I told her. 'And look what happened. That meant I was able to become your wet nurse, and here I am, still with you all these years later.'

'Was it God's will that my mother died?' she asked.

I looked at her in surprise. She had always been so docile, so obedient. I couldn't believe that she was asking me such a question.

'You know that everything is God's will,' I told her, a little more sternly than I intended. 'Including this wedding. You should be grateful and happy, and looking to the future, not raking up the past.'

'I don't want to die,' she said again as though she hadn't heard me. 'And then at times I think I do, as long as it's soon.'

I gently put a finger across her lips. 'That's enough talking. You should be asleep.' I snuffed out the candle by her bed. 'Remember, I'm just in the next room if you need me.'

When I went back to my own room, I couldn't settle. I picked up my rosary, but found it impossible to pray. What was happening to my little dove made me question what I had just told her. Was it really God's will that she should marry Lorenzo Canestri? It seemed that it was more the Duke's will. And the Duke had shown little respect for God's will with his cavalier treatment of the Archbishop. Although I was a member of the Duke's household, I didn't feel that my thoughts made me disloyal, since all my loyalty was to my little dove.

I will never understand why, but that night I felt I shouldn't go to sleep in case she needed me. I wasn't concerned about Lorenzo Canestri. He wouldn't dare approach her before the ceremony, and I was sure the Duke would have posted his own men near Lorenzo's rooms just in case he decided to go wandering.

It must have been a good angel who kept me awake and alert because I suddenly heard a faint noise from my little dove's bedroom. Footsteps. The creak of the door as it opened. She was running away. Perhaps I should have raced out and confronted her, or even raised the alarm, but instead I decided simply to follow her. I grabbed an unlit candle, draped my cloak round me and crept into the corridor, well-lit with torches, just in time to see my little dove, wearing nothing but her night-chemise, disappear round the corner.

To my amazement, she headed down the servants' stairs towards the kitchens. I wondered whether she had an unexpected craving for some wine or a sweet pastry. But in that case, why hadn't she ordered a servant to bring it to her?

Down here was darker, and she was so intent on her mission that I had no fear of her seeing me. She reached the low-ceilinged sleeping quarters for the scullions and kitchen maids, and stopped at the open door of the room where five girls were curled up on straw pallets, several of them snoring gently. The place stank of grease and smoke. She knelt beside the nearest figure and gently shook her shoulder.

From my vantage point, I saw the girl stir and then sit bolt upright as she realised who had wakened her. I couldn't hear what was said – my little dove stayed close to her and whispered in her ear. She gave the girl something – a coin, I deduced, by the way the girl bobbed her head in gratitude before standing up and stripping off her woollen kirtle. I supposed it was understandable to sleep in your clothes if you didn't have a bed with sheets and blankets, but I wondered how sanitary the dress was that even now my little dove was pulling over her night-chemise. The girl helped to lace it up and pointed to a hooded cloak hanging from a hook in the wall. My little dove snatched it, and put on the pair of leather shoes the girl handed her.

I had never seen my little dove act like this, decisive and

resolute. She was always such a meek, submissive child. She must be driven by desperation, and I was in terror of what she planned to do. I hid myself in an alcove as she passed by me to go back upstairs and then I followed again at a discreet distance. She reached up to one of the flaming torches and lit a tallow candle she had hidden in her sleeve. Then with an effort she pulled aside a massive tapestry of the Triumph of Diana, depicting the goddess standing beneath a canopy of cypress oaks.

She would know that the image symbolised chastity and independence. But I had no idea that she knew what the tapestry concealed: a narrow door. It was so perfectly designed that it was unnoticeable to the naked eye. You had to push in exactly the right place. She pushed in exactly the right place, releasing a spring bolt buried in the jamb, and the door panel sighed ajar.

I knew that once she had stepped through, the panel would drift shut with a muted thud, never locking, only latching. A returning hand could open the panel from within as easily as from the corridor. I couldn't waste any time. I slipped behind the tapestry and through the door panel before it closed, but let the glow of her candle move ahead before I followed.

I wondered how often she had made this journey, but my question was answered almost immediately. She was completely uncertain about this path, hesitating after every step. She pressed her free hand against the wall, her fingertips splayed, as though for balance.

I already knew the way – I had walked it fourteen times. The first time was mere weeks after I had been taken into service as wet nurse for my little dove, the Duke's wife scarcely cold in her grave. The ancient chief steward, a man who had served three successive Dukes, had summoned me and asked a series of extraordinary questions:

- If the Duke ordered a physic I knew would harm the little one, would I obey, delay or defy?

- If a palace guard asked where I slept last night, and the truth would compromise the family's safety, what would I say?
- How long would I cradle a feverish child before calling a physician? And whose permission would I seek first?
- Which was the greater betrayal: selling a secret, or speaking it to save my own life?

I can scarcely remember how I answered, but it must have been to his satisfaction, because he then entrusted me with one of the palace's darkest secrets. He took a lantern and led me by back ways to an unguarded narrow corridor where he pulled aside the tapestry of the Triumph of Diana. He showed me how to open the concealed door, and together we stepped into the hidden passage.

'Wars are not always fought on distant fields,' he said as the door closed behind us. 'If enemies or assassins breach the palace, you, not the guards, will be closest to the child. This gives you a route to avoid the danger and leads to a maze of streets on the edge of the town.'

Thanks to the saints, I never had to escape with my little dove, but every year, I would go unseen to the tapestry, press open the door and walk the length of the passage to remind myself of the route until I no longer needed a lantern to guide me.

Now, as I watched my little dove feel her way along the wall, I knew what she would touch: pitted limestone, moss-cool moisture, the ragged seam where one builder's chisel gave way to another's. The staircase plunged straight and narrow, a cramped descent built for haste, but she moved with fearful caution, even when the passage straightened out. She had no idea that it was now a level path to her destination.

Mortar dust trickled from the low ceiling, and a gurgle of water echoed through unseen culverts. A sudden draught almost snuffed out the candle, and she cupped her hand round it, remaining stock-still until the wick steadied. In the flickering light she was at last able to see the oaken door ahead of her. When she reached it, she stretched out her hand, skimming the wood. Her faint gasp told me she had reached the iron emblem in the shape of an hour-glass. I imagined rather than saw her press her thumb on the upper bulb and forefinger on the lower, the plate turning on a hidden spindle so that she could push the door open.

I waited in the blackness for some moments so that she wouldn't know she was followed. She could only go in one direction when she emerged, so I would be able to catch up with her quite easily. In my turn, I felt for the metal hour-glass and opened the door.

The ossuary was no bigger than a cobbler's shop, a low-vaulted chapel with every cubit of wall sheathed in relic racks, illuminated by candles regularly replenished by the monks. Narrow shelves, six tiers high, were laden with skulls, with vertical stacks of femurs and tibias between them. Smaller bones were pressed into mortar as decoration.

The whole place was a *memento mori*, somewhere to meditate on the fact that in time we would all lay aside our bones, just as these forbears had done, and come with naked souls before our Maker. But I had no time for meditation. My concern was with the living. I quickly crossed the worn flagstones and came out into the lane between the tenements, relieved to find that no clouds obscured the full moon and I could see my way along the paving stones that glimmered like damp fish scales. I moved silently but quickly, invisible in my dark cloak, and soon saw my little dove ahead, her candle doused.

The lane bent left, then funnelled into an older quarter where trades the city preferred not to name kept watch through the night. My little dove stopped in front of a narrow open door-way, moonlight catching her profile.

I almost cried out. I knew the place, but how did she come

to know of somewhere so dreadful? I prayed she had mistaken her destination, but she pushed open the door to the dimly lit interior and didn't re-emerge. I fought the urge to fling the door wide and drag her back out. Unwanted words thudded in my head: *the shop that sells silence in vials, the shop that sells silence in vials*.

I concealed myself in the passageway opposite and waited for her to step back into the street after bargaining for murder. I watched her disappear down the lane and then I crossed over and thrust the door open. The air tasted of wormwood and almond, candles floated in bowls of dark oil, and the shelves were crowded with stoppered vials.

The apothecary, dressed in the black robes of a scholar, was gaunt and watchful. Not giving him the chance to greet me, I approached the counter and commanded: 'The girl who was just here. What did she want?'

He gave an apologetic shrug. 'I have so many patrons. I find it impossible to remember what they all ask.'

I fished out the household signet ring that I keep on a ribbon round my neck and saw that he recognised it.

'Ah,' he said with an insincere smile, 'you needn't trouble yourself about her. A serving wench who was in need of a medicinal tincture. Nothing to do with the Duke's household.'

I realised then that my little dove had used her bridegroom's ring as a token, allowing the apothecary to lie as he did. I dropped my voice to a hiss. 'You think I don't recognise one of our scullery maids? I asked you what she wanted.'

His lips pinched, calculating. 'My trade depends on privacy.'

I slammed my palm down on the counter. 'You want to continue your trade? I've not come unaccompanied. Three of the Duke's men are at hand and will take very little time to break all these pretty bottles and a great many of your bones.'

The apothecary's shoulders sagged.

'Very well,' he muttered. 'She was here with a commission from the bridegroom that's to wed the Duke's daughter. Lorenzo

Canestri. He was clear in his request. A poison with no antidote. Enough for one person.'

I made my way back to the deserted ossuary and lit my candle from one of the many there. As I returned through the hidden passage, I could think of nothing but death. The bones lying in the ossuary reminded me of judgement to come. I thought again of the ancient steward's questions, and for the first time began to see what their purpose could be. Could a mortal sin ever be forgiven or did it mean eternal damnation?

Little point in asking the Archbishop. On principle, he had no firm answers: he was swayed by any passing breeze if it came from the direction of the Duke's palace. His homilies always drifted into careful vagueness, trailing off whenever doctrine risked pricking a powerful conscience. But perhaps there was something to be said for his approach. I had always believed there was a firm division between right and wrong. But now I could see that there could be a case for doing wrong in order to prevent a greater wrong.

I reached my room unnoticed, took off my cloak, and then went to check on my little dove. She lay rigid beneath the embroidered covers, breathing too evenly, a curl of her dark hair stuck to her forehead with the damp of recent haste. Feigning sleep.

I went over to the fine-grained walnut cabinet with its tiers of drawers as though finding somewhere to set my candle, in case she was watching me through her eyelashes. One drawer hadn't been pushed fully home. I had no doubt what it contained – a vial of poison for which there was no antidote.

I looked round as though satisfying myself that all was well despite knowing that it was not. I whispered goodnight and a blessing to my little dove, who still pretended to be asleep. Then I went to my own room and attempted to say my prayers.

The Wedding Day: 2

I snatched a feather from one of the mountebanks and held it in front of my little dove's lips as she lay on the marble floor. For a long moment, there was nothing – and then the feather quivered, lifted, and settled again. A breath, shallow but certain. Not dead, merely in a faint.

I ordered her to be carried to her bedchamber, where I loosened her bodice and wafted a household pomander packed with clove, musk and rosemary under her nostrils.

Her nostrils flared as though jabbed from within, her eyelashes fluttered, and her eyelids opened. She turned her head away from the pomander, her gaze unfocused and drifting. Then she found my face and, murmuring something unintelligible, tried to sit up.

'Hush now, lie back,' I said, gently pressing her shoulder. But with sudden resolve, she pushed against the mattress until her back met the carved headboard. She paused there, her face ashen.

'I must speak,' she managed, her voice husky and unsteady.

I set the pomander aside and reached for a linen cloth, dabbing her clammy forehead. 'Your head's reeling. Words can wait.'

'They cannot. Nurse, I have done something very wicked.'

She raised a trembling hand as though to forbid any contradiction.

'One day,' she said with an effort, 'I followed you and saw you go behind a tapestry and disappear.'

I had always been so careful not to be observed. My little dove was slyer than I had imagined.

'I tried for months until I discovered the secret of opening the door,' she said, her voice strengthening. 'But I was too afraid to go into the hidden passage. Until last night. I disguised myself as a scullery maid and I. . . .I went to an apothecary I had heard of.'

'How did you come to hear about this apothecary?' I asked.

'People talk in front of me. They think I don't understand.'

I had little doubt that one of those people was the Duke.

'Nurse, I pretended to be there on behalf of Lorenzo Canestri. I bought poison, poison without an antidote.'

'Why did you do such a thing?'

'Because I was afraid. I was so afraid of marrying Lorenzo Canestri. I drank the poison just before the ceremony, Nurse, drained it to the last drop, and now I'm going to die.'

I caught her in my arms. 'No, my little dove, you're not. The poison would have worked long before now. God has saved you. He's saved you from committing a mortal sin. It's His will that you live a long and happy life.'

She began to cry, tears of relief, her head against my shoulder.

I thought of how, when Lorenzo Canestri heard of her gift of gloves, I saw his expression change. I knew he would convert her small courtesy into a stage for his own magnificence. He would commission even finer gloves for the Duke and eclipse my little dove's gesture, displaying his vast wealth.

When I went this very morning to collect the gloves my little dove had ordered, I praised the glove-maker's expert handiwork and he couldn't resist telling me about his other, grander, commission. I begged to see the gloves, and he opened the carved cypress box to show me. At that moment, I claimed to see a pickpocket in the lane outside. When the glove-maker went to investigate, I took the vial I had removed from my little dove's cabinet, and emptied the poison over the Duke's gloves. The leather darkened a shade and then paled again as the solvent fled into the air, leaving tiny crystals in the fibres, ready to re-awaken at the first sheen of sweat.

On my return to the palace, I cleansed the vial thoroughly and filled it with harmless rose-water for my little dove to drink.

And I waited for the Duke to pull on the gloves, for the

poison to begin its work, for the Duke to believe his assassin was Lorenzo Canestri. But his eyes were already dimming. I positioned myself beside Lorenzo Canestri and screamed: 'No.'

My cry enabled the Duke to detect his quarry and dispatch him.

Nestled against me, my little dove whispered: 'It's really true? It's God's will that I live?'

I stroked her hair. 'Everything is God's will,' I said.

Author Bio:

Olga Wojtas is the author of the "Miss Blaine's Prefect" series of comic crime, featuring Shona McMonagle, a time-travelling librarian from Morningside. She also writes the "Bunburry" series of cosy crime novellas set in the Cotswolds, featurning amateur sleuth Alfie McAlister and his elderly friends Liz and Marge.

Chapter Three

RED HEART SUMMER

Sheila Dene' Lawrence

It's 1919, and a jubilant homecoming turns deadly when a mob crashes the celebration for returning servicemen.

The dust settles, but one fallen soldier doesn't get back up. It's left to his fiancé to untangle the secrets, lies, and jealousies that led to murder.

August 1, 1919.

It was the hottest day of what was being regarded as Red Summer in the Deep South as well as other hotspots throughout the states that were supposedly united.

Sweat mingled with tears as people lined up alongside the road, taking a respite from jobs and household chores.

A raggedy rendition of The Stars and Stripes Forever announced the parade celebrating brave brothers, sons, boyfriends, and husbands who had returned upright.

The band performed on makeshift drums, washboards and any object that made a lyrical racket. They escorted the demobilised from the train depot, through the streets until they prematurely disbanded upon recognition of their beloveds on the sidelines, armed with arsenals of hugs and kisses.

Strutting like bantam roosters, the uniformed soldiers proudly marched in their final formation. Frenzied children tossed flower petals; they swirled and danced. Their yells contended with the pounding rhythms.

There weren't many cars, but an abundance of flags and streamers adorned creaky wagons ambling along. A choir sang 'When Johnny Comes Marching Home, Hoorah, Hoorah', 'Over There', 'Keep the Home Fires Burning', and concluded with 'Glory, Glory, Hallelujah'.

Sadie Atkins had her shift covered at Mercy Hospital so she could be in the welcomers' circle. She searched the rows of soldiers marching in time. No one she'd ever known strolled with the swagger of Roosevelt Booker. He'd be easy to spot.

She prayed that Uncle Sam hadn't altered that.

Clem Jones sidled up next to her. He said, 'Of course, you'd be here looking for Roosevelt, wouldn't you?'

Sadie swung around to see her childhood friend had joined the fanfare.

'Of course. I've been counting the days until his return.'

Clem moved in closer to protect his conversation from

listening ears. 'I'm twice the man he is. We could've been having ourselves a good time while you was 'round here waiting on him.'

'I don't want to hear it, Clem. He's a good man; he loves me. And I'd rather my fiancé not see you all stuck up under me, so please go away.'

'Sadie.'

At the sound of his voice, Sadie began to scream. 'Roosevelt, it's really you?'

The soldier broke formation and his lips met hers, full force. Lifting her and spinning her around, Roosevelt shed competing tears.

Pausing, he leaned aside and broke into an even wider grin. 'Ruben?'

She echoed him, 'Ruben? You're back?'

'Nothing could keep me from joining this celebration to welcome my little brother back on U. S. soil.'

Like bookends, the brothers sandwiched Sadie in-between with matching grizzly hugs.

Everyone celebrated except a sombre Clem who looked on with the corner of his lip twisted, resembling a stroke survivor.

Suddenly, the cadence of the procession was thrown into arrythmia as word rippled through the lines, 'Run. Take cover. Trouble done showed up.'

No one had to explain.

The crowd scattered.

Mayhem ensued.

Shots rang out.

Glass shattered.

Celebrants ducked into doorways, inside shops, and behind anything broad enough to shield them from the disturbance.

When all but the dust had settled, heads popped up and out. Neighbours helped neighbours that needed to be tended to, mainly due to trampling.

Seems the shots fired were aimed at the sun and only discharged to disrupt the revelry.

Sadie was among the first to put her nurse's training into action. She tore shirts and bound bleeding wounds. She worked feverishly until she noticed her friend and co-worker standing over her.

Edna stared but didn't speak. The one nurse Sadie had never seen cry was now drenched in tears as she reached for Sadie's hand. She guided her to the other side of the road, still in silence.

Sadie watched her closely because she seemed to be in shock. It was only when they came to a halt that Sadie diverted her attention to what blocked their path.

'Roosevelt,' she screamed before dropping to his side.

The police came, not because they cared but because it was customary in the case of death. A few paraders waited around to assist, while others loitered to be able to accurately recant the story.

Sadie was inconsolable. 'All these people and only my Roosevelt ends up dead.'

A policeman uncovered him to make a hasty pronouncement of cause of death.

'Here,' he said, handing Sadie a sheet that read, 'Coloured male found deceased on Main Street following a community disturbance. Cause of death: blunt force trauma.'

'He wasn't shot?' she asked.

'Not that I can see. Ask the undertaker for anything else you want to know. He may discover other wounds, but it's hard to miss that gash on the back of his head.'

Sadie, along with her comforters, glanced quickly enough to wince and agree.

'So, you'll be doing an investigation?'

'Nope, not for a riot. Be glad only one person was killed.'

'But those men had no reason to show up here. Someone needs to be held responsible for this.'

'Did anyone here witness this man being clubbed?' He looked into the smeared faces.

No one could say they had.

The officer concluded, 'Then, ain't nothing more I can do.'

He took the paper back and added, 'No witnesses. Perpetrator unknown. No further action to be taken.'

He said, 'Case closed. And I advise y'all to bury him and just leave it be. Unless you want more funerals.'

A camera flashed, and the officer looked as if he would charge the photographer; however, the cameraman's cohort quickly stepped in and raised his credentials.

'Levi Cane. We're from the Defender.'

The muted officer backed away, leaving a cheerless crowd with more questions than answers.

The next day everyone except Sadie huddled to read the newspaper article.

She reasoned, 'I know what happened. I was there, remember? And I've relived it a hundred times over.'

She began a fresh sob.

Finally, unable to resist, she told Edna, 'Hand me that paper so I can see how they done dismissed the murder of my sweetheart.'

The article read, *'The streets were alive with pride and purpose as a community gathered to honour the return of their brave loved ones from the battlefields of war. Black soldiers in uniform marched with dignity and received applause from onlookers lining the streets and waving flags.'*

Sadie said, 'Yeah, yeah. And whatnot.'

It continued, *'Tragically, the celebration was marred by the sudden arrival of a group who clashed with the celebrators. They never got close enough for hand-to-hand combat, but people were hurt in the mad rush to escape danger and protect themselves.*

'Sadly, Private Roosevelt Booker, a veteran of the Meuse-Argonne campaign, was found lifeless on Main Street after the melee. There were no eyewitnesses, and police reported it as a casualty of unrest. Subsequently, no investigation or arrest will be made.'

With a heavy sigh, Sadie folded the paper across her lap and stared into nothingness.

Before passing it along to the next reader, she picked the paper up and read it again.

She repeated the action a third time as if she couldn't trust her eyes to read the same thing three times in a row.

'What did that reporter say his name was?'

She looked back at the article to answer her own question before retreating to the front desk and picking up the candlestick phone.

'Gladys, please get Mr. Levi Cane at the Defender.'

Instead of doing her job, the operator struck up a conversation that Sadie had no interest in participating in. She responded in cryptic phrases, 'Yes, as well as can be expected.

'Yes. Unbelievably sad.

'Yes. Some real devils.'

She interrupted, 'I really need to contact Mr. Cane. Can you please put me through?'

'No need,' a voice said behind her.

Sadie spun around to see the same clean-shaven reporter that'd been at the incident.

'Mr. Cane.'

'I take it you've read my article?'

'Yes, sir.'

'Can we talk?'

'Yes, sir.' Sadie led the journalist to the outside stoop.

'You've heard from the undertaker?'

'Yes, sir.'

'And were there other wounds?'

'No, sir.'

'So, I take it we've come to the same conclusion?'

'Yes, sir.'

Although Levi was her age, Sadie was careful to show the proper respect to this White man who was courageous enough to return to a volatile, grief-stricken environment. Moreover, to return and confidently avow, 'Miss Sadie, Mr. Booker wasn't killed by them White men.'

Sadie nodded as the reporter confirmed, 'Your fiancé was killed by one of your own.'

Through muffled tears Sadie said, 'Yes, Sir. I figured that much out. And I intend on finding out who did it.'

Instead of returning to her post, Sadie strolled aimlessly toward Main Street, repeating the parade route. Not exactly knowing what she hoped to uncover, she looked from side-to-side instead of ahead.

'What you doin' out here looking all lost?'

She stopped short of stepping on Clem's toes.

'Last time I checked there was nothing illegal with taking a walk.' She side-stepped him to pass but he grabbed her forearm, tighter than necessary.

'You know how I feel about you, Sadie Mae. I'd sure hate to see harm come to ya.'

Sadie looked him in his milky eyes. 'Why would any harm come to me?'

'Word on the street is, they accusin' us of killing Roosevelt instead of them mob fellas.'

'That's the word, is it?'

'Yeah, and it's crazy because Roe was sort of a hero to these folks just by making it back alive. Everybody loved him.'

Sadie yanked herself free.

'At least one person would disagree. And I intend on finding out who. Go tell that to whoever's spreading this talk on the streets. Now, if you'll excuse me, I gotta get back to work.'

Sadie had barely gotten a block away when she heard her name called.

'Miss Atkins.'

It was the journalist.

When he caught up to her, he asked, 'You okay? That didn't look too friendly.'

She sighed. 'I was almost concerned, too, but I'm fine. What you still doing here?'

'I saw you leaving work, so I followed you because I don't think you realize how dangerous this could be.'

'Dangerous?'

'Yes, ma'am. If someone had something against your fiancé, it's reasonable to think you may be in danger. If it was important enough to kill once over, it's important enough to kill again.'

He added, 'You seem like a real nice lady, and I don't wanna see this end badly. Take my home number in case you need me and I'm not at the office.'

'Thanks, any advice before you go?'

'You're doing it. Repeat Roosevelt's steps. Go wherever he went, leading up to the parade. See whoever he saw. And keep your ears open. People like to talk around here, and oftentimes they'll talk too much. Pay attention to any and all gossip.'

'Thanks. Will do.'

'And most of all, look for motive. In this case, I think it must be personal.'

'Motive?'

'Yes, most common are jealousy, betrayal, secrets, scandals, inheritance. Find the motive, find the murderer. Meanwhile, trust no one. Be careful that you find him before he silences you.'

He added, 'I'll ask around, too.'

Sidling up next to Sadie, Ruben appeared. 'We don't need your help. I'll help Sadie. Roe was my flesh and blood. The last family I had. I owe him to find out the truth. Besides, I don't trust no White man no further than I can throw one.'

'Ruben, please.'

Sadie escorted the reporter a few feet away and explained, 'It's not for lack of trust but I must agree, Mr. Cane. Folks 'round here won't be too quick to talk to you.'

'Understood. But I still think I can assist, so don't hesitate to call. I got connections in a lot of circles, but I'll leave for now. Don't wanna cause a stir. Be safe.'

The entire community showed up to pay their respect for the slain soldier. They lingered afterwards to fellowship and enjoy the feast prepared consisting of each cooks' specialty.

Frock-wearers and hat-donners spread the table with crispy, golden chicken, fried to perfection, hamhock-seasoned collards, okra-strewn black-eyed peas, sliced tomatoes resembling wagon wheels, and syrupy candied yams with cornbread for sopping.

Lemonade refills kept the ladies' conversations flowing, while moonshine fueled the men who huddled underneath a not-too-distant Weeping Willow.

Activity seemed to pause at the arrival of journalist Levi Cane.

Sadie intercepted him on the outskirts of the gathering. 'Why you back? A funeral's not news and this one's not safe for you. Most folks don't know yet that it wasn't them White men that killed Roosevelt. Thankfully, I got the undertaker's report in person 'cause if he'd called and Gladys or somebody on the party-lines got a whiff of it, the whole county would know by now.'

'That's why I came,' Levi said. 'I was thinking since the killer could still be lurking, you might need some assistance. You won't know who you can trust here.'

'That's mighty thoughtful, Mr. Cane, but what's in this for you? You just curious or chasing a story or what?'

'Guess I'm guilty of it all - being a little nosy and a little ambitious. I'm trying to land a job up north with a bigger press. I need to write a piece that'll get their attention. And I think this could be it. But most of all I believe in justice and want to see it done.'

'Thanks for your honesty, but I don't wish to be your big story about how an irrational Black woman who loses her fiancé refuses to believe it wasn't murder.'

'I can promise you that wouldn't be the angle. More like - A decorated soldier, destined to marry his sweetheart, have a family, and work his land. Who would want him dead?'

He pulled out a large envelope and extended it.

'I also thought this may help, if you can bear to look at them. My photographer always takes more pictures than we'd ever use. We only used one of the parade and one of the aftermath. Maybe there's a clue somewhere in these.'

Sadie took the package gingerly as if it contained a bomb.

Levi whispered, 'I'll leave now because all eyes and ears are on us, and that's the last thing you need when trying to catch a killer.'

As soon as he drove off, Edna hurried over.

'Did he say one of our folks killed Roosevelt?'

She spewed, 'You know he's lying. He's a devil, too. Seems to me he sees this pretty coloured widow-woman and he's trying to cross the line. I can get Clem to run him off; he'd go to the ends of the earth for you. You got that effect on men, but they don't pay me no nevermind.'

Edna chuckled half-heartedly, 'Guess some's just got it, and I don't. But best you watch out for him. He seems a little too curious.'

Sadie sighed before agreeing, 'He is curious, wondering since I take care of other folks, who's gonna take care of me now.'

Their eyes locked; however, Edna didn't speak.

Sadie said, 'Exactly. That was my answer as well.'

Sadie picked up the phone for the third time within the hour, and the same conversation was in-progress on the party line. This time, she heard her name, so she decided that rubbernecking was justified.

She listened.

'I think she done lost her mind with grief. I hear she 'round here looking for a killer. She gone mess around and get herself dead.'

'Yeah, 'specially if that White man keeps sniffing round her.'

'She light-skinned enough to pass though if she went where folks don't know her.'

Sadie cleared her throat. 'Harrumph. Gonna be much longer ladies?'

They ended the call without saying as much as 'so long'.

'Gladys, can you dial Ruben, please?'

After a pause, she came back. 'No answer, Sadie.'

'How about Edna?'

Same pause. Same response. 'No one answering there, either.'

'Thanks.'

Gladys said, 'They probably headed to church. Guess you can catch them there, if you going today.'

'Thanks, Gladys.'

'If you're going, you might wanna get a move on, or you gonna be late.'

'Thank you, Gladys.'

Sadie hung up before the operator could offer any more unsolicited advice.

Making her way inside the church house, Sadie had scarcely settled onto the unforgiving wooden pew when someone next to her leaned in to ask, 'Hey, how you gettin' on, Sweetie Pie?'

Her answer was a quiet nod and a smile.

'Bless your heart. What you gone do now?'

Sadie humped her shoulders like a kid caught without an alibi.

The start of the sermon saved her from further inquisition.

However, immediately after the benediction, the curious churchgoer and an equally nosy friend caught up to Sadie on the walkway.

'Any chance you can still move in the Booker's farmhouse since you was almost married?'

'Ain't it rightfully Ruben's? He is the only Booker left?'

'Is that why he's back?'

'Can't be. Roosevelt was still alive when he got here.'

Edna scurried over to rescue her friend. She said, 'Excuse us, ladies, but you don't really need her for this conversation, do you?'

When they were a polite distance from the busybodies, Sadie covered her mouth and snickered. 'I cannot believe you said that to them.'

'Well, they jaw too much 'bout stuff that don't concern them.'

'Wonder where they got all that from?' She looked sideways at her confidante and raised a brow.

'What? Not me. I haven't been talking to nobody about what we discuss.'

'Nobody?'

'Uh, well. Not them.'

'But everybody knows everybody. Tell one and it's done.'

'Right. I'm sorry. I'll remember that. But I hear Ruben been talking a lot around town, too. Any idea how long he plans on hanging around?'

'Nope. Is you wondering 'cause you want him to stay, or you want him to leave?'

Edna giggled. 'You know pickins slim around here and he's nice to look at. Although, a city slicker like him wouldn't be interested in a plain Jane like me.'

'Don't sell yourself short. You're a good person. Got a good profession. Cook real good. Keep a clean place. What's not to love?'

'Also, got nappy hair, a broad back and strong as an ox. Men prefer soft women, like you.'

'Different men like different kinds. Just keep searching.' Sadie gave her friend a quick hug and said, 'See ya, later. Got errands before the sun goes down.'

'Concerning Roosevelt?'

'Concerning me.'

'Okay, don't get none on you.'

'Back at you.'

Sadie left walking. She returned to Main Street and darted into the only business open, the funeral home.

Somehow, like blood seeping from a wound, the daylight drained to darkness before Sadie headed home. She'd scarcely made it down the isolated dirt road when she heard the clip-clop of hoofs.

Though too dark now to see, the speeding up of the hoofs was unmistakable.

It was getting closer.

Sadie ran.

She ducked behind a huge oak and crouched low until she heard the pursuer's steps wane. She remained until she heard nothing but stillness.

Instead of going home, she backtracked to the safety of the hospital, where she occupied a bed there until daybreak.

Edna woke her. 'Why're you here? Thought you were off today.'

Sadie explained, 'I narrowly avoided a potentially bad situation last night. I thought it best not to go home, just in case whoever was after me might show up there to finish the job.'

She went to the phone and called Levi Cane.

When he answered, she said, 'I need to see a man about a horse.'

She hung up and left.

Understanding this meant 'meet me as soon as possible', Levi showed up at the abandoned barn they'd decided on as a rendezvous spot whenever discretion was needed.

Once Levi processed what Sadie shared, he said, 'My God. This just got hotter.'

Sadie could only nod.

'Just a thought -a man wouldn't have to sneak. He'd have the strength to overpower you. Maybe, you should expand your investigation to include women as well.'

'And children.'

She showed him the note she retrieved from her door before meeting him. 'Looks like a child wrote it.'

The two stared at the words, *'Stop or Die.'*

A tear fell as Sadie said, 'I don't know what to do and seems like no one cares.'

Levi said, softly, 'I do.'

Refusing to let her walk back alone, he dropped her off close to the hospital.

When she turned the corner towards home, Clem stepped out of the shadows.

'Nice evening for a ride.'

Sadie paused but didn't acknowledge his comments. She didn't stop until she was safe inside her room.

❧

Saturday morning, Sadie called Ruben. 'I've got to clear Roosevelt's things from his room. Thought you might wanna join me.'

'What things? Hadn't he just arrived?'

'Yes, but his trunk and duffel were sent ahead to the boarding house when he got in. I'm sure it's probably just papers, letters, and clothes.'

Ruben agreed, 'Sure, I'll come. It's bound to be hard for you. We can go to the picnic afterwards and make a nice bonfire while we have a good cry.'

'And hear the latest gossip.'

❧

The gossipers gathered beneath a tree. They sipped sweet tea and did what they were best at, on a Saturday after chores were completed —snacking and yacking.

'Yep. I reckon folks got tired of returning soldiers taking jobs they didn't want anyway. They just didn't want to see no Negroes working and trying to have something besides babies and the blues. They just suffering from pettiness.'

'Nobody had to worry 'bout Roosevelt though. He wasn't bothering anybody, and he just took that room at the boarding house till them tenants got off his daddy's farm. Then he and Sadie was gone have some property of their own.'

'Guess she gone have to rethink her whole life now.'

'Or find herself another man.'

'That would be easiest. Ain't a man that pass her and don't glance back for another gander.'

'Clem would marry her tomorrow. He got it bad for her.

52

Always have. He thought he was gonna slide in on her after Roe got shipped out. But she act like he ain't good enough.'

'I think she was just trying to be faithful 'cause she know it would get told if she wasn't. Didn't keep ole Clem from trying, though. I know he ain't much, but he's better than nothing. I'd take him over this fool I got.'

'Welp, just in case she hollerin' trouble when there ain't none, better make sure you lock your doors till this killer nonsense dies down.'

'All this fuss over an accident with everybody running over each other, trying to escape.'

Like the deep-rooted tree she stood beside, Sadie's feet were planted as she heard conversations going on around her about her.

'Sadie, there you are,' Ruben shouted, and all chatter abruptly ceased. 'Let's go have a sit down.'

Edna hurried over to join them.

No sooner had they settled before Levi showed up.

'Who invited you?' Ruben asked, planting his fists on his waist.

Leaving a safe distance between them, Levi said, 'Just wanted to say bye to Miss Sadie.'

'You got the job?'

'No, but I'm headed north anyway and taking a chance.'

Ruben thumbed his suspenders like banjo strings as he sneered at Levi.

'Yep, a man such as yourself ought to do well up there. Ain't nowhere safe for a Black man during this Red Summer, though. That's why I came back. Figured being here couldn't be no worse than trying to survive up north.'

'It wasn't to be with your family?'

'Not many left. Just Roe, who I thought had a little more time overseas. And lo and behold, I got back in time to see him return like some kind of hero. Guess managing to not get himself killed over there was his great feat. Then, what a shame this happened. Like DuBois says, 'We *return from fighting. We return fighting*'.

'It's unfortunate, indeed. So, what's the next turn on the trail for you?' Levi asked.

Ruben frowned at him. 'You ask a lot of questions.'

'Just small talk. Job hazard. Think you'll stay south? I hear it's a lot of opportunities in Detroit, Chicago. How long ago were you up north?'

Ruben looked sheepish as he admitted, 'Years, until 'bout a month or so ago.'

'Really?' Sadie said, 'I thought you came in with the soldiers. I didn't know you'd been here for a spell. Ain't nobody told us nothing.'

Edna joined the inquisition, 'Gladys says you been getting lots of calls from Chicago. Is that where you were?'

'Yep. They want me back, but I had business down here, so I've been busy figuring out my next.'

'Wow,' Sadie said, 'I wish I had a roaming spirit like y'all since the fact is, there's not much left here for me. All my family's gone. Roosevelt was my last hope for a new start. Starting over in a new place might do me good, too.'

'Ain't nothing to it, but to do it,' Ruben said. 'I gotta run. Edna, you need to bring Sadie with you to the juke joint tonight.'

After he left Sadie whispered, 'You been going to the juke?'

'Just when I can't sleep. They're so close and how else I'm gonna get married unless I find me a man?'

'Calm down. I just asked 'cause I was surprised that I didn't know, that's all.'

Edna exhaled, and they enjoyed a laugh.

Levi waited around for Edna to leave but she didn't take the hint and seemed determined to outstay him.

'Well, I need to go,' Levi finally said. 'I need to see a man about a horse, and, for the record - anywhere you go would be lucky to have a Nurse Sadie. Take care, ladies.'

As he drove off, Edna said, 'Oooh, anywhere would be lucky to have a Nurse Sadie.'

Sadie retorted with, 'Oooh, you been hanging out at the juke?'

'Okay, you win. Excuse me while I use the facilities,' Edna said.

Sadie slipped off as soon as Edna walked away.

She met Levi at the barn.

'Just wanted to say, I have your address. I'll write and let you know where you can contact me because I really want to know how things work out. Promise?'

'Promise.'

After Levi hugged her, she raced back to make sure she was seen saying her goodbyes so no one could say she disappeared with the newspaperman.

Later, Sadie settled in her room and began the grievous task of going through Roosevelt's footlocker.

She found a bible that she'd offer to Ruben tomorrow.

Flipping through the pages she found several documents tucked away at Genesis 25. She rifled through military papers; she would save those. She found letters she'd written; she would save those, too. He'd bound them in the order they were received.

She came upon some unopened letters. The first was from Ruben.

And from who else?

This lumpy one was from town, but it wasn't from her. Her fingers trembled as she unfolded it, not knowing what to expect. She didn't have to read the words because she recognized the writing.

Nevertheless, she read and reread until the betrayal hit her. She found three more in the stack, all unopened.

Roosevelt hadn't bothered to read them. But why not?

Since she couldn't very well ask him, she'd have to go to the source. She stopped by a phone to place a call on the way out.

'I need to see a man about a horse right away. I'll be at the juke joint.'

Before she disconnected, Gladys asked, 'You going into raising horses? Does that mean you gone be moving to the Bookers' farm?'

'No plans yet. Good-bye Gladys.'

She headed out to ask some tough questions. She only hoped Levi got there in case she needed help. She wasn't sure if she could count on anyone else to save her. Perhaps she should call the police, too.

Sadie heard the music thumping before she strolled up to the juke. She gathered her courage and stepped inside.

'Hey' Edna shouted. 'You came.'

Clem added, 'Do my eyes deceive me? It's about time you let your hair down.'

Ruben just grinned like a Cheshire. He intercepted, 'Let's shake a leg, Sis.'

Sadie yelled over the noise, 'Can we step outside for a minute?'

As the group exited, Levi pulled up.

'Am I ever glad to see him,' Sadie mumbled.

Like the town crier, Levi announced, 'I was just leaving for Chicago but found something you need to see. I did some digging and found a document recently filed that may interest you.'

Ruben turned to make a break, but Sadie said, 'Don't leave yet and miss the real party.'

Clem stepped in his pathway and blocked his exit.

Levi continued, 'It would appear that the land and family house promised to Mr. Booker was petitioned for by someone else. Someone down on his luck up north, who returned recently because seems he had no other choice.'

'The will states, should there be a spouse, it goes to her. Next in line would be Ruben. But this is what's interesting. Ruben filed for the land days before Roosevelt's death.'

'What does this mean?' Sadie asked.

'It means motive. Although, I'm not clear why. He's the oldest, so he should automatically get it.'

'Maybe this explains it.' Sadie handed Levi one of the documents from Roosevelt's bible.

'Ruben Atwood's birth certificate. He wasn't Roosevelt's legal brother?'

'Nope, another letter in there explains that the Bookers took him in and raised him after his parents died but there was no official adoption, just kind-hearted folks doing the right thing.'

A crowd began gathering outside, and the music quelled on the inside, enabling them to also hear.

'I think it's time to call the police,' Sadie suggested.

'I already did. They're not interested unless we deliver a killer and a confession.'

Ruben growled, 'All I know is I didn't kill him. I loved him.'

Sadie said, 'As happy as I am that we finally have a motive, I got a personal bone to pick right now with my so-called friend. So, hold onto that thought because we're just about to hear Edna explain these.'

Edna looked at the letter Sadie extended toward her, but she wouldn't reach for it.

Sadie flicked it open and read it aloud, evoking gasps from the bystanders.

'Guess you weren't the only one who loved him, Ruben,' she added.

All eyes were on Edna, who just dropped her head and said nothing.

'You certainly are some kinda friend.'

Breaking, Edna began to scream and cry. Like an eruption, she spewed, 'You don't know what it's like, 'cause men always making a fool of themselves over you. Roosevelt was nice to me.

He treated me like I mattered, and I guess I just thought if I could get him, you could choose someone else. You had choices. I didn't. I'm sorry, Sadie Mae. I wasn't trying to hurt you. I just wanted someone too. When I saw him at the parade, all he could ask was where's Sadie? And once all hell broke loose, he was only concerned with finding you, like I wasn't standing there holding a pipe, ready to fight alongside him. He made me feel like garbage. I was crushed. I didn't mean to hit him like that. I swear. I always say I don't know my own strength.'

The policeman stepped to the front of the crowd. A killer and a confession had been hand-delivered, so he arrested her.

The next day the headlines read, *Veteran's Murder Solved.*

'Miss Edna Louise Samples has confessed and been arrested for the murder of Roosevelt Booker. This is the final article by Levi Cane for the Whatley Defender.'

Tucking the paper away, Sadie went to her room and packed all her belongings. Then, she walked over to the hospital to drop off a letter and make a call.

'Gladys, please connect me to Whatley-518.'

'Shole will. I can't believe your own friend went and killed your man. You doin' okay?'

'As well as can be expected, thanks.'

Sadie heard Levi pick up, but she never heard Gladys put the phone down, so she spoke quickly and hung up.

'I need to see that man about a horse I've decided on. I'll be at home waiting.'

When Levi arrived, he looked confused.

'Hey, I didn't quite understand. I wasn't sure that you meant for me to come here. What'll folks say if someone sees me?'

'It won't matter. They can say what they want. We won't be around to hear them. With Roosevelt, I felt I had no better choice. With you, I'm making my heart's choice. Help me with my bags?'

He hugged her first.

Author Bio:

Sheila is a member of Sisters In Crime, Alabama Writers Forum and a board member of Alabama Writers Cooperative.

When she is not writing cozy mysteries and her Danni Cobb series, she is problem-solving as an Application Developer and soul-saving as an ordained minister. She makes her home in Birmingham, Alabama.

Chapter Four

CADAVERS AND CONSPIRACIES

Wendy H. Jones

When Professor John Wilson enters his anatomy theatre at Surgeons' Hall in 1840s Edinburgh, he expects to find a cadaver on his dissection table, not an empty slab and a room full of confused medical students. With their course under threat and suspicion mounting, a trio of students vow to uncover the culprit of this apparent prank. But as they delve into the dark corners of the school and the secrets of its staff, they discover that the disappearance may not be a prank at all. Atmospheric and steeped in Victorian intrigue, "Cadavers and Conspiracies" is a cozy mystery with a surgical twist.

Astonished didn't even begin to cover Professor John Wilson's feelings when he stepped into the anatomy theatre that morning. With a flick of his frock coat tails and a nod to the serried ranks of students packing the seats of the lecture theatre, he strode towards the anatomy table, which took pride of place in the room, and carefully placed his dissection logbook on the table allotted to it. He pulled on protective cuffs, checked his instruments – all present and correct – and pulled back the cover. The reason for his astonishment quickly became apparent to the remainder of the room. He seemed to be missing a partially dissected cadaver. His trained eye had known something was amiss, but he was not in any way expecting a pig and two severed legs. Even more astonishing, the legs were from different bodies. It did not need a trained anatomist to deduce this; a drunk beggar could have done so, as one leg was white and the other black. As they only had one black cadaver on the premises, it was apparent where that leg came from. He assumed, with no evidence to support it, the other came from his own misplaced corpse.

Students gasped. A quiet murmur turned into a full-throated crescendo interspaced with some extremely misplaced giggles. With reactions such as this, the gigglers may have a very short career in medicine.

'Quiet.' His commanding voice cut through the clatter. Hush fell.

Drawing himself to his full height, he looked around the room with a frown which signified an impending ten force gale. Students shrank in front of his eyes; his frown deepened. He expected laughter or, at the very least, smug looks. Nothing.

'Sirs.' His students ceased lounging and straightened their backs. The professor paused before adding, in a tone more menacing than enquiring, 'Where is my cadaver?'

Silence reigned.

Once the silence was way past comfortable and his audience started squirming, he said, his voice low, 'Whoever did this will be removed from this course with immediate effect.' The calmness with which he said this had the students quaking in their highly polished boots. Surgeons' Hall was the top medical school in the country, with students travelling from all corners of the world to attend and learn from the world's best, so this was no mean threat but a life-changing warning. 'In fact, if this cadaver is not returned, your course will be *terminated* with immediate effect.' He paused to allow the serried ranks to take this in, then added his final proclamation. 'None of you will qualify.' The calmness with which he said this highlighted the seriousness of the situation.

He was presented with two hundred stunned faces and a fair scattering of gasps.

'You are dismissed. You will be informed when, or if, you can return to your studies.' With another flick of his frock coat, he turned and strode from the room, his figure commanding until the second he disappeared.

Cue another crescendo as notebooks were stowed and students arose. This was the most exciting thing that had happened since they arrived in Edinburgh. It was also the most shocking, bordering on devastating. Cadavers were hard to come by and if one disappeared it was likely to seriously interrupt their studies if not end them. Although most came from backgrounds which could afford the fees, delay meant loss of earnings when entering private practice late. Also, medical training at Surgeons' Hall was the most prestigious in the world and would open many doors to them. Those aiming to serve in the military would no longer be eligible, as this was the only route acceptable to military doctors. Shoving and jostling commenced as accusations flew.

'I bet it was you, Hamish. You've a nasty streak about you.'

Hamish scowled at his friend. 'And why would I do that? I'm as keen as you to pass anatomy.'

'Fat chance of that with no corpse.'

'You can count me out.' Jacob wore the Jewish Kippah, so the likelihood of him handling a pig was negligible to nothing.

'We're going to have to find that damn corpse or our student days are numbered.' Alexander had a look in his eyes which invited no opposing viewpoint.

Two pairs of eyes swivelled towards him. A heartbeat of silence later, Hamish asked, 'How do you propose we do that?'

Alexander Stuart, bookish, observant, and used to being obeyed, pushed his spectacles up his nose and said, 'Meet me in The White Hart Inn for luncheon and we'll set out a plan of action.'

The others, used to obeying him, nodded and dispersed.

'A cadaver? How could you lose a cadaver?'

John stared at his colleague as though he were a particularly interesting specimen. 'If I knew that, I wouldn't be standing here talking to you about it.' He smoothed his already pristine coat. 'I'd be instructing my assistant to return it to its rightful place.' He could not quite help wondering if Hugh Jones was losing his faculties.

Hugh, still as sharp as a dissecting knife despite advancing years, said, 'Well, you do rather appear to have lost one. Or rather, had one stolen.'

'Don't you think I know that?' John was not in the mood for pleasant chit chat.

'I can't help thinking this is a student prank.'

'If it is, it is a particularly odious one.'

'Indeed.' Hugh's tone turned soothing. 'It will probably be decorating your dissecting table by lunchtime.'

'If it is not, the consequences will be dire.' John stomped off, glowering and muttering to himself about students in general and the wastrels who had stolen his corpse. He strongly suspected students were the culprits but not his current cohort. They were either genuinely flabbergasted or should be gracing the stage at the *Theatre Royal*. He fully intended applying his finest grey cells to the matter. His grey cells did briefly wonder if he should call the police but dismissed the idea as foolish. Involve anyone else and Surgeons' Hall would be splashed across the pages of *The Scotsman*. It would not do to bring this esteemed establishment into disrepute. It would also harm his reputation if the world knew he couldn't keep track of the cadavers handed into his care.

The trio of amateur sleuths jostled for a table in the crowded tavern, eventually swiping one from under the nose of a furious medical student.'

'Gentleman should wait their turn.'

'Gentleman, who are juniors, should know their place,' Hamish said, his voice quite cheery. He wasn't up for debating the finer points of tavern or student etiquette, having more pressing matters on his mind.

Once settled with plates of cold mutton and pickled vegetables in front of them and the aroma of stale ale swirling around them, debate opened as to how they could retrieve the missing corpse and bring the perpetrator to justice.

'If we're to do this quickly, we must split the tasks and work simultaneously.' Hamish, the doer and most practical of them, was keen to get on with the task.

'Slow down, Sir.' Jacob, in his usual meticulous manner, pulled on the cuffs of his jacket sleeves. 'Instead of dashing off with no thought to the matter, let us decide what paths to take.'

'He's right,' Alexander pulled his glasses off and polished them on a pristine handkerchief before placing them neatly on the bridge of his nose. The handkerchief was meticulously folded and placed back in his pocket. 'A plan of action is what we need.'

Hamish sighed but, giving in to the inevitable, pulled a notebook and graphite pencil from his pocket. 'Jacob, you're always asking questions. You can interview staff and students.'

Jacob swallowed before choking out, 'What? Wait—'

'No time for arguing.' He moved on, leaving Jacob blinking like a startled owl.

'Alexander.'

Alexander adopted a haunted look, wondering what was coming at or for him.

'Examine the theatre for any signs of foul play.' He scratched his chin and added, 'Wouldn't hurt for you to search the theatre records while you are at it.' He took in the bullish look on Alexander's face. 'No time to waste.'

Jacob swallowed his last mouthful of mutton and pushed his plate back. 'And pray, what are you going to be doing?'

'Searching the highways and alleyways. Talking to the common man. They are the ones who will have seen a corpse being spirited away.'

'Corpses are always being spirited away around these parts. It's like a national sport.' Alexander risked a small smile.

'But usually towards Surgeons' Hall, not away from it.' As far as Hamish was concerned that settled the matter. He jumped up. 'As I said, gentlemen, there is no time to waste. May I remind you bodies are difficult to come by and deteriorate fast if not stored correctly.' Hamish took in their faces and added, 'Even with embalming.' He elbowed through the crowds in the direction of the pub door. The others trudged in his wake, Alexander wondering how power had been wrestled away from him in so gentle a manner. He shrugged. There would be time to debate relational dynamics once their studies had resumed. Right now, finding the corpse was all that mattered.

The professor, scowling and muttering, stomped around the corridors of Surgeons' Hall like a demon in training for a major event. 'Get out of my way.' An unfortunate anatomist assistant scurried off before he lost his job or something even more personal. Wilson, in a good mood was bad enough; in a bad mood, no one could imagine the consequences. He'd once thrown a scrap of newly dissected liver at a student who had the audacity to sneeze in his theatre. The only reason he was still working was his reputation as the greatest anatomist the world had ever known. Students flocked from all corners of the earth to study under him.

Having moved on from his initial thoughts it might be a student, his acutely analytical brain focussed on those lower on the food chain. His stomping took him all the way to the basement and along corridors he very rarely frequented. He threw open the door with such vigour it knocked an unsuspecting cleaner off his feet. The man pulled himself up and wrung his hands as he cringed in front of his superior. 'Sir, what...what...'

'In the name of God.' He looked the man up and down and said, 'Do you know anything about my missing cadaver?' He paused. 'Well?'

Another man stepped forward. 'He means body, Angus.' He turned and looked Wilson dead in the eye. 'We dinnae know nothing.' His gaze did not waver. 'Ye'd be better aff speaking to your so-called pals. Or getting the peelers in.'

'Don't be so impertinent, man.' Despite his words he turned and stomped off again. Good anatomist assistants were hard to come by, and Fergus was the best in Scotland. There was no use making a dire situation even worse.

Fergus muttered, I wish his deid body was on the table,' bringing a smile to his friend's face.

Blissfully unaware of what was being said behind his briskly retreating back, the Professor's thoughts turned blacker and faintly murderous. *If I find the person responsible there will be a fresh body ready for dissection.* Not that this would help. The dissection would need to be started from scratch and there was no room for manoeuvre. Dead bodies did not keep indefinitely.

Someone strode past him, banging into Wilson as he did so.

'Watch where you are going, Sir.' Elias Murdoch, quite vehement in the fact he was in the right, glanced at the person he had charged into. His face paled. 'Professor Wilson. Please accept my humble apologies. I thought you were a student.'

'Do I look like a student to you, you imbecile?'

Elias, a new anatomist on the team, trembled.

'Do you know the whereabouts of my cadaver?'

'Sir.' The man blinked several times. 'No, Sir.' Then, remembering he too was an anatomist, pulled back his shoulders, looked Wilson dead in the eye and said, 'Why would I jeopardise training? My son is looking to join this school, as you well know.'

Wilson, who had no remembrance of this being the case, said, 'As God is my witness, I am without any credible reason as to why they employed you. Go about your business.'

His colleague scuttled off in the direction of the anatomy vaults, all his bravado having disappeared in a withering cloud of disapproval.

Wilson frowned. *What business would he have going there? He was not scheduled for any lectures and there were no new bodies. Addle-pated fool.* He performed an about face and followed, determined to find out if it had anything to do with his missing body. He would not put sabotage past him or any other one of his colleagues. A vice clutched at his heart. *Surely no one would stop so low as to interfere with medical training to get back at him.*

Hamish, ebullient and enthusiastic, was having the time of his life interrogating the population of Edinburgh in what he thought was a subtle manner. Or at least the ones who frequented the vicinity of Surgeons' Hall and its environs.

'Andra, you're the eyes and ears of Hospital Street.' He took shallow breaths against the smell emanating from the local tramp. He might be used to noxious vapours from patients, but this was a whole new level.

Andra grinned and expectorated phlegm through a mouthful of broken teeth, missing Hamish's leather ankle boots by a whisker. The student took a step back. Keen as he was to complete his studies, he drew the line at ruining his apparel.

'Aye. Yir right. Money fir a wee dram might loosen my lips.'

'Loosen those lips first and then I'll see if your information is worth the price of a dram.'

'There's been activity that's no' quite legal up by Blackfriars. Although I'm convinced it's a load o' havers.'

'What do you mean, not quite legal? I'll decide if it's nonsense or not.'

'Bodies making their way fae yon cemetery to your school.' He whipped off his hat. 'God have mercy on them.'

Hamish wasn't sure if he meant have mercy on the corpses or the grave robbers. The news, though not pertinent to his investigation, was still a surprise as grave robbing was meant to have been dead and buried following Robert Knox's departure. Interesting. He flipped a penny in the direction of Andra, who expertly caught it and scrambled to his feet. He shouted after the man and threw him another coin. 'Buy yourself a meat pie as well.' He was sure the money would be sidelined into more alcohol, but he was willing to give the man the benefit of the doubt.

Further subtle, and increasingly less subtle questioning, led him nowhere. As the light faded, he turned to wend his weary way back to his lodgings, passing lamplighters on his way. A coal fire and candles awaited. Despite Edinburgh being one of the first cities to have the newest coal gas lamps, this dazzling technology had not yet made it to his lodgings. Coal and candles had barely made it to his lodgings, his termagant of a landlady being a believer in temperance in everything, including creature comforts. With a face that would haunt gargoyles, her one redeeming grace was the cheapness of her sparsely furnished rooms, hence the reason he could toss coins at beggars.

Jacob, the most moral and upright student in the history of Surgeons' Hall, was not having such a good time of it. The thought of questioning his superiors, or even his equals, had his blood running cold. The confidence that often came with his heritage had skipped him completely. Except in his abilities as a doctor which were seeped into his bones, taking root in his very marrow. Nor did idle chatter sit easily on his frail shoulders. Yet, for the sake of his studies, he searched for the deeply sleeping lion of his meagre confidence. His questioning elicited a titbit of information in that Mr Durnley, one of the lab assistants, had been seen looking shifty that morning.

Jacob took out his handkerchief and mopped his brow as he stood before Durnley. 'I am sure you have heard the news of our missing cadaver.'

'Aye.'

'Have you any idea of its whereabouts?'

'Are you blamin' me fir that?' The man grew to his full height, exuding menace and the threat of imminent bodily harm.

'Not at all, Sir. I just thought you might have heard something.' Jacob decided he was in so much trouble already he might as well continue. He too pulled himself to his full height. 'What did you do in the lab this morning?'

The man shrank, his eyes darting right to left. 'How do you know I did something?'

'That's of no matter to you. What did you do, and does it have anything to do with our missing body?'

'Your body's no' my concern. I dropped a jar o' ethanol.' He glared at Jacob. 'No' that it's any business o' yours.'

Whilst unfortunate, this was not a matter of severity. 'Go about your business.'

Durnley glared but did as he was bid. Upsetting students was not in his job description and he'd weans and a wife to feed.

Jacob, astonished at his newfound bravery, wandered off before realising he was now hopelessly lost. His usual haunts included the anatomy theatre and lecture rooms, and the bowels of the building were like a foreign country. Peering into one room, the use of which was lost on him, he noticed a trail of linen bandages on the floor. Frowning, he hurried over. Not only was this anathema to his neat and tidy upbringing, it was also a waste of supplies, something not tolerated in this august institution. He followed the trail of bandages, hoping it would lead to a partially dissected body, and they could all return to their studies. Unfortunately, the God of Abraham, Isaac and Jacob was not shining fondly on him as the bandages led to nothing more than a cupboard full of embalming fluid. Putting one foot in front of the other, he resumed his search for a way out of the subterranean abyss.

Alexander's search started and finished in the same way – with nothing to move their impromptu case forward and no cadaver to cheer the situation up. Mooching around an anatomy theatre, which was currently out of bounds, was not lifting his mood any higher. The only fortunate part of the whole proceedings was the dissection logbook had been left out. This never happened as the Professor kept it closer to him than a mother suckling a newborn. His brows drew close together. Where was the page from the previous day? Every other page was meticulously completed with the date clearly annotated but not 13th March 1843. Wilson would not leave out the recording of a day's lecture and dissection. He gave a thorough sweep of the room whilst keeping a close eye on the door, then turned to leave. As he was about to go, he spotted something odd at the edge of one of the benches. Further investigation elicited a piece of paper stuffed in a crack between the bench and the supporting wood. It was tough to retrieve but judicious, yet gentle, pulling and tugging rewarded him. Opening it, he was the next one to be astonished on this perplexing day. It was the missing page but with some of the words obliterated by scribbling. *Who would go to the trouble of folding a page so neatly, then stuffing it in such a stupid place? It was shouting out to be found.* Whilst he could not answer that question, he fully intended applying some vulcanised rubber to the pencil marks to ascertain what was so important it must be hidden. At least he might work out one small part of the puzzle.

The three huddled around a meagre fire in Hamish's room. There wasn't enough in any of their coffers to justify eating out twice in one day, their fathers being of the opinion too much money hurled in their direction would take their eyes off the main goal of qualifying as doctors. Plus, they didn't want anyone looking on with interest. They never knew who might be following them around given their attentiveness to this case.

They were most interested in the mysteriously hidden page from the dissection logbook.

'It seems a lot of trouble to fold up and hide like that.' Hamish rubbed his hands together then threw caution to the wind and placed another piece of coal on the fire. Flames flickered at its edges, giving the impression heat was imminent.

'Have you got any rubber?' Jacob didn't take his eyes off the paper.

Hamish rifled around in his writing desk and handed it over.

Leaning over the small desk he gently applied the rubber to the pencil markings, moving slowly, yet methodically.

Alexander peered over his shoulder before saying, 'I'd do that a bit faster. The cadaver will have rotted to the skeleton before you are finished.'

Jacob, as unflappable as always, continued without changing

tack. 'Going too fast will rub the ink underneath.' He glanced up. 'Where will that get us?'

Alexander sighed and threw himself into the one armchair which graced the room. He wriggled around but finding a soft spot proved impossible. He wriggled some more, unsure whether it was comfort he was seeking or it was mere impatience. One never knew under these circumstances.

At last, Jacob leaned back in the rickety chair and said, 'Not my best work, but—'

Alexander and Hamish, who had leapt from the bed and armchair, crowded around him. 'Never mind the quality. What does it say?'

Jacob pushed his glasses up his nose and said, 'It would appear our professor is not keen on his junior associate, Mr Murdoch.'

His friends peered over his shoulder and their eyes widened.

Mr Murdoch's work is sub-par.

'I wasn't expecting that,' Hamish said.

'I'm more curious as to why he would write it in an anatomy logbook.' Alexander's face said he thought the professor was a ha'penny short of a shilling.

Hamish raised an eyebrow. 'He pretty much owns the place, he can write what he wants anywhere he wants, and they will not dismiss the esteemed professor.'

The others nodded their agreement.

'We need to speak to Mr Murdoch and find out his opinion on the matter.'

Alexander followed boldly with Jacob shambling behind, shoulders hunched and a dejected look on his face. Interrogating anatomists, no matter how junior, was not something he relished.

Gloominess had settled over Surgeons' Hall like a mouldy blanket, bringing a general air of dereliction. This from the number one medical school in the world. Usually buzzing, a noisy silence enshrouded its hall. Rather than finding Murdoch, they found Professor Wilson marching down the corridor a glint in his eye that promised trouble for anyone who came into his orbit.

He stopped in front of them. 'I thought I made myself quite clear. You were to leave the premises and not come back until my cadaver was found.' He glared at them. 'Am I to dismiss you from your studies, gentlemen?'

Jacob, his fear of losing his place studying medicine overcoming his fear of the professor, blurted out, 'We have news of interest regarding the missing body, Professor.'

Hamish and Alexander were stunned into silence.

Wilson swivelled to face the speaker and stared. 'Well. Out with it.'

All three fell over themselves to tell the story of what they had been up to, eventually screeching to a halt and handing over the torn-out logbook sheet.

The professor frowned and peered at the sheet. 'What have my jottings got to do with my missing cadaver?'

Jacob had once more entered frightened rabbit mode. Hamish stepped into the breech. 'We think Mr Murdoch may have taken it in revenge for you...' He took in the professor's face. 'Any imagined slight he may feel you had cast in his direction.'

The professor's eyes took on a more hopeful glint. 'Follow me. I don't want you three out of my sight. Who knows what you might do if I leave you to your own devices.' He strode off, his long legs powering him forward, leaving the young men scuttling to catch up. They did so without delay. No one would dare cross the professor. Except Murdoch, it would seem.

They found Murdoch hiding in his minuscule, yet spotless, office. He cringed when the door flew open and the professor barged in.

'Where is the cadaver?' Wilson leaned over the desk, causing Murdoch to flinch.

'Sir, I told you previously. I have no idea. I have nothing to do with your missing body.'

'Do you deny tearing this from my dissection logbook?'

Murdoch read the sheet and grew a backbone. He stood. 'I have seen neither your corpse nor this sheet. The reason I appear sub-par, as you put it, is because I am terrified of you.' He folded his arms and glared at the astonished professor. 'You criticise me at every turn. Dismiss me. I no longer care.'

Before the professor could open his mouth, Hamish stepped in. 'Sir, who is that at the door?' His voice shook. Even the ebullient Hamish had his breaking point.

They all swivelled to look.

The young man said, 'Maybe not all dead things remain where they are put.'

No one was quite sure whether he was talking about the missing cadaver or the graverobbers who were rife in Edinburgh.

The professor opened his mouth to speak, but before he could utter one word his colleague interrupted.

'Amos...'

The young man bolted before Murdoch could finish. The five men took off in hot pursuit, the young students leading the pack. 'How do you know him?' The professor's words were surprisingly vibrant given the rapid pace. 'I don't recognise him as a student.'

'He's my son.'

Wilson shook his head as he kept up the pace.

Amos bolted into one of the rooms. He'd spent hours exploring the entire building and knew where every nook, cranny, door and corridor was. This particular room had a door to a hidden corridor meant only for those in the know. He reached for the handle but had only just clasped it when he was pulled to a halt by a judiciously placed hand. Alexander, who boxed to keep fit, pulled him around to face them.

The anatomists screeched to a halt beside the boys. Silence hung in the air. No one seemed to have words worthy of the enormity of the situation.

After mere moments that seemed to stretch into a number of minutes, Murdoch said, 'Amos, what have you done?'

The young man looked at the shoes he was scuffing on the floor. He was the vision of a two-year-old child rather than a fifteen-year-old man.

'What have you got to say for yourself?' Wilson's voice was low but there was no mistaking the underlying hint of menace.

The silence continued.

'Speak up, boy.'

Amos's father's tone brooked no argument, and years of obeying loosened the boy's tongue. 'He's vicious to you, Pa. You come home each night dreading going back to work again.' He glared at Wilson. 'I wanted to teach you a lesson, so you would know how my father felt.'

For once in his life, Wilson had no words. He took a few deep breaths before saying, 'This is no excuse for halting medical training or interfering with a body which was donated to this medical school.' He paused to allow the young man to take in the enormity of what he had done.

Alexander, watching with interest thought, given the absence of any policemen in this case, the body may have been purchased illegally rather than donated. For the sake of his future medical career, he kept his own counsel.

Wilson was not finished. 'Your behaviour is abhorrent.'

Murdoch said, 'I fully agree.' He nodded in Wilson's direction. 'Do what you will in the way of punishment.'

'Your son will not attend this institution to complete his studies.'

'I feel that is fair. He must face the consequences of his actions.'

Alexander was now convinced the body was illegal, as there was no intention of handing the culprit over to the police.

Amos paled and slunk against the wall.

'What have you done with the body? We need to retrieve it so we can resume anatomy lectures.' Wilson turned to the three students. 'Thank you for your assistance, gentlemen. You are free to go. Report to my office at 7am tomorrow.'

The boys trooped off not knowing whether there was trouble or honour ahead. You never could tell with Professor Wilson.

The anatomists contemplated the events of the day before Wilson spoke. 'I may have been quick to judge you. Please accept my apologies.'

Murdoch held out his hand. 'All is forgotten, Sir. A new start. I must also apologise for my son. He was not raised that way.'

The men shook hands.

'Amos, take us to the body.'

He trudged off with Wilson and his father in pursuit.

The next morning brought serried rows of medical students eager to resume their anatomy lessons.

They held their breath as two men walked through the door to the anatomy theatre.

'Today, I will be assisted in my dissection by Mr Murdoch.'

Murmurs ran through the ranks as the students took this in. A strange turn of events indeed.

'For the next three days, I will be assisted by Brown, Stuart and Frankel in turn. This is in reward for helping find our missing cadaver.' He waved a hand over the dissecting table which once more was graced by a partially dissected cadaver.

Gasps filled the auditorium as they all looked at Hamish, Alexander and Jacob. Then spontaneous applause broke out.

Their professor allowed it for a few moments before saying. 'Quiet. Let us begin.'

Author Bio:

Wendy H. Jones is a multi-award-winning, best-selling Scottish author of crime thrillers, cozy mysteries, children's picture books and non-fiction books for authors. She is the winner of the Books Go Social Book of the Year at Dublin Writers Conference and the prestigious Scottish Association of Writers, Janetta Bowie Chalice for best non-fiction book She is also an acclaimed international public speaker, teaching writing craft and marketing, worldwide.

In addition, she is the Editor in Chief of *Writers' Narrative eMagazine*, a partner in Auscot Publishing and Retreats and owner of Scott and Lawson Publishing.

She is also proud to serve as the Co-Chair of the Membership Committee on the board of Sisters in Crime, an organisation which supports writers worldwide.

Chapter Five

THE DOLLMAKER'S DEMISE

Marti M. McNair

When landlady Agatha Linton discovers her peculiar lodger, dollmaker Henrietta Wren, slumped lifeless at her worktable with a silk ribbon knotted around her throat, whispers of murder spread like shadows. With scandal threatening her household, Agatha turns to her nephew Edwin, a sharp-eyed writer with a taste for mysteries. As Edwin follows a trail of broken promises, poisoned glasses, and eerie porcelain brides, he unravels a chilling plot of betrayal, obsession, and deadly ambition. But in a world where every ribbon hides a secret and every doll's eyes seem to watch, truth may prove more terrifying than lies.

Outside, the city seemed to hold its breath. Inside number forty-seven Penumbra Lane, the gloom seeped through the keyholes. Mrs Agatha Linton, a stout and sharp-eyed landlady, shuffled along the narrow corridor, clutching a steaming pot of beef stew to her chest. Her wool shawl flapped with each step, breath curling in the chill air as she approached the attic flat of her most peculiar lodger - Miss Henrietta Wren, the dollmaker.

At the top of the stairs, Agatha paused. The door stood ajar, its edge nudged by a draught. Her brow puckered. Miss Wren never left the door open - not even a sliver.

'Miss Wren?' Her voice wavered, barely above a whisper.

The atmosphere hung still, cloaked in a deadly hush.

'Miss Wren,' she called, this time a little louder. 'Are you home?'

Agatha pushed the door wider. Hinges groaned. The stew sloshed ominously in its pot. Inside, the cramped room lay silent, bathed in amber lamplight. Rows of dolls, in various stages of assembly, lined the shelves, their painted faces eerie in the dimness. Her gaze caught a spill of copper curls draped across the worktable. She blinked. A breath caught. Henrietta lay slumped at her worktable, cheek pressed against the wood. Her fingers dangled, limp. A half-finished doll stared skyward from beneath her arm, its blue glass eyes fixed in eternal surprise.

'Oh, merciful heavens,' Agatha gasped, her heart thudding as she edged closer. Around Henreitta's pale neck, a silk ribbon had been tightly knotted. Pink. Delicate. Unmistakably the kind she used to tie around her doll's throats.

Staggering back, Agatha dropped the stew pot. A gasp clung to her throat as her wide eyes fixed on the horror before her. She turned and fled, her skirts clutched in her fists. She had to fetch Edwin. Her nephew would know what to do. He'd seen dark things before and had written about them.

Edwin Linton stood by the threshold, notebook in hand, eyes narrowing as they swept Henrietta's room. The stench of the lamp oil mingled with faint traces of lavender and the spilled, overcooked stew. His aunt hovered behind him, her lips moving in silent prayer.

Henrietta's body remained untouched, still slumped over the table. The knotted ribbon at her throat was too exact, too careful to be kind. Ceramic limbs, doll heads, and spools of thread littered the worktable. Yet, among the chaos, a few details stood out.

Just beside her hand lay a porcelain doll, its face fractured in a jagged line from chin to brow. The doll wore a miniature wedding gown - hand-stitched lace, satin trim. Exquisite craftsmanship. He jotted down every detail in his notebook.

'Perhaps, dearest Aunt,' Edwin said, his tone cautious. 'You should bring in the constabulary at once. Such a grievous matter surely demands their attention.'

Agatha wrung her hands. 'No, Edwin . . . please. Not yet. If word spreads that murder has occurred here, I'll lose every respectable lodger I've got. The scandal alone would ruin me. We must be discreet, just until we know more.'

Edwin paused before the small, cracked sink in the corner, his gaze dropping to an empty glass resting inside. He lifted it carefully with his handkerchief, bringing it close to his nose. A faint, bitter scent lingered - sharp and unsettling. He set the glass down.

His eyes fell to the floor. A fine layer of dust clung to the uneven boards. Starting beneath the window, he spotted a line of tiny shoeprints, perhaps a child's - pressed clearly into the powder. They started at the sill, as though someone had stepped down from the open window, and crossed toward the worktable. The prints continued, unbroken, tracing a diagonal path across the room before vanishing beneath the tattered curtain − right where they had begun.

Edwin blinked. The steps were too precise to be random. There was no smudging, no drag. Whoever had walked here had done so with intention. Edwin lifted the edge of the curtain. Nothing beneath but a stack of old crates and a mousehole chewed into the skirting board.

He straightened and scanned the floor again. Near Henrietta's foot lay a scrap of paper, curled at the edges and jagged along the tear. It had been ripped clean through the middle of a word, leaving only the letters Sie. Edwin frowned. A name? A fragment of something more? It meant little on its own, yet something about it felt important. He slipped it into his notebook, realising he would have to show and explain it to the constabulary later.

Behind him, Agatha cleared her throat. 'Henrietta often quarrelled with the gentleman on the landing below, you know,' she murmured. 'Mr Clarence Thorne. A playwright. Always pacing, always muttering. He and Miss Wren argued something fierce last night.'

Edwin turned to look at her. 'About what?'

She hesitated. 'Money, I think. He came storming down the stairs, shouting, *You'll regret this.* Heard it with my own ears. A few others heard it too.'

Edwin nodded once. 'In the meantime, we must make sure no one finds out about Henrietta's demise. Not until we have an explanation.'

Descending the small flight of steps, Edwin crossed a narrow landing and, after a moment's pause, knocked tentatively on the playwright's door. A pause. Then, creaking floorboards. The latch lifted. Clarence Thorne filled the doorway - tall, unshaven, eyes bloodshot. Ink stained his fingers. He blinked as if dragged from sleep.

'Yes?'

Edwin inclined his head with the utmost civility. 'Mr Thorne, I beg your pardon for disturbing you at such an hour, but I wondered if I might have but a moment of your time? It concerns Miss Wren.'

Clarence's jaw tightened. 'Henrietta,' he muttered. 'Why? What's she done now?'

'I believe you were acquainted. My aunt heard raised voices last evening - something about a financial disagreement?'

Thorne snorted and raked a hand through his dishevelled hair. 'If by disagreement you mean her failure to honour a professional agreement, then yes - there was contention. I furnished her with every material required for the commission - oak, silk thread, glass eyes . . . all at my own expense.' He clenched his fists at his side, his jaw tightening. 'She was to craft a troupe of bespoke marionettes for my forthcoming play. Time was agreed upon. Terms were set. Yet she delivered nothing. Not so much as a carved limb. I daresay she lost interest the moment my coin changed hands. Perhaps she never intended to see it through. You would have to ask her.'

Edwin's pen scratched softly across the page. 'And last night, how did she seem after you confronted her?'

'She laughed in my face. I left before my temper betrayed me. I told her she had one week to produce the goods or she'd be sorry.'

Edwin paused, tapping the spine of his notebook. 'Had she ever done the like before? Promised work and delivering nothing?'

Thorne gave a dry chuckle. 'More than once, I assure you. Miss Wren had a knack for making elegant promises only to abandon them before a stitch was sewn. Just ask Jasper Bell - one of the regulars down at the Fox and Fig on Coal Lane. He warned me, but I didn't listen. She had been commissioned by him to craft a mechanical puppet for his niece's christening. She took his coin too, sampled his gin, and that marked the end of it. I hate to admit it, but she had a way with words and I fell for them. Giving her the benefit of doubt is my wrong doing.'

Edwin tilted his head. 'Why did Mr Bell not report her

deception to the police? Surely, he had grounds if she took his money without producing so much as a sketch or spindle.'

Thorne leaned in, lowering his voice to a near-whisper. 'But the tale grows murkier. Bell was seen ascending to her attic on more than one moonless night. When his wife - formidable as a thunderclap during Sunday service - came hammering at the door, chamber pot in one hand and a rolling pin in the other, Henrietta denied all impropriety. Claimed Jasper had never paid her a farthing, and that they were only acquaintances through his desire to make a purchase of a puppet.' Thorne shook his head. 'Truth is, the man was likely tangled in her petticoats. She played with hearts the way she played with porcelain. I must admit, I'm rather shocked at Jasper. His wife is as comely as she is clever. Why would any man turn from a fine roast to cold mutton. I may be mistaken, but I thought I heard Madam Bell's dulcet tones last night.'

Edwin hailed a hackney carriage and directed it eastward through the winding lanes towards the modest outskirts of Highgate. The Bell's cottage crouched behind a thicket of ivy and crumbling brick. Moss thickened the garden path, and a thin plume of smoke curled from the crooked chimney. He rapped twice on the door with his gloved knuckles.

A moment passed. Then another. Just as he raised his hand to knock again, the door creaked open to reveal a slender woman with keen, intelligent eyes. Her layered woollen garments, though worn, were arranged with care, and the drape of her time-softened cardigan lent her an air of quiet elegance.

'Yes,' she said, eyeing Edwin from head to toe.

Edwin bowed slightly. 'Madam Bell, I presume. Forgive the intrusion. I am Edwin Linton, the nephew of Mrs Agatha Linton. I've come with urgent news regarding Miss Henrietta Wren.'

'Miss Wren? What of her?'

'Might I come in? The matter is delicate.'

'Jasper is unwell,' she said, though the door was already swinging open. 'But if it concerns Henrietta Wren. . . well, then you'd best come in. My husband and I have had no end of trouble with that one.'

Edwin stepped across the threshold into a parlour cluttered with faded taxidermy under glass domes. Heavy drapes muffled the light, and a fire sputtered low in the grate. Jasper stirred in his armchair by the hearth, a knitted blanket slouched across one shoulder.

Madam Bell gestured to a lumpy settee. 'Sit, if you please,' she said, lowering herself into a high-backed chair, crossing her ankles. Her skirts shifted, rising enough for Edwin to glimpse the slender feet encased in thick woollen stockings – elegant in shape, though a touch too long and narrow to match the delicate, childlike prints on Henrietta's attic floor.

Edwin folded his gloves and tucked them into his coat pocket. 'There has been an incident involving Miss Wren. She too is unwell, and presently unable to speak for herself. I've been asked to make quiet enquiries into her affairs - the people she dealt with, promises she made and any misunderstandings which may have arisen of late.'

Madam Bell inhaled sharply. 'You'd need more than one notebook for that.'

Jasper stirred uneasily, a shudder running through him as a cough escaped. 'What are you implying, Emmaline?'

'I imply nothing,' she said, her eyes darkening. 'But if folk she cheated start knocking on our door, I won't pretend surprise. Now calm yourself and take more of your medicine.'

'I was not cheated,' Jasper said, spooning liquid from a small glass bottle. 'I was robbed, plain and honest. Paid her three pounds and six - all up front - for a mechanical marionette. She said it would sing the old classic hymn, you know the one, "Rock of Ages". I waited six weeks. When I went to her door, she denied ever having been paid. Said she'd never even drawn up the design. She called me confused, or worse. Accused me of all sorts. It felt like she'd mistaken me for someone else.'

Edwin caught the faint, lingering scent of the medicine - the same bitter, greenish note that clung to the glass in Henrietta's room. Had Henrietta been ill too?

'Did you retain a receipt or a sketch?' Edwin asked.

'It was a handshake and a promise, like gentlemen used to do. She toasted it in gin and drew the thing on my napkin . . . which she took with her, now I think of it.'

Edwin made a small note, then asked carefully. 'Had you any knowledge of other commissions she was working on recently?'

'None she named,' Jasper said. 'Only muttered once she'd been approached by someone foreign, a man with an accent. He wanted her to build something grand. Said she'd outdo herself this time. She looked pale when she said it, like the thought of it frightened her.'

Edwin probed further. 'Did she mention his name?'

'Something with an S,' Jasper said. 'She said it while wrapping her scarf over her face, so I couldn't hear properly. Signore or senore or something or other.'

'Have either of you ever seen inside her lodgings? Apart from your visits, Mr Bell?'

Jasper gave a grunt. 'Only the once. Dolls lined the shelves like a church choir - all watching. Made my skin prickle.'

Edwin was silent for a moment. 'Forgive me, Madam Bell, but may I inquire where you were last evening?'

Madam Bell bristled. 'Home, of course. With my feet in mustard soak to help with blocked sinuses and a penny dreadful in my lap. Why do you ask?'

Edwin's eyes flickered to her crossed ankles again. He stood and bowed once more. 'No real reason. Thank you both for your candour. If anything else comes to mind, I ask you to send word at once.'

Coal Lane wound narrow and uneven, its cobbles glazed with cold rain and the stench of coal smoke clung to the alley walls. Edwin pulled his coat tighter as he approached the Fox and Fig, a squat, timber-framed tavern leaning slightly as though drunk on its own liquor.

Inside, the air was thick with pipe smoke and fried onions. Low voices hummed beneath the clatter of mugs and the scratch of a fiddle.

Edwin approached the bar, where a bald man with bristled side-whiskers and a grease-smeared apron wiped tankards with a grimy cloth.

'Good evening,' Edwin began. 'I'm told this is where one might find Mr Jasper Bell, from time to time.'

'Aye.' The man replied without looking up. 'Jasper and his rickety knees haunt that corner table more regular than the gaslight. His wife dragged him home three nights ago, she did. She may have the face of an angel, but she has the temper of the Devil himself. Poor man didn't stand a chance. I've not seen him since.'

Edwin gave a thin smile. 'I'm not here about Bell himself, but rather about a woman he knows. Henreitta Wren. Do you know her?'

'Not personally,' the barkeep said, lowering the tankard. 'But I serve her when she comes in from time to time. Usual sort. Polite enough.'

'Did she ever meet anyone here? A foreign gentleman, perhaps?'

The barkeep scratched his temple. 'Might've done. A few months back, she came in with a man – dark coat, darker eyes, silver on his cane. His accent weren't local. I'll say that. Eastern European, I reckoned. He ordered expensive wine and didn't touch it. Just sat there watchin' her talk.'

'Did you hear what was said?'

'Not clearly. Something about parts. She kept gesturing with her hands, like this . . .' He mimed delicate turns and winding motions. 'Like she was describing gears or mechanisms.'

Edwin scribbled notes quickly. 'Would you happen to recall his name?'

'No, but he left behind a glove. Black kid leather, stitched with some sort of crest. Miss Henreitta came back the next day asking after it, said it belonged to Mister Sige or Seeg . . . something foreign.'

A pause. Then, as Edwin pocketed his notebook, the barkeep added,' She also bought something off of Tilda Blackstone. She sells ribbons and lace scraps. Henrietta needed pink ribbon, the good kind.'

Edwin froze. 'Pink silk ribbon?'

'Aye. If memory serves, it was the last length Tilda had on the reel. Miss Henrietta said it were for doll trimming - some special project – but she looked uneasy, like she weren't telling the whole truth. Best ask Miss Henrietta yourself. Far as I recall, Tilda wasn't too keen on handing anything over, what with money still owing from the last purchase. Miss Henrietta had a way of acquiring credit.'

Edwin's mind leapt back to the ribbon - the deliberate knot around Henrietta's neck. Silk. Pink. Unmistakable. 'Where might I find this Tilda Blackstone?' he asked.

'Her stalls in the market place off Bellweather Court. She'll be there tomorrow if it's dry. Ask for the lace woman with the green bonnet. She never stops flapping her gums.'

Edwin nodded, offering a coin in thanks. 'Sorry, one last question. Had Miss Wren ever spoken of being . . . frightened?'

The barkeep hesitated. 'Once. When Bell was drunk and bleating on about his puppet order, she looked a bit shaken. She actually came in last week, wanting to return his money - had it wrapped in an envelope. Asked me to tell him she had it for him and that he should call round. She looked out of sorts, and I asked her if she was well. I'll never forget her answer.'

Edwin's brow lifted. 'And what was that?'

'She said, it's not the coin I owe that scares me. It's the ones with darkness where their soul should be.'

Then she smiled like it was a joke, but her hands shook when she clasped them on the bar.'

Edwin stepped back into the street, the fog rolling in thick, softening the edges of buildings and blurring footsteps behind him. He stared at the ground for a moment - pink ribbon, an unfamiliar foreign man, debts demanding repayment, and the delicate shoeprints pressed into the dust on Henrietta's floor. One thing he was certain of - until now, none of those he had spoken to appeared to know that Henrietta was dead. Or so he thought.

The Tea room was quiet - just two widows whispering over their Victoria sponge and the clatter of a kettle behind the counter. At the table by the window, Edwin stirred his tea absently as his aunt poured sugar into hers with a steady hand. 'You look tired,' she said, eyeing him over the rim of her cup.

'I feel it,' he replied. 'Henrietta has left more knots than thread behind her.'

His aunt leaned forward. 'Have you learned anything. We can't afford to wait much longer before alerting the constabulary. The body will start to decompose.'

Edwin offered a clipped summary. 'Henrietta had disputes with Thorne and Jasper Bell. Promises broken. Money taken. I get the impression Mrs Bell is not keen on her. Henrietta also met with a foreign gentleman, perhaps Eastern European. She purchased some pink ribbon from a lace seller named Tilda. I'll seek her out next.'

Agatha reached for his hand. 'Do be careful, Edwin. This isn't just ink and scandal. Something about this . . . it frightens me.'

He squeezed her fingers gently and rose, buttoning his coat all the way to his throat. 'Then let's hope I find only ribbons and gossip.'

Bellweather Court seethed with colour and clamour. Barrowmen bawled beneath soot-blackened iron awnings, their cries rising above the rattle of cart wheels on cobbles. Draught horses fidgeted in their harness, flanks steaming in the morning chill. Children slipped like shadows between crates of plums and wicker hampers writhing with eel. Roasted chestnuts and the faint tang of burning coal filled the air.

Edwin made his way through the crush of petticoats and bootheels, scanning stall signs. Beneath a ragged green canopy, a petite woman in a brilliant green bonnet stood among bolts of lace and silk. She was speaking to a customer in a tinny sing-song voice. Something about taffeta and bridal gloves. Edwin waited until the woman departed, then stepped forward.

'Madam Tilda Blackstone?'

She turned - narrow faced, quick eyes, with a nervous flutter at the corners of her mouth. 'That's me. Ribbon or lace today, sir?'

Edwin removed his hat. 'My name is Edwin Linton. I believe you sold some pink silk ribbon to a Miss Henrietta Wren not long ago.'

Tilda's hands stopped mid-fold on some cloth. 'Did I?' she said, her voice neutral.

'She's a dollmaker,' Edwin said. 'Red hair. Frequented the Fox and Fig now and then.'

Tilda's eyes flitted to his face. 'Yes . . . yes, I remember now. Bought the last of the pink. Asked if I'd more in stock. I didn't.'

'Do you recall when that was?'

'Oh, weeks ago. Two, maybe three.' She was speaking too fast. 'I've had no more since. Even if I had, I doubt I'll be selling her anymore. It's a shame she met such a horrible demise.'

He cleared his throat. 'May I ask . . . how did you know she was dead? It's not been reported to the constabulary yet.'

Tilda blinked. The colour drained from her face. One hand landed shakily on a basket of buttons, sending them skittering across her stall. Her mouth opened, shut again. She looked as though she might bolt. 'I didn't . . . I didn't do anything,' she said, the words catching in her throat. 'I swear to you.'

Edwin held up both hands. 'Then speak with truth. Before someone else asks less kindly.'

She glanced to either side, but no one seemed to be paying them any mind. Still, she lowered her voice to a rasp. 'I didn't kill her. I didn't touch her. I swear on my life.'

'Then who did?' Edwin asked.

'I don't know. I only . . .' She looked down, tears springing to her eyes. 'I climbed through the window.'

Edwin's eyes narrowed.

'I'd no other choice,' she said, almost pleading. 'She owed me six shillings for that ribbon and more besides. I gave her fine lace on a promise of a bulk order. Said she'd sell dolls before Michael-mas, swore it on her mother's grave. She'd have the sum to pay me back, but she never did.'

'So, you entered her flat, through the window?'

'I knew she kept it unlatched. Her attic overlooked the roof of Cobbler's Row. I'd done it once before, to drop off a parcel when she weren't in. . .I thought . . .I thought I'd take something small. Worth the cost of what she owed. A brooch maybe. Or one of those glass-eyed dolls.'

Edwin said nothing.

Tilda shook, clutching her table for support. 'But when I got in . . . she was already there. Slumped over the table. Her hair was all down, like she'd nodded off sewing, but then I saw it. The ribbon. Tied tight around her throat. Pink. The same one I'd sold her. *My* ribbon.' She swallowed. 'I called her name, but she didn't move. I didn't check her pulse, I couldn't. I was frozen. The lamp was still burning. The dolls all watching. I . . . I climbed back out. I didn't take a thing.'

'Why didn't you go to the police?' Edwin asked.

'Who'd believe me? A ribbon-seller crawling through a lady's attic window in the dead of night. They'd say I did it - strangled her with my own silk.'

A silence passed between them. Tilda's shoulders sagged. 'The last time I saw her properly, she looked frightened. I'd asked for the money, and she went pale. Said she'd have it soon. That she had a new buyer, someone wealthy. Foreign. But she didn't sound proud. She sounded terrified.'

Edwin drew in a slow breath. 'Did she say his name?'

'No. Only that the doll was a present for his bride to be.'

Rain battered against the windowpanes. Edwin sat at his aunt's kitchen table, the torn scrap of paper spread before him, the remaining letters smeared but legible - *Sie*. He had nearly dismissed it as meaningless. The barkeep at the Fox and Fig had said Sige or Seeg . . . something foreign. And Tilda, advising the doll was for his bride-to-be.

He climbed the stairs to Henrietta's attic. The constables had still not been summoned; his aunt had made certain of that. The room remained the same. The ribbon still knotted at her throat, the fractured doll staring blankly, and the air thick with the fading scent of lavender and lamp oil.

Edwin re-traced Tilda's footprints from the window to the worktable. Then, crossing to the hearth, he dropped to his knees. He shifted aside the stack of crates and ran his hand along the floorboards. One yielded with a soft creak. Beneath it, wrapped in oilcloth, lay a wooden box. Inside – a beautifully made bride doll. She was exquisite. Pale porcelain limbs, articulated joints, silken blond hair. Her mouth half-open as though ready to speak. A wedding gown of fine lace, the same cut of pink ribbon already tied delicately at her throat.

Edwin stared, a slow dread coiling in his chest. Nestled within the doll's box lay a piece of thick cream paper. Embossed at the top was an unfamiliar crest - a stag rearing between twin serpents, their tongues entwined. Beneath it, a name unfurled in fine, slanted ink – Signore Seigbrecht. Just below, printed in narrow, severe lettering, was and address. Hotel Imperium, Room 3B, Chancery Lane, London. Edwin read the rest of the note carefully, then folded it and slipped it into his pocket.

The Hotel Imperium stood over Chancery Lane like a mausoleum with delusions of grandeur. Its façade, once white, was now the colour of soot. A pair of wrought-iron lanterns flanked the door, their flickering gaslight barely penetrating the London fog.

Inside, the lobby was hushed and dim, the floor tiled in black and cream. A clerk dozed behind the front desk, spectacles askew. Edwin passed him with a polite nod, then made his way up the main staircase, its plush runner faded to the shade of dried blood. He paused before Room 3B. The corridor was silent, save for the faint hiss of the gas lamps along the walls. Edwin rapped. No answer. He tried again. Still nothing.

He reached into his coat pocket and withdrew a small velvet pouch - not something he carried often, but an inheritance from his father's old desk. Inside, a skeleton key filed thin, a wire hook, and a miniature tension wrench. Victorian lockpicks, fashioned for drawer locks but adaptable in a pinch.

He cast a quick glance to the left, then to the right - nothing but still shadows and the faint creak of floorboards in the far distance. Satisfied, he dropped to one knee, slipped the wrench in first, and felt it catch against something solid. Then, with nimble fingers, he eased the hook in beside it until he heard the lock click. The latch gave way. He stood, heart thudding, and eased the door open.

At once, the scent struck him. Not cologne. Not tobacco. Mustard. A heavy, heady tang that curled behind the nose and settled deep in the sinuses. He'd smelled it in Madam Bell's lounge. The hotel room was dark, the curtains drawn. A small case lay on the bureau, half packed. On the table, a folded silk handkerchief embroidered with the initials E.B. He stopped. Drawn across the bed was Emmaline Bell's cardigan, the one she had worn when she answered the door in Highgate. A glass bottle stood on the marble sink-top, cloudy with a drying residue at its base. On smelling it, he recognised the same earthy scent found in Henrietta's glass, and in Jasper's medicine. Without delay, Edwin wrapped the bottle carefully in his handkerchief.

Edwin stepped through the grand arched entry of St. Bartholomew's Hospital, the corridors heavy with the scent of carbolic acid. He found Jonathan Preece in the anatomy theatre, his sleeves rolled up to the elbows and a smear of chalk dust across his waistcoat. The young doctor looked up from his notes, a flicker of surprise in his eyes. 'Edwin? What brings you here?'

Edwin pressed the cloth-wrapped bottle into his friend's hand, lowering his voice. 'I need your expertise, Jonathan. Quietly, if you please. There's been a death . . . and I suspect it was no ordinary ailment.'

Hours later, Jonathan returned, his face pale. 'It's poison,' he said, with a curt nod. 'Conium maculatum, otherwise known as Hemlock. Enough to daze a man, distort his faculties. Taken over weeks, even in small doses, it would disorient the mind – cause hallucinations, paranoia, until, at last, the heart simply stops.'

Edwin sighed. 'Henrietta was not strangled after all. The ribbon was staged. She was being poisoned long before the end. They must have been watching and waiting in order to stage her death so dramatically.'

Edwin summoned his aunt, who in turn sent for the constabulary - no longer able to supress the storm Henreitta's death would unleash. When Archibald Thackery arrived, a great slab of a man with a crimson nose and a handlebar moustache - he filled the parlour like a looming giant.

'So, you're saying, Edwin,' Archibald growled, 'That Miss Wren's demise weren't from a struggle, but slow calculated murder?'

'Precisely,' Edwin replied. 'The pink ribbon was staged, a theatrical flourish, perhaps to incriminate Tilda who sold her the pink ribbon. The truth is more chilling. Henrietta suffered bouts of fear, and perhaps episodes of confusion. It was the poison – hemlock – administered over time. The same poison, I believe, that Emmaline Bell is feeding to her husband, Jasper.'

'Lord preserve us,' muttered Archibald, running a thick thumb beneath his collar.

Edwin folded his hands. 'I believe Emmaline wants to free herself, you see. Jasper was an obstacle. But it wasn't just escape she desired – it was elevation. Love had already knocked at her door. A foreign gentleman, Signor Seighbrecht – wealthy, aloof, and obsessed with a commission for a bridal doll, for his fiancé. But that was before he met Emmaline Bell.'

Archibald narrowed his eyes. 'You're saying he and the Bell woman were entangled?'

Edwin nodded. 'They met at the Fox and Fig. He must have saw her while waiting for Henrietta. Emmaline bewitched him. And together, they began whispering plans. First, to be rid of Jasper. Then, to silence Henreitta Wren. Perhaps his next victim would be his intended bride.' He withdrew the letter from his pocket - Henreitta's scribbled note, scrawled upon the very crest-paper bearing Seigbrecht's seal. 'Henrietta knew,' Edwin said. 'She had uncovered their affair - their plan to elope. So, she created not one doll, but two. The real commission, she buried beneath her floorboards with this letter and one of Seighbrecht's gloves. The second doll - the decoy - she worked on at her table.' He picked the doll up and handed it to Archibald. 'Look closely, and you'll find the lace has tiny uneven stitching on it forming words. They read, his soul is black and he will stop at nothing to have his heart's desire. The message is unmistakable.'

There was silence for a moment before Edwin continued. 'Signor Seigbrecht, though smitten with Emmaline, would never risk a scandal. His reputation, his fortune - would all burn if Henrietta exposed the truth. So, with Emmaline's help, he chose the quieter path. They silenced the dollmaker.'

'And now?' asked Agatha, as she warmed her hands beside the fire.

'Now,' said Archibald, in a steely voice, 'They shall be arrested while I look into the murder of Henreitta Wren, and the attempted murder of Jasper Bell.'

'You'll find Signor Seigbrecht has not checked out of the Imperium. And Emmaline Bell, well, she left behind her cardigan in his room, but not her guilt. Let them be found. Let justice be done.'

Archibald nodded solemnly. 'By thunder, Mr Linton. You ought to be with Scotland Yard yourself.'

Edwin offered a weary smile. 'I'll settle for a pen and paper, Constable. Though I daresay this story may yet be worth publishing after all.'

Author Bio:

Having had a passion for reading and writing since an early age, this passion has only grown over the years. Marti M. McNair has been writing since she could pick up a pen and after her children flew the nest she turned to writing seriously. Her main focus is writing for a YA audience, and her books feature dystopian settings, dark political undercurrents and places her characters in precarious situations which tests them to the limit. She was the winner of the prestigious Scottish Association of Writers, Barbara Hammond Prize. She is also a partner in Auscot Publishing and retreats and a graphic designer for Writers' narrative eMagazine.

Chapter Six

SECOND SIGHT

Lisabeth Earley

Nineteen-year-old Gwen Henderson has a secret: she can glimpse the final memories of the dead. When a beloved small-town singer vanishes, Gwen teams up with Barry Lawson, a sharp-eyed skeptic with more charm than she expects. Together they uncover the truth hidden by the river – and discover a connection neither of them saw coming.

Spring 1989

I stepped out into the sunshine with a check in my hand and a pit in my stomach. Payment always felt strange. Like I'd sold something I shouldn't have. A piece of someone's grief, maybe. Or a truth that didn't want to be found.

Barry Lawson followed me down the walkway, hands in the pockets of his jeans, a hesitant half-smile on his face. I knew the type. Clean-cut, smart eyes behind those horn-rimmed glasses, college ring flashing on one hand. Probably wore suits to class presentations. Now he looked like he was trying to figure out what to do with his hands.

'I have a question,' he said.

I kept walking. 'Only one?'

He laughed, quick and surprised. 'Okay, fair. One for now.'

I unlocked my car door and turned to face him. 'Shoot.'

'How'd you know my uncle was cheating on my aunt?'

There it was. No warm-up, no easing into it. Straight to the real question.

I slid the check into my bag and shrugged. 'Sometimes people leave trails they don't realise.'

'That's not an answer,' he said. 'You knew the name of the woman he was seeing. You knew what hotel they went to. You even knew the kind of dumb perfume she wore. My aunt confirmed it.'

I didn't say anything.

He studied me, squinting a little like sunlight alone couldn't account for how hard it was to see me clearly. 'You're a psychic, aren't you?'

I laughed, mostly to buy myself a second. 'Is that your theory?'

'Look, I don't know what you are. But that wasn't luck. You knew. And I think you could help a lot more people if you stopped solving little side cases for spiteful relatives.'

'You calling your aunt spiteful?'

'I'm calling her wealthy, bitter, and newly empowered,' he said. 'And grateful to you, by the way.'

I leaned against the roof of my car. 'You came out here to thank me?'

'I came out here to propose something.'

'Marriage?'

He laughed again, nervous this time. 'Business.'

I waited.

'There's a missing persons case that's gone cold. Young woman named Sarah Taylor. You probably know the name.'

'Small town. Of course I do.'

'She went missing a few weeks ago. Last seen after a performance at the rec centre. Left behind her guitar and her bag, but no one's seen her since. Her family's not rich, but there's a community reward and some media interest. If someone could help crack it... that could open up more cases. More clients.'

'And more money?'

He smiled. 'I majored in business. I'm not ashamed of that part.'

'And what would you do in this little arrangement? I'm guessing you don't have a supernatural gift of your own.'

He opened the passenger door of his car but didn't get in. 'I have research skills. People skills. Logic. And gas money.'

I considered. Then: 'You're offering to be my Watson?'

'Only if you get to be Holmes.'

I closed my car door and crossed my arms. 'You want to talk details?'

'Burgers and fries at Palmer's?'

I glanced back at the house. The curtains had shifted. Barry's aunt was probably watching, making sure I didn't get roped into anything else. 'Fine,' I said. 'But I'm not psychic.'

He grinned. 'You're something.'

I got in the car and pulled out slowly, watching him in the rearview mirror as he jogged to his own. He didn't know it yet, but he'd just signed up for something much stranger than gas money and logic could account for.

Palmer's was quiet for a Friday afternoon. A couple of booths were full, mostly older folks nursing coffees and watching the world go by. The air smelled like fryer oil and sweet pickles, and the waitress behind the counter gave Barry a smile like she knew his usual.

We slid into a booth near the window. He let me take the side with the better view, which I appreciated even though I didn't say it. I liked knowing what was around me. Who was coming. Who was watching.

He opened his menu like he needed to think about it. I didn't bother.

'You said Sarah Taylor?' I asked.

He nodded. 'Twenty-two. Local celebrity. Sang at every town event. Pretty much everyone in Piney Hills knew her name, even if they didn't know her personally.'

'She disappeared after a concert at the rec centre.'

'Right. Her guitar was still there, along with her purse and coat. No signs of a struggle. No one saw her leave.'

The waitress stopped by and took our orders. Cheeseburgers, fries, iced teas. She winked at Barry on her way back to the kitchen.

'Friend of yours?' I asked.

He ignored the bait. 'There's a five-thousand-dollar reward for information. Her family put it up. Her parents are gone, but she lived with her aunt. The local radio station's run a couple of segments on it, so it's getting attention.'

'That doesn't mean there's anything left to find.'

'You haven't tried yet.'

I sat back. 'What's your angle, Barry? You want to get rich off missing persons cases?'

'I want to work with someone who's not afraid to look where the police won't. You see things, Gwen. I don't know how, but I watched you crack a case in under a week that had lawyers stumped for a year. I'm not asking you to explain it. Just to use it.'

I glanced out the window. The town square was just beyond the diner's parking lot. Everything was blooming, too bright, too alive for a conversation about a girl who might be dead.

'I can't promise anything.'

'I'm not asking for promises. Just a chance.'

The waitress returned with our food. The smell of hot grease and salt broke the moment, and I was glad for it. Barry doused his fries in ketchup and didn't push me to speak.

I picked up a fry and dipped it in his ketchup without asking.

'I'll need to go where she was last seen,' I said. 'And I want to talk to the aunt. Alone.'

His expression said he hadn't expected a yes, at least not this easily. He leaned forward, smiling. 'We can do that.'

I met his eyes. 'We?'

'You're going to need backup. Someone to take notes. Look things up. Keep you grounded.'

'You offering to be my intern now?'

He grinned. 'Only if I get to add it to my résumé.'

I ate another fry. The truth was, I didn't like doing this alone. And I hated being wrong. If Sarah Taylor was out there, alive or dead, I wanted to know what had happened. And something about the way Barry looked at me, like I wasn't crazy, like I might even be useful, made me think it might be less awful to have someone along for the ride.

I nodded toward his fries. 'Finish those and let's get to work.'

When I got back to the house, Gran was on the porch with a bowl of butter beans in her lap and a worn dishtowel across her knees. The screen door creaked behind me as I stepped out to join her.

'Palmer's again?' she asked without looking up.

'Barry Lawson bought me lunch.'

She gave a little hmm and popped another bean into the bowl. 'The aunt's boy.'

'Sort of. He's her nephew, not her kid.'

'I know who he is. He was here this morning.'

That stopped me. 'What?'

'Dropped off a basket of pears from his aunt. Said thank you, and that he hoped you'd be willing to work with him on something else.'

'Did he say that?'

She nodded, smiling to herself like she knew a joke I didn't. 'He's got curious eyes. The kind that don't stay where you put them. Told him he ought to be careful poking around in places most folks stay out of.'

I leaned against the porch post. 'You didn't scare him off, did you?'

Gran chuckled. 'Didn't seem scared. Just intrigued. I expect you know the type.'

I thought about his grin over fries and the way he'd looked at me when I'd said yes. Like he knew something was starting and wasn't sure yet if it would be big or dangerous. Maybe both.

'He wants to help with the Taylor case,' I said. 'Wants to work together. I haven't told him anything.'

'Yet.'

'Yet.'

Gran flicked a bean into the bowl. 'Just remember, baby. Some folks come looking for answers. Others come looking for you. Don't get the two mixed up.'

I didn't say anything to that. I just watched the sun slide down the edge of the pine trees and tried not to feel like something had shifted.

Gran always knew things before I did.

We met in front of the rec centre the next morning, just after eight. The place was locked, but Barry had called someone who knew someone, and within five minutes, a sleepy-eyed janitor let us in and told us to lock up when we left.

The gym still smelled faintly of popcorn and warm plastic chairs. A banner from the spring talent show hung half-crooked over the bleachers. Sarah Taylor had sung here last. I remembered the flyer. Acoustic set. Local favourite. Final song around nine. And then nothing.

'She usually set up here,' Barry said, walking toward the low stage. 'Same spot every time.'

I nodded and stepped up, scanning the space. There was still a music stand in the corner. Some leftover tape on the floor where the mic cords used to be. I closed my eyes and let myself breathe her in. Not her perfume or her presence, but the echo of something left behind.

And there it was. That tug.

I knelt beside the stage. A single bobby pin was tucked into the crack between two floorboards. I reached for it. The metal was cool, ordinary. But when my fingers closed around it, I felt it.

Not sound. Not sight. Just sensation.

Grief. Heavy. Muffled. Like a song played underwater.

'She was sad,' I murmured.

Barry looked up. 'You feel something?'

I nodded. 'It's faint. Not violent. Just... weighted. She didn't run. She drifted.'

He didn't ask how I knew. Just waited, his eyes steady on mine.

I stood slowly and brushed my hands on my jeans. 'I need to see where she would have walked. If she left on foot.'

He stepped aside. 'Back door's this way.'

Outside, the morning sun hit the pavement in streaks of

gold. I followed the sidewalk down the side of the building, pausing where it curved toward the street. Barry stayed quiet, letting me think.

'She went that way,' I said finally, pointing toward the path that led to the riverwalk.

He glanced at me. 'You sure?'

'No,' I said. 'But my gut is.'

He gave a little smile. 'I trust your gut.'

Something in his voice made me look at him. He wasn't humouring me. He wasn't afraid either.

'I don't know why,' I said. 'You barely know me.'

He held my gaze. 'That may be true. But I'm already sure of one thing.'

'What's that?'

'You don't pretend to be someone you're not.'

I looked away first. The path to the river stretched ahead like a dare.

'We'll check it out,' I said, my voice a little steadier than I felt. 'But I go first.'

He smiled again. 'Of course you do.'

The riverwalk was quiet, the morning mist still clinging to the trees. The air smelled damp and earthy, a sharp contrast to the warmth of the rec centre. I pulled my jacket tighter around me as Barry walked beside me, the gravel crunching under our boots.

We followed the winding path that hugged the river's edge, searching for anything Sarah might have left behind. The leaves rustled with each step, but no other sounds stirred.

About halfway down, an elderly man sat on a bench, feeding pigeons. He looked up as we approached, eyes sharp despite the wrinkles.

'Morning,' I said.

He nodded but didn't speak.

Barry stepped forward. 'You live around here?'

'Been here all my life,' he said, voice gravelly. 'Seen a lot of things pass through.'

We exchanged a glance. I motioned gently. 'Did you see anything unusual the night Sarah Taylor disappeared?'

His eyes clouded over. 'Maybe. I thought I saw her get into a car by the old mill. Didn't think much of it then.'

Barry frowned. 'A car? That doesn't fit with the story we've been hearing.'

I felt a cold prick inside me. That kind of witness account could send us chasing shadows.

'Did you see the driver?' I asked.

He shook his head. 'Nope. Too dark, and I wasn't paying close enough attention. Just seemed odd.'

I thanked him and we continued down the path, the old man's words hanging in the mist like smoke.

Near a cluster of willows, I spotted something half-buried in the dirt. A guitar pick, worn and scratched. I picked it up and let the weight settle in my palm.

The moment I touched it, Sarah's sorrow came rushing in, sharp, suffocating. She was standing there, at the edge of the river, trembling like she wanted to run but couldn't move.

I closed my eyes to steady the wave. Barry's hand brushed my arm, warm and grounding.

'Gwen?' His voice was soft.

I swallowed hard. 'It's heavier than I thought.'

He nodded. 'I'm here.'

The ache in my chest was raw, but Barry's presence made it bearable.

'We should keep going,' I said. 'But I need to rest soon.'

He offered a small smile, one that said he understood without pressuring me.

At the end of the path, the river curved wide and dark. The sun had burned away the mist, leaving a glare on the water.

'Think she was here?' Barry asked.

'I do,' I whispered.

'We'll find her,' he promised.

For the first time since this all began, I believed him.

The small house on Elm Street smelled of lavender and old books, the kind of place where memories seemed to stick to the wallpaper. Barry and I stepped inside quietly. The front door creaked softly behind us, and I felt a weight settle in the air, like grief that hadn't quite loosened its grip.

Ms. Turner, Sarah's aunt, met us in the living room. She was a woman shaped by years of worry, her hands rough but gentle, her eyes tired but sharp. A faded silver locket hung from her neck, catching the late afternoon light as she offered us chairs.

'I'm so glad you came,' she said, voice steady but edged with sorrow. 'It's been hard, not knowing.'

Barry nodded respectfully. 'We're here to help.'

Ms. Turner took a deep breath and began. 'That night, Sarah had just finished her set at the rec centre. She was radiant, like always, but I could tell something was off. She seemed... distant. After the show, she left her guitar and her bag at the rec centre. She said she needed some air, went out for a walk, but she never came back.'

I listened closely, picturing the scene in my mind. A young woman haunted by invisible shadows.

'I waited up for her,' Mrs. Turner continued, voice trembling slightly. 'But she never walked through that door again.'

Barry and I exchanged a glance. The pieces were beginning to fit, but the picture was still blurry.

Ms. Turner stood and led us down the narrow hallway, the floorboards creaking beneath our feet. Sarah's room was at the end, bathed in fading sunlight through lace curtains. The walls were covered in posters of bands and faded newspaper clippings from her performances. A guitar rested against the bedpost, silent and waiting.

I stepped inside slowly, my fingers brushing over a stack of notebooks on the dresser. The room smelled faintly of jasmine and old paper. On the nightstand, a small velvet box caught my eye.

Ms. Turner watched me carefully. 'That was Sarah's most treasured possession. She wore it every day.'

I lifted the lid, revealing a delicate silver locket, its surface worn smooth by years of touch. Inside was a faded photo of a young woman with kind eyes. Sarah's mother, I guessed.

Holding the locket, I felt a flicker of something. A whisper of emotion, like a half-remembered dream. Not a full vision, but enough to tell me this was more than just a keepsake.

Barry stepped closer. 'Looks like you found your key.'

I nodded slowly, slipping the locket into my pocket. The room seemed to hold its breath, waiting.

Ms. Turner's voice broke the silence. 'If there's anything you need, just ask. We all want to know what happened to Sarah.'

I met Barry's eyes. There was a quiet understanding between us. This case was bigger than we thought. And somehow, I felt the weight of that locket pressing against my side, a silent promise that Sarah's story wasn't finished.

Back at my place, I sat cross-legged on my bed, the locket warm in my palm.

Barry was at my desk across the room, flipping through one of Sarah's notebooks we'd borrowed from her aunt. His brow was furrowed, lips moving slightly as he read lyrics or maybe diary entries, piecing together the girl we never got to meet.

I turned the locket over in my hand. The photo inside, still grainy and soft at the edges, showed Sarah and her mother, cheek to cheek, smiling like nothing bad could ever touch them. But it had.

I closed my eyes and let the weight of it sink into me.

At first, nothing.

Then...

A tug behind my eyes. A drop in the air pressure. And the sound of breath.

Sarah's.

I wasn't looking at her; I was her.

I felt the worn wood of the bridge railing under my fingers, cool from the night air. The moon glimmered on the water below. My chest ached, not from cold, but from something worse. Loneliness. Exhaustion. That hollow kind of sorrow that didn't even need a reason anymore.

I can't do this forever. The thought wasn't spoken, but it echoed like a bell.

Someone had shouted her name earlier that night. Too loud. Too sharp. Her manager. Angry that she'd walked off after the show. Accusing her of wasting potential. 'You think your voice is all you need? You think that's going to get you out of this town?' Words like fists.

And she had walked. Just walked. Not to run away. Not to die. Just to escape the noise, the weight.

But at the edge of the bridge, the river whispered something different. Something quiet and dark and strangely peaceful.

I gasped and dropped the locket.

It hit the quilt with a soft thud, but it felt like thunder.

Barry was at my side in an instant. 'Gwen?'

I pressed the heel of my hand to my forehead. 'She didn't plan it. She didn't pack a bag. She just... broke. And no one noticed.'

His hand hovered just above mine, like he didn't want to startle me but didn't want to leave me alone either. 'You saw her?'

'I was her.'

We sat in silence for a moment, the room too still.

'I've never seen it that clearly before,' I said finally.

Barry's voice was quiet. 'Are you okay?'

I nodded, but my throat felt thick. 'It's not just knowing what happened. It's feeling what she felt. It stays with me.'

He moved his hand and, without speaking, took mine gently in his. His touch was warm, grounding.

'You shouldn't have to carry that alone.'

I looked at him. His expression was open, no trace of curiosity or fear, just concern. Maybe even something more.

'You're not what I expected,' I said.

He smiled, a little crooked, a little shy. 'Neither are you.'

The sky was overcast when we returned to the river. The wind carried the scent of damp pine and something colder underneath. We parked near the walking trail and hiked past the old willows, following the same path Sarah had taken.

I held the locket tightly in my pocket. It had cooled overnight, but it still carried weight. I couldn't stop thinking about that last moment on the bridge. The calm before the silence.

Barry kept pace beside me without speaking. He didn't need to ask what I'd seen. He trusted I would tell him what mattered when it was time.

We reached the spot where the river curved, just beyond the edge of town. The water was slow here, dark and still, like it had secrets to keep.

'She was here,' I said quietly.

Barry scanned the trees. 'You're sure?'

'I felt it.'

We walked along the bank, stepping carefully through brambles and wet grass. The earth had softened from recent rain, and my boots sank with each step. I moved slowly, searching for a sign. A piece of clothing. Jewellery. Something the current might have spared.

Then I saw it.

Caught between a fallen branch and the muddy shore was a scrap of fabric. Pale blue, nearly the same colour as the sky when it clouded over. I knelt and reached for it.

A wave of sorrow washed over me again, sharp and unmistakable. My breath caught.

'She's here,' I whispered.

Barry crouched beside me. 'We need to call someone.'

I nodded. My voice didn't want to work.

He touched my shoulder, gentle and steady. 'You found her, Gwen. You did it.'

Tears welled in my eyes, unexpected but not unwelcome. I hadn't realized how heavy the search had become until it ended.

'It's not just about finding her,' I said, my voice cracking. 'It's about understanding why she never came home.'

'And now people will understand,' he said. 'Because of you.'

I turned to him, wiping at my cheek. 'Because of us.'

His hand lingered a second longer, then fell away. We stood together as the breeze stirred the leaves, both of us staring down at the quiet water.

I pulled the locket from my pocket and held it in my palm.

'You're going home, Sarah,' I said softly.

Barry didn't speak, but I felt him beside me. Solid. Present.

We walked back the way we came, slower this time. Neither of us said much, but I didn't feel alone.

Ms. Turner met us at the front door before we could knock. She must have seen the car pull up. Her hands were trembling, clasped tightly in front of her chest.

'You found her,' she said. Not a question. Just a statement, quiet and sure.

I nodded. 'We called the police. They'll send someone to recover her. But we stayed until we were sure.'

Tears pooled in her eyes, and she reached for the doorframe to steady herself. 'Thank you,' she whispered. 'I didn't want it to be true. But I needed to know.'

'She didn't suffer,' I said gently. 'She was overwhelmed. She didn't mean to disappear. She just... didn't know where else to go.'

Ms. Turner let out a soft sob and covered her mouth with one hand. Barry stepped forward and offered her his arm. She took it, and together we guided her to the living room.

The house felt different than before. Still full of grief, but not the same sharp-edged kind. It had softened now, like sorrow with a place to go.

Before we left, Ms. Turner pressed the locket into my palm.

'She would have wanted you to have this,' she said. 'You brought her home.'

I tried to give it back, but she closed my fingers around it. 'Keep it. Just don't forget her.'

'I won't.'

Barry and I walked out into the late afternoon light. The sun had broken through the clouds, slanting gold across the front yard.

He leaned against the car and looked at me like he wasn't quite sure what to say. I wasn't either.

'You okay?' he asked.

'I will be.'

He nodded, thoughtful. 'You did something real. Not just... whatever it is you do. You gave that woman peace.'

I looked down at the locket, its surface warm in the sunlight. 'I've spent a long time thinking my ability was more of a burden than a gift.'

He studied me for a moment. 'It's both. But you don't have to carry it alone.'

I looked up at him then. Really looked. The worry in his

eyes, the softness in his smile. The way he had stood beside me without asking for anything in return.

'I'm not used to people sticking around,' I said.

'Well,' he said, grinning slightly, 'I've got nowhere better to be.'

A laugh caught in my throat, but it felt good. Lighter.

We stood there a minute longer, the quiet stretching between us, not uncomfortable. Just full of possibility.

I slid into the passenger seat without another word.

Barry got in and turned the key. 'So,' he said, backing out of the driveway, 'what do we do now?'

I smiled out the window, still holding the locket in my hand.

'We wait for the next case.'

A few days later, I was on the porch shelling peas with Gran when Barry's car pulled into the driveway.

She looked up without missing a beat. 'You expecting company?'

'Not exactly,' I said, but my heart had already started to skip.

Barry climbed out with a bag of takeout in one hand and a crooked smile on his face. 'Thought you might like a burger. And maybe a new case.'

Gran gave me a sideways glance. 'That boy's going to keep you on your toes.'

I stood to meet him at the steps. 'A new case already?'

He handed me the bag. 'Lady down in Pine Creek swears her husband's haunted. Figured it was either a ghost or a jealous mistress. Either way, sounds like a job for us.'

I raised an eyebrow. 'Us, huh?'

Barry looked down at me, his smile softening. 'Unless you're planning to go solo.'

I shook my head. 'No. I think I work better with a partner.'

He gave a quiet, satisfied nod.

From the porch, Gran called, 'He can stay for dinner, if he peels potatoes.'

Barry grinned. 'Deal.'

I stepped aside and let him follow me into the kitchen, the locket still tucked safely in my jacket pocket. I wasn't sure what this was yet. This partnership, this friendship, this pull I felt when he looked at me like I was more than the girl who could see the dead.

But I was willing to find out.

Author Bio:

Lisabeth Earley, the architect behind enchanting cozy mysteries, weaves tales as intricate as her crochet patterns. With a knack for crafting suspenseful plots, Lisabeth invites readers into a world where the intrigue is as warm and comforting as a hand-made blanket. When not penning captivating mysteries, she indulges in the soothing rhythm of crochet hooks, creating masterpieces that mirror the intricacies of her storytelling. Lisabeth's love for family shines through in her characters, inspired by the joyous chaos of spoiling her grandchildren. Her mysteries aren't just whodunnits; they're invitations to curl up with a cup of tea, a cozy blanket, and lose oneself in a world where every thread unraveled leads to delightful revelations. Lisabeth Earley, a wordsmith and yarn whisperer, crafts mysteries that unravel seamlessly, leaving readers hooked from the first stitch to the final clue.

Chapter Seven

BLACKMAIL BY DEGREES

Gareth Williams

The year is 1920. The place Cambridge. An idyllic college is thrown into turmoil by a spate of escalating thefts. Joseph Bidwell is as dedicated as his father who was head porter before him. Having survived the First World War and a global pandemic, he will do anything to protect this place of safety. With the college's reputation hanging in the balance, obstructed by eccentric professors and distracted by concerns for his own family, Joseph draws on his compassion and the support of his shrewd wife to investigate. Is there one thief or several? Is the motive love, greed or something more political? As Cambridge prepares for a vote that may change the face of the university forever, the late spring air is full of questions but precious few answers.

Joseph looks out from the Porters' Lodge at a procession of yellow ducklings waddling after their mother towards the river. His face creases into a smile and his big hands fold yesterday's *Cambridge Daily News*.

He approves of women receiving degrees alongside the boys who think they are already men. High time. He doesn't like the thought of trailing Oxford.

At least the resumption of the boat race saw the Light Blues win by four lengths in March. Five years without a race. Five years ruined by war. The smile drops from between his mutton chop whiskers.

Joseph eases the weight off his left leg where splinters from a shell ripped his thigh apart. A familiar figure appears from Tudor Quad onto the high-backed bridge.

He raises a hand, confident Ethel's sharp eyes will spot the gesture. Sure enough, she returns his wave with a feather duster as if brushing away the last of the morning mist, and he is smiling again. She moves easily across the court in a defiantly floral housecoat.

Where would he be without Ethel? Certainly not worrying about Ronnie, a red-headed junior porter, and his intentions towards Agnes. As Ethel's head appears through the door, he admires everything she has gifted their daughter. She is slight but strong, poised and alert, her blonde hair silvering, but still too beautiful to have said yes when he proposed.

Ethel has a twinkle in her blue eyes. 'Have you heard, Joe?'

For a moment Joseph is confused. He shrugs, playing the part he was made for, to be the other half that makes them whole. 'Heard what, my love?'

'Professor Pocklington's fob watch is missing. He's making a fearful fuss, clucking like a chicken whose beady eyes see the axe.'

Joseph rubs his crisply shaven chin as he absorbs this image. 'Did you help him search? You know how absent-minded he is.'

Ethel's expression warns him not to second-guess the

college's senior housekeeper. 'It's gone, all right. Maybe left in the mathematics faculty? He's in a right state, no matter. The watch was a gift from his father when he graduated Senior Wrangler.'

Joseph grimaces. There will be no rest until the watch is found. Gaining the top first-class degree in mathematics endows legendary status. Rupert Pocklington lives entirely in a world of numbers since his ancient father was subtracted by the Spanish Flu last year. The loss hit him hard. Without Ethel, he would likely walk around the quads in his underdrawers. He cannot abide any disturbance to his routine, although this only randomly includes remembering to sleep or eat.

'Will he let me handle it?'

Ethel looks over her shoulder, waiting for a pair of lanky students in matching college scarves to finish scrabbling in their pigeonholes for post that isn't there.

'The professor is a genius but it will take him days to reach the conclusion most of his colleagues would leap to immediately.' Ethel's measured delivery invests her insight with pathos.

'Which is?' Joseph is afraid he already knows the answer.

'That one of us took it, of course.'

'A college servant? That would be a disaster,' Joseph muses, absentmindedly tracing the masthead of his newspaper before pressing a perfect thumbprint on his forehead.

'If any of us were guilty, it would be,' Ethel counters, using a licked corner of a rag to remove the ink.

'I must get onto this right away,' he says, reaching for his bowler hat on a hook above his head. 'There'll be an almighty furore until blame is firmly pinned somewhere.'

'Below stairs, you can be certain,' Ethel reiterates before heading out to check on her team. Joseph follows her from the lodge and watches her disappear into the embrace of honeyed neo-classical buildings.

Joseph loves the symmetrical poise of New Court but he is not sorry to cross the bridge, doffing his hat to a giggling group in pleated skirts punting waywardly down from Scudamore's Boatyard.

He passes through the weathered brick arch into a tunnel beneath the Master's Lodge. The corridor is so gloomy even a man of barely five foot nine inches hunches his shoulders.

As he limps into Tudor Quad, the sun is a gauze-veiled orb hovering above vibrant grass. He recalls the college gardener's reply when asked by a visitor how to achieve such an immaculate lawn.

'Four hundred years.'

The professor's rooms are in the far corner, up a turning staircase of creaking wood that smells of ancient damp and stale tobacco. Joseph is sure the smell inhabited this stairwell long before the professor. No doubt it was well established, even before his father joined the college staff.

The sign at the foot of the stairs indicates Professor Pocklington is currently in, so Joseph grasps the curve of the rail and begins to climb, wincing with every other step. He knocks three times in quick succession and composes himself.

'Enter,' comes the muffled reply.

Joseph operates the latch and steps inside. There is little light in the compact hall but a door is open ahead, revealing stained glass celebrating an early benefactor to the college. Weak shafts of refracted sunlight dapple the dark floorboards with shards of the spectrum.

Joseph does not spot the professor until he shuffles from behind his corner desk to stand quivering amidst the kaleido-scopic display. A tattered cardigan hangs awkwardly on the mathematician's gaunt frame because he has misaligned its leather-covered buttons.

'Ah, Bidwell. Your good lady has told you?' The professor's voice is as unsteady as his stance and his parchment-dry skin rustles against his checked shirt.

'Most regrettable, Professor. Can you tell me when you were last in possession of the fob watch?'

'It was a gift, you know? From my father.' Pocklington's dull-brown eyes are moist and he is shaking so much that Joseph reaches out. The professor does not resist as he is guided towards the safety of his desk chair.

'His passing was a great sadness.' Joseph spots a tendril of smoke emanating from the professor's cardigan pocket. 'If I may, Professor?' He leans across the desk to pull a well-chewed briar-wood pipe free before patting discreetly at the smouldering tan-wool garment. Professor Pocklington regards his pipe with surprise before reaching out tentatively. Joseph watches blood-less lips puff until the bowl's maw glows orange, and an aroma of sweet citrus fills the air.

'Ogden's St. Bruno flake?' Joseph asks, remembering the distinct smell of his father's pipe tobacco.

The professor frowns and reaches for a round-edged tin sitting atop notation more impenetrable than hieroglyphics to Joseph's eyes. He picks up the tin, peers at the label, and sets it down again without comment.

'Your fob watch, Professor? Do you recall where you last saw it?' Joseph asks gently.

'Why, on its chain, right here,' a heavily veined hand pats his left side. Fumbling fingers laboriously unbutton the scruffy cardigan to reveal a herringbone waistcoat.

Joseph notices the third button is missing. 'Was this where you fastened your chain, Professor?'

'Yes, I think that's right,' comes an unconvincing reply.

'On a T-bar chain?'

A hesitant nod as a yellow nail runs down mother of pearl buttons to the gap.

'Is it possible the chain came loose or a button failed?' Joseph prompts.

A crease puzzles across the mathematician's high forehead like an unbalanced equation, before retreating into his hairline.

'Well, yes. Quite possibly. I suppose I must just accept it is gone? You must think me a fusspot but it did mean such a lot.'

Tears drip from surprisingly fine lashes and a shaking hand withdraws a crumpled white handkerchief from a trouser pocket.

'I will alert my team. Hopefully, we will discover it somewhere in the precincts of the college.'

❀

Walking towards the Porters' Lodge, Joseph cannot help thinking of his own Pa, dead from the same epidemic that left the professor so alone. Apprenticing to his father was as natural as breathing and cheering on Rovers against Granta on the grass of Parker's Piece. He suspects the professor knows nothing of football but he does understand the loss of a parent, which is what his fuss over the fob watch is really all about.

He spots Ronnie yawning like a hungry fledgling as he exits the Porters' Lodge. The junior porter senses the scrutiny.

'Chasing that night climber really wore me out,' Ronnie explains cryptically.

'You were doing what last night?' Joseph barks.

'I entered it in the logbook,' squeaks Ronnie.

Joseph scowls. He has let his interview with Professor Pocklington shake his routine and he is paying for it. 'Sorry, Ronnie. Tell me about this trespasser. Some chancer up from a London gang, stealing to order?'

Ronnie looks doubtful. 'A whippet in black, I saw, spidering over Butcher's Lane gate, and up a drainpipe. He scuttled across the roof. Picked him up disappearing over the wall into the Fellows' Garden. Flushed him out and he legged it along the river path. He dived into the Cam where the boundary wall blocks the way.'

Joseph rubs his chin. A London gang would surely target one of the college treasures? 'Well, he couldn't have taken the professor's fob watch, could he? Not if he swam for it. Perhaps he was testing our security for some future larceny?'

He has yet to hang up his bowler after an absent-minded brushing when the rosy cheeks of his daughter appear.

'Dad, you won't believe it, but there's a mob on its way. Someone has stolen a ring belonging to Mr. Bottomley and all The Boars are up in arms.'

'Make yourself scarce, my girl. We don't need you mixed up in this,' Joseph's avuncular face struggles for the requisite sternness but he replaces his hat and walks out into the courtyard to await the dining club's delegation.

The son of a viscount, Percival Bottomley is a chinless misogynist and a coward but with a dozen followers at his back, he stomps across the bridge belligerently.

'You there, Bidwell,' he brays, 'one of the college servants has stolen my birthright.' Joseph holds his tongue. 'My ring, damn you, always worn by the heir.'

Several hulking fellows in loud waistcoats crowd close, smirking, but Joseph doesn't flinch as he regards Percival Bottomley's puny profile. Could one of them be playing a trick on the unlikeable dullard?

'Mr. Bottomley, that is a serious allegation. If you would accompany me into the Porters' Lodge?'

'Never mind that, I want the culprit dismissed immediately.' Cheers of inebriated support fill the court although it is barely mid-morning.

'Naturally, Mr. Bottomley, if there has been any wrongdoing.'

'What are you, some mealy-mouthed Labour politician? Get on with your job.'

'Of course, Mr. Bottomley but I will need to investigate. It is hard to dismiss a thief until they are apprehended, wouldn't you agree?' As head porter, he should know better. What would his father say? It never pays to confront entitled Old Etonian poll men who fill their days with fox hunting and wine, pranks and jaunts to houses of ill repute without any expectation of an honours degree.

Joseph cannot help a fleeting smile. The Hon. Percival Bottomley deserves no honours and will go down with no more than a pass degree, just like his father.

'What are you grinning about?' shrieks Bottomley, spittle flying. Joseph stiffens his back as if still on the parade ground and fixes Percival with a steely gaze.

'Very well, let's get on with it,' Bottomley concedes.

He has missed lunch. He has endured the prattling of a boy who publishes pamphlets railing against awarding women degrees while his own presence is an affront to the very concept of a selective university. Bottomley pointed the finger not only at college staff but also several grammar school boys on scholarships.

The aimless heir even suggested Agnes might be responsible as she cleaned for him before Ethel moved her daughter beyond the unpleasant attentions of the dining club set. Joseph was prevented from spluttering defiance by an insidious thought. Might besotted Ronnie have been so foolish? Stealing a ring to dazzle his sweetheart? He was a light-fingered lad before Joseph took him in hand and offered him a job.

He faces a difficult interview with the master of the college this afternoon. Rummaging in his desk drawer, he finds the remains of a pasty wrapped in greaseproof paper. He inspects grey meat suspiciously before throwing the stale husk into the bin. He does track down a paper bag containing three Everton mints in his coat pocket. He sucks black-and-white stripes aggressively, seeking the soft centre.

At least the denizens of the dining club are unaware of Professor Pocklington's missing watch. Should that news leak there will be a witch hunt where all questions of proof or guilt will be jettisoned.

Ethel appears with a plate of cold cuts covered by a tea towel.

'Agnes tipped me off, thought you could use a bite.'

'Do you think anyone on the staff could have stolen Bottomley's ring?' He doesn't mention Ronnie. He knows Ethel thinks the boy isn't good enough for their daughter. If he has taken the ring, then she is right.

Ethel perches on the corner of his desk. 'How did it go with Professor Pocklington?'

'He won't be any trouble but Bottomley...'

'Will make a stink because his father will disown him if he doesn't retrieve the family heirloom. Are you going to involve the Bulldogs?'

'He will accuse Agnes if we don't get the thing back,' Joseph confesses as he considers summoning the university police force.

Ethel's supple body freezes and her blue eyes glint. 'He will lose more than a ring if he threatens my daughter.'

'Who is threatening Agnes?' pipes a squeaky organ pipe of a voice from a blushing face.

'Never you mind, Ronnie,' Joseph tells the junior porter more gruffly than he intends. He studies the freckled youth's fiery hair spilling over his collar. 'Take your bowler off indoors,' he adds, spotting Ethel appraising Ronnie critically. She is still bristling about the threat to Agnes.

'Calm yourself, Ethel. I can handle Bottomley. What brings you back to the lodge half way through your rounds, Ronnie?'

Ronnie twists the narrow rim of his hat nervously. 'I was about to leave Copper Birch Court when the bursar caught me. He is in a right state. There's been a theft. He sent me to summon you.'

Joseph exchanges a morose look with Ethel.

'What's happening to this place?' she laments.

As he crosses the turgid river once more, Joseph tries to make sense of three alleged thefts in a single day. When was the last report of stealing? Not since he came back from the war. The skulking night climber. Did he steal the ring? Easy to transport and unaffected by a dip in the dirty river but hard to fence.

'Bidwell, thank heavens,' a bony finger extends in his direction. 'The college's First Folio, the Lansbury Bequest, has gone missing.'

Joseph has little formal education but he treasures his leatherbound copy of Shakespeare's plays with marbled facings and a book plate for the mathematics prize in Form IVB. The year he left school to work at college.

Hesperus Walker, the bursar, hurries Joseph into his pedantic office. 'We have to get it back, it's worth more than my house.'

Joseph's eyes settle on a shiny brass lectern set beside an armchair angled in the corner of the room to catch the afternoon light.

The bursar shuffles awkwardly, turning his pinched face away from the empty stand. 'Well, yes, it was here. I have an unofficial understanding with the librarian.'

'When did you last see the volume?' Joseph suspects the understanding is so unofficial that the librarian knows nothing about it. Is this what the night climber was looking for? If so, he must have hidden it to retrieve later.

'I was reading from it just yesterday. *The Merchant of Venice*,' the Bursar replies without irony, fingering half-moon spectacles. 'I found this note in its place this morning.'

Joseph scowls. 'The master will tell you how to vote,' it says in spidery script. Is this about degrees for women at Cambridge? Surely the master favours the status quo?

'Leave it with me, Bursar,' Joseph declares with considerably more confidence than he feels. 'I have my weekly meeting with the master, but I will give the matter my full attention.'

The Master's Lodge is a half-timbered pavilion set atop a brick cloister seemingly too narrow for the task but Joseph pays the building no mind as he traverses the Long Gallery. Sir Appleby Montieth rises from his wing-backed chair, a patrician figure with salt-and-pepper hair and a hook nose.

'Bidwell, on time as always. I trust everything is running smoothly?' A tenuous voice.

'I am afraid it has been a rather trying day, Master,' he replies, seeing no way of softening his news.

'Really, Bidwell? Never mind. I am sure you will handle everything admirably. As you know, the whole university is on tenterhooks as the vote approaches. I am lobbied day and night by fellows and students, past and present. It is exhausting.'

Joseph dismisses any thought the master is orchestrating matters for some political purpose; he lacks both the inclination and imagination. Accepting a delicately flared glass of sherry, he sips slowly, savouring the tangy yeast and almond. He is about to elaborate the spate of disappearances when Lady Millicent Montieth enters through a side door.

'Ah, Bidwell. I thought I heard your voice. Mind if I join, Appleby?' She sits beside her husband without waiting for a reply. Joseph cannot help a smile. The queen and her consort. She appears every week. The daughter of the Bishop of Ely, she is cleverer and better read than her husband. Elegant without haughtiness, she wears a day dress of muted purple and green layers accented with white lace.

'I was informing the master of recent developments.' Joseph notices a folded piece of paper held lightly in Lady Montieth's left hand.

Sensing his attention, the master's wife hands him the note. 'This was left in the master's pigeonhole.'

Appleby Montieth gives his wife a look of surprise. 'I have not seen this missive,' he declares, trying to sound affronted but Lady Millicent ignores his petulance.

Joseph unfolds the middling quality paper and reads aloud.

'Unless the master declares his support and votes in favour, I shall continue my campaign.' A thin, angular, awkward hand and the slightest smudge.

'Continue with what?' asks the master, desperately trying to catch up.

'The thefts, darling,' Lady Montieth explains in a soothing voice, laying a firm hand on her husband's arm. Joseph frowns. How does she know?

'The bursar caught me crossing the bridge. He was most agitated. I gather it was you, Bidwell, who told him of the other incidents?'

Joseph is glad to leave the Master's Lodge. Lady Montieth sees him out with a wry smile. Tall, poised and unbowed at sixty, she is a graduate of University College London, and entirely responsible for her husband's rise.

He decides to take a spell in The Grove, a wood with glades of wildflowers and winding paths. He loves daffodils but even their trumpeting colours cannot cheer his mood.

Someone is trying to blackmail the master by stealing from residents of the college. These are politically motivated acts. Agnes and all the other college servants are off the hook. Why would any of them risk their job so that privileged women might obtain degrees?

Joseph limps past a cheerful stand of orange-nosed daffodils without noticing. He knows the master has influence but would his support be sufficient to sway the vote? Who in the college stands to benefit? He is getting nowhere when Ronnie thunders along the path, limbs arcing awkwardly, nostrils flaring with effort.

'Mr. Bidwell,' the boy pants, 'you won't believe what's happened now.'

Joseph waits patiently. Still nothing. 'Well, how can I tell,

Ronnie?' he eventually asks. The junior porter looks puzzled. 'What has happened?'

'Oh, right, of course. It's the chapel,' blurts out Ronnie. Joseph sighs with relief. At least it isn't another theft.

'What about the chapel?' he prompts more patiently.

'The thingy on the altar, you know, with the three religious paintings, it's gone. This was left in its place.' The junior porter extends a familiar-looking folded piece of paper.

'Let me guess,' Joseph starts in a resigned voice, 'they demand the university awards degrees to women?'

Ronnie stares open-mouthed, shaking his head so hard his bowler is dislodged, releasing the full force of his red hair to put the spring flowers to shame. 'How did you know?' he asks.

The chapel holds a special place in Joseph's heart. The dean secured an archbishop's dispensation to conduct his wedding to Ethel. Agnes was baptised at the font. He steps through the pointed arch that features in all their wedding photographs and turns right through the rood screen. Sure enough, the altar is denuded.

The Annunciation by The Master of Bologna, painted between 1460 and 1480, at about the time the college was founded, is priceless. He stares down the aisle between rows of inward-facing pews at the painful absence. The incongruously sweet spice of peonies fills the high-raftered space.

Joseph considers the two wrought-iron stands, occupying the north and south transepts, supporting lyrical displays of purple and white flowers offset by artful sprays of greenery. Unmistakably the work of Lady Montieth. Might she have seen anything? When does she arrange flowers? Always in the cool of morning.

'Ronnie, did you see the master's wife when you were patrolling this morning?'

'I don't think so, but I was a bit tired after chasing that night climber, so I might not have noticed.'

❦

The clock in the library tower chimes nine o'clock. Joseph should be off duty but he cannot leave. Ethel understands. She has sent Agnes home.

'Do you want to talk?' she asks gently. He pushes back in his chair and finds his last Everton mint. He sucks intermittently as he watches Ronnie lighting the gas lamps. The boy has done a double shift without complaining. Agnes could do a lot worse.

'Why was Bottomley's ring taken? It doesn't fit the pattern,' he ponders aloud.

'Now, I might know the answer to that,' Ethel offers. 'You know I clean his set since it got uncomfortable for Agnes?'

Joseph nods attentively. His wife is the only person better informed than he about college business.

'Well, I was turning down the wastrel's bed just now, while he entertained his cronies in the living room. Talking as if I wasn't there, as always. Anyway, what does he say? Only that the thief left a note. Let me see, yes, that's it: if your father votes for women's degrees, your ring will be returned.'

'So, everything is connected. That's a relief.' Joseph chews cautiously at the toffee centre of his mint and eases his stiff leg beneath the desk.

'Why do you say that?' asks Ethel.

'Because there is only one person to apprehend.'

'And if you don't catch them?'

'More things will go missing,' Joseph admits.

'Have you noticed anything about the objects taken?' Ethel prompts.

'They are escalating in value?'

'Yes. What's worth more than a priceless painting?'

The couple look at each other.

'There can only be one more theft, if the thief sticks to the pattern,' Ethel suggests.

'The Foundation Gift,' Joseph agrees. 'The Regent's Silverware.' The fine tableware which graces the Founder's Day Feast. Probably worth less than the First Folio or the triptych but context is everything. Without the silver, the college cannot fulfil its annual obligations to their founder.

'How would someone manage to steal it?' Ethel mimes the scale of the collection.

'Plus, it's locked in the cellar strongroom. Still, let's go and check on it, right now.'

The big key grates in the lock and the strongroom door complains as Joseph hauls it open. A bare bulb yields a sickly yellow glow that barely dispels the shadows from cobwebbed corners.

Ethel sucks her teeth. The shelves along the river-facing wall are empty bar a folded piece of paper. Joseph hesitates, so she steps inside and retrieves the note.

'You read it,' he says tiredly.

'Hah,' Ethel exclaims. 'Last chance.'

Joseph reaches out and takes the note. Two words. Not much of a clue. But an eloquent ultimatum. How he wishes he was still searching for absent-minded Professor Pocklington's watch.

'Maybe the professor was robbed? But why didn't he get a note?' he asks.

'Have you checked his pigeonhole? He never remembers his post.'

Joseph nods. He has no doubt there will be a note. The professor knows nothing about women. No doubt, he will forget to vote. But if he did? Likely he would vote against.

'When the fob watch went missing, I was sure the professor had just lost it. When Mr. Bottomley accused all and sundry, I suspected a prank by one of his ilk. But when the First Folio was taken, I couldn't deny a crime had been committed. The note left no doubt why. Still, I was fairly sure the watch and the ring would just turn up.'

Joseph aims a slap at his forehead but catches the brim of his bowler, sending it flying. Ethel deftly catches it. She holds it out to her husband but he ignores it. 'But then Lady Montieth handed me the second note, addressed directly to the master. I need to speak with her again.'

'Why?' asks Ethel.

'Peonies,' Joseph replies.

Lady Montieth shows him into a room he has never seen. She looks tired in the bright morning light angling craftily through a small window.

'This is my hideaway,' she explains, looking affectionately around the book-lined space. 'I doubt my husband knows it exists.'

Joseph accepts a straight-backed chair and studies the master's wife. 'I couldn't sleep last night,' he admits.

'Because you had worked it out?' Lady Montieth rejoins calmly.

Joseph nods. If he is wrong, he will lose his job. Ethel and Agnes will surely be dismissed as well.

'I am in the right place, then?' he asks reluctantly.

Millicent Montieth tucks a wisp of hair into the carefully constructed coiffure piled atop her head. 'You are, I judge, precisely where you ought to be.'

Joseph wonders if this is a coded message telling him his job is safe?

'No one notices a woman, you know, unless she breaks a window or chains herself to railings,' Lady Montieth observes. 'That's what made it so easy.'

'But you are the master's wife,' objects Joseph.

'Even so. There is nothing remarkable about my presence on a staircase, crossing a courtyard, entering the chapel or checking inventory in the cellar.'

'You paid Professor Pocklington a visit?'

'I was lobbying for the upcoming vote. He proved intransigent. Despite his bereavement, I found I was angry with him but we shared a sherry nevertheless. He nodded off. I noticed his button hanging by a thread. It was the impulsive action of but a moment to loosen it completely and slip the fob watch from his pocket.'

Joseph kneads his left temple. 'Forgive the impertinence but how did you get beneath his cardigan?'

Lady Montieth laughs heartily. 'He was surprised by my appearing unannounced; he couldn't shed the scruffy thing fast enough.'

'And the student's ring?'

'That took a bit of guile. His father has great influence amongst non-resident members. If he changes his vote, many will follow.'

'I understand you were a suffragette?' She is not wearing purple, green or white but a deep blue today.

'I still am. Why should women not have the vote on the same terms as men? Degrees too, even here.'

'Indeed, but how did you acquire a ring that hardly leaves Bottomley's little finger?'

'Have you watched him play cricket? He really is quite a talented batsman, although prone to running out his partners.'

'He takes the ring off to bat?' Joseph asks, feeling out of his depth.

'I was a decent player as a student. Appleby didn't approve. That's the last thing I gave up on his account.' There is a soreness to this last sentence. 'I help with tea in the pavilion. I overheard Viscount Bottomley ask after the ring. His son admitted he always put it on his mantelpiece for safekeeping.'

'So, all you had to do was slip away from the game and rifle his rooms?' Joseph pauses. 'How did you obtain a key?'

'You shouldn't blame yourself. No one sees a woman, remember? You always hang your keys on that hook in your office when you go off duty.'

'So, I am complicit?'

'As a man? Or head porter?' quips Lady Montieth. 'I dedicated my married life to this university. I won the right to help choose the government but my granddaughter must still go elsewhere for a degree?'

Joseph thinks about Agnes. She was good at school but left at fourteen, as he did. One step at a time.

'I cannot fault your motive, Lady Montieth. I hope the vote is carried,' Joseph admits. 'I suppose I will find the triptych hidden in the vestry?' He receives a graceful nod. 'And the silverware?'

The master's wife opens a hidden door in the book-lined panelling to reveal a secret cupboard crammed with ornate salvers and tankards, cups and goblets, cutlery, candlesticks, and condiment sets.

'How did you transport it all?'

'Have you forgotten the dumb waiter that runs up from the cellar? Two journeys transferred the whole lot.'

Joseph imagines the ageing activist hauling on ropes in the depths of the night. He shakes his head in admiration.

'I think you should return to the Porters' Lodge and telephone the constabulary,' Lady Montieth advises with equanimity. 'I have been in a cell before.'

Joseph leaves Professor Pocklington's study with a smile on his face. He has never enjoyed a lie more. The watch was handed in by a student. Found in a lecture hall.

The mathematician cried copiously before insisting they

share a sherry while he extolled his late father's virtues, never once letting go of the watch.

He knocks brusquely on the door of C3 Copper Beech Court.

'What?' brays a needling voice.

'It's Bidwell, Mr Bottomley. I have something of yours.'

The door is wrenched open and a dishevelled figure stumbles out amongst a fug of cigar smoke. 'You caught the thief, then?'

Joseph fixes the rat-like student with his steeliest stare. 'Not exactly, Mr. Bottomley. The police apprehended a doxy. This,' he produces the blood-red ruby ring, 'was in her possession. The officers traced the coat of arms. Would you care to explain how your family heirloom came to be in such unlikely company?'

Percival Bottomley is flushed and furtive as he snatches the ring from Joseph's outstretched hand and slams the door. A second lie and just as satisfying.

'Well, that's that,' Joseph chuckles. He saunters through the venerable quads as the early May sunshine sits warmly on his shoulders.

He glances over at the chapel, where *The Annunciation* by the Master of Bologna is back on the altar.

Across the courtyard, the library's leaded windows keep watch, Shakespeare's First Folio now a permanent fixture in the collection. The bursar was too overjoyed at its recovery to grumble.

Ahead, the limewash of the Master's Lodge is bright with the promise of summer, the Foundation Gift secure once again in the basement strongroom.

Lady Millicent Montieth has publicly called out her husband in the local press. The master has responded in the only way he knows, capitulating entirely by declaring support for Cambridge's female students.

As Joseph reaches the bridge, he sees Agnes at the college gate, leaning into Ronnie's shoulder. Ethel appears from New

Court and he waves. She raises her duster, and he knows all is as well with the world as he can make it.

Author Bio:

Gareth Williams is the author of the Richard Davey Chronicles and is currently working on the fourth instalment, a sequel to *Needing Napoleon*, *Serving Shaka* and *Rescuing Richard*. After studying history at Cambridge, he enjoyed a long and happy career as a history teacher. Now retired, he lives on the Isle of Skye with his wife Helen and has almost finished 'bagging' all 282 Munros, the Scottish mountains over 3000 feet.

Chapter Eight

CURTAIN CALL

Dianna Sinovic

When an actual dead body turns up onstage during a high school production of an Agatha Christie play, drama coach Angela Trigg is shocked and baffled. At first, she's concerned not only about the untimely death (a school custodian) but also for her students when the subsequent performances are cancelled. When the police blame the death on her and issue a warrant for her arrest, Angela realizes her very future is at stake. She'll lose her teaching job, yes, but the evidence of poison points to her guilt, and with it, the prospect of prison . . .yet, she knows she's innocent.

Sir Claud, coffee cup in hand, addressed the others in his home library. 'Please, let's all take a seat.'

Angela Trigg nodded approvingly from the sound booth at the rear of the auditorium. John Chase, as usual, commanded the stage. The audience below her became more alert as John/Sir Claud sank onto an armchair, and the butler locked the room behind him.

This was the set-up for the 'murder' in *Black Coffee*, the play Angela had fought with the school principal to produce.

'A murder on stage is hardly appropriate for high school students,' Lindel Pierce had scolded. 'Especially here in the Missouri.' He wagged a finger. 'People expect something more traditional.'

And now, on opening night, with every seat filled, and SRO folks lined up against the back wall, she felt vindicated. This was the 1970s after all. TV was full of crime shows like *Kojak* and *Columbo*.

Mark, the senior playing Richard, Sir Claud's son, delivered his line flawlessly. 'What do you mean by this?'

And the scene progressed: Sir Claud explaining as he sipped his coffee that they were all locked in the room and would remain so until the detective Hercule Poirot arrived. Or until someone returned the secret nuclear formula that had been stolen from his safe.

The clock on the library's mantel struck nine, and on that cue, the lights flipped off, plunging the stage into darkness.

Angela signalled to her sound engineer to roll the recorded effects over the PA: heavy breathing, metallic clinks, tearing paper. She frowned as she caught an ambient sound of dragging. That wasn't part of the scene.

When Nicole, playing Richard's wife Lucia, screamed on cue, the lighting tech flipped the stage lights back on.

With the cast focused on the arrival of Agatha Christie's sleuth Poirot, acted by Tim with a fake beard, monocle, and as close to a Belgian accent as he could muster, it was Angela who first spotted the change that forever altered her life: John/Sir Claud was no longer in the armchair. In his place was someone far too old to be a student, doing a fabulous job of playing dead.

Was this a joke? Who would do such a thing on opening night? She fingered the folded envelope in her pocket and her pulse quickened. Onstage, the action continued and she watched, both horrified and fascinated, to see what would happen when the cast discovered the change.

Mark/Richard turned to Sir Claud. 'Father...' Mark hesitated on his line as he took in the new person in the chair, then rallied. 'Father, you must dismiss M. Poirot. We no longer need him.'

As expected in the scene, Sir Claud remained collapsed in the chair, offering no response.

'Heavens.' Mark/Richard rushed to the chair, as rehearsed. 'Doctor.'

Tim/Poirot likewise moved to Sir Claud to feel his pulse, as the script ordered. If Tim was shocked by the newcomer, he didn't let it show. 'Yes, I'm afraid...' he paused for effect, as Angela had coached him. 'I'm afraid I am too late for Sir Claud.'

And so went the rest of Act 1, which continued with Sir Claud silent in the chair as the rest of the characters interacted as they had practiced. Once the cast's initial surprise passed, the lines flowed smoothly and the audience chuckled at the appropriate places. Angela exhaled; she finally recognised the newcomer as Pete Withers, school custodian. Why wasn't John in the chair?

When the curtain closed between acts, Angela radioed the stage manager to delay the start of Act 2. She hurried backstage to give the custodian a piece of her mind, but before she was halfway there, a shriek echoed through the auditorium, followed by a murmur of voices behind the curtain. The audience took up the sound, as people whispered and shifted in their seats, waiting for the play to continue.

Backstage, Angela was immediately accosted by the cast.

'Mr. Withers...is unconscious,' Tim said, his Poirot monocle dangling on its ribbon.

'He's dead,' hissed Nicole. She was putting on a brave front but seemed close to tears.

'Now, now. I'm sure he's fine.' Angela stepped to Withers, checked for a pulse, and steeled herself. 'Gary,' she said to the stage manager, 'find Mr. Pierce and ask him to call an ambulance.' Was Withers was passed-out drunk? Rumour had it that he liked to imbibe, even during work hours. She leaned forward, pretending to examine his well-lined face, and caught no whiff of alcohol.

'People,' she said in a low voice, stepping away from the chair, 'I'm sorry. We've worked so hard on this, but we're going to have to end the performance right now.' Disappointment immediately etched itself across their faces. That and worry. 'There's still tomorrow.' Angela reached out a hand to either side of her and the group gathered their traditional cast huddle. 'Go change, clean up...hug your parents.'

In front of the curtains, Angela looked out at the packed house. Alive with the hum of conversation, the space quietened to silence, providing her cue.

'I regret to tell you tonight's performance is ending early because of a medical emergency.' As she expected, the audience gasped. She added quickly. 'It's not a student. The cast and crew are all fine. I'd like to ask you all to exit the auditorium.' The crowd rose to its feet, chattering. Raising her voice, she made one last update. 'We'll make an announcement about tomorrow's performance, but we hope to hold it as planned.'

Once again she wondered, where was John Chase?

Angela was glad she'd shooed the cast off to their dressing rooms. She'd also sent Gary, the stage manager, and the crew home. It was best to leave the set exactly as it was, she decided. The ambulance crew tried but failed to revive Peter Withers. He was declared dead and taken away. The police were called, and she braced herself to face Lindel Pierce, who was sure to castigate her once again for pushing to produce the play.

She was deep in thought when Mark Hatfield appeared at her side, his eyes wide.

'We found John,' he said softly. 'He's in the prop room. His hands and feet are wrapped in duct tape.'

She followed Mark behind the backdrop to the poorly lit backstage area, bounded by black curtains. A small knot of students crowded around the prop room entrance. They moved back as Angela approached.

In the light of the small room's naked bulb, John Chase sat, in his Sir Claud costume, bound in tape and seemingly asleep.

No, no, Angela thought. *Let him be alive.*

As though hearing her silent plea, John blinked and shifted slightly.

'John.' Angela knelt beside him. 'What happened?' She motioned to Mark, and the two of them slid John out of the space. Multiple hands worked to remove the tape. He rubbed his face, as though trying to wipe away whatever had befallen him.

'I don't know,' John said, his voice froggy. 'I remember sitting in the chair when the lights went out…And now I'm here.'

Her mind turning over the sequence of events, Angela landed on the obvious next step. 'Go find Principal Pierce,' she told Mark, 'and have him contact John's parents. We need them here.'

'I'm fine,' John protested. 'Don't call my folks. They don't care about any of this acting stuff.'

She sighed. 'Let's get you up. The police will be here any minute. They may want to talk to you.'

'Police?' His face reflected puzzlement and confusion.

'Mr. Withers died on stage,' Mark said. 'He had a heart attack or something.'

'On stage?' John continued to look confused.

'He was in your chair. We don't know how he got there.'

Principal Pierce eyed Angela with annoyance as the police detective stood on the stage with them. The curtains were open again, this time on a now-vacant auditorium.

'Interesting,' Detective Ward said. He flipped through his palm-sized notebook, in which he had written vigorously for the last ten minutes. 'The custodian ends up on stage, even though he's not part of the play, and your student, who should have been on stage, ends up in a closet, and no one knows anything about it.'

'I told you this play was a mistake,' Pierce murmured to Angela.

Ward must have caught the words, because he followed up without delay. 'Mistake?'

Keeping her tone light, Angela explained. 'Oh, Mr. Pierce and I didn't see eye to eye on this production.'

'The play is about *murder*,' Pierce said, whispering the last word. 'It's just not the right topic for high school students to represent, in my opinion.'

Ward smiled. 'Agatha Christie, right?'

Surprised, Angela nodded. 'Yes, *Black Coffee*. You know it?'

'I'm a mystery fan, and Dame Agatha is one of my favourites.' He seemed to remember the seriousness of the situation and erased his smile. 'No one's saying anything about murder, Mr. Pierce. The victim most likely had a heart attack. But the fact that your student was secured in an offstage room does add... *complexity* to the situation.'

Pierce threw up his hands as though warding off the detective's words. 'You know kids. They play tricks on each other. Break the rules, horse around. It was probably a prank taken too far, that's all.'

John Chase was one of Angela's most dedicated students,

touring colleges that offered a major in theatre. Not the type to put his performance at risk. But Pierce had made up his mind, so she stayed silent.

The detective left to interview John, waiting in the school lobby.

'I assume you'll cancel this production,' Pierce said, once Ward was gone. He rocked back on his feet and peered down on her.

'No,' she said, returning his stare with steel. 'The cast has worked hard on this play. You saw the auditorium tonight: It was packed. What happened this evening was unfortunate, but, as they say, 'the show must go on'.'

Pierce was the first to blink in the showdown, but he got in the last word. 'I'll speak to the superintendent. He may have another opinion on the matter.'

At her home, Angela slipped off her flats and blazer and changed out of her production dress, the long-sleeved blue shift she wore to every opening night for good luck. Her cat padded out from the bedroom and jumped onto the couch, curling into a ball next to her.

'Ginny,' she said, stroking the grey cat's head, 'what are we going to do?'

Her teaching career had been on a steady rise for the last five years, as she pushed the envelope with challenging plays, plays she wished she could have acted in back when, and drew avid students into her wake. She considered whether Pierce's push-backs stemmed more from feeling upstaged than concern over the content she was presenting. Maybe it was time for curtains here, and a search for a more welcoming role. Get a doctorate, teach at the university level.

Ginny, intent on grooming, ignored her, so, with a sigh, she dug into the fridge for leftover takeout. She turned on the radio, moving the dial until she hit on a favourite, 'Ain't No Sunshine,' and reheated the lo mein on the stovetop.

Carrying her plate back to the living room, she settled back on the couch and propped her feet on the coffee table, next to the framed photo of her and her first husband. How she wished she could share tonight's events with him, but he was long gone. She saw again the stage lights popping on and the custodian sitting in the chair where John Chase should have been. Someone had sabotaged the production; she felt that in her bones. But why?

She set down her plate and retrieved the folded envelope from her blazer. It had arrived two days ago, addressed to her with no return address; inside, just a slip of paper and the words: *found you*. She refused to consider the obvious sender. It couldn't be; she'd covered her tracks.

Early Saturday, the superintendent overruled her insistence that the play be presented as planned that evening. Pierce called her, waking her from a dream in which Jim O'Toole had miraculously recovered from the hit-and-run, meaning she never had him cremated or had to endure a short-lived and disastrous second marriage to Ian McMaster. Groggy, she mumbled something into the phone.

'Angela, make sense,' Pierce said, his words clipped in anger. 'You'll need to inform the students right away. Then we'll put out a general notice on local radio about the cancellation.' Pierce was at his best commanding his troops in an emergency.

'You're right,' she conceded. The cast would be upset enough with the custodian's death, especially happening when it did. They would reunite now, if she asked them to. Instead, she privately vowed to work doubly hard to pull off the next play.

Pierce continued to talk in her ear, and when he paused, she knew he was waiting for a response.

'Sorry, I missed that,' she said. 'Still waking up.'

His harumph spoke for itself. 'I said, the police detective will be stopping by your home this morning.'

'Oh?' She moved to the kitchen table, opening her notebook that held the list of phone numbers for the cast. It would be a painful undertaking, passing on the news of the aborted performance, holding virtual hands over the phone line while the kids vented.

'Pete Withers died of poison, not a heart attack.'

A quick intake of breath was her immediate reaction.

'You might want to call a lawyer.' Then he hung up.

When the phone rang again five minutes later, she assumed it was Pierce, tossing another grenade into the sudden chaos of her life.

Instead, she heard only breathing and then a click.

Angela made it through the entire cast list before Detective Ward showed up. For each phone call, she kept the news brief and reminded them of the cast party. Even if they couldn't go through with the performance, she would make sure they came together to celebrate their hard work.

Ward stepped into Angela's living room slowly, as though reluctant to disturb her, but once seated on her easy chair, notepad in hand, he was all business.

Yes, the coroner had released his report, noting that the custodian had indeed died from poisoning. That's why Ward was at her house, to hear again the progression of last evening's production and its aftermath.

Angela tapped a finger on the side of her coffee mug. 'Do you think Pete's death, the poisoning, was intentional?'

Ward gripped his pen. 'Do you?'

'No.' Ginny rubbed against her legs, and she reached down to scratch the cat's ears. 'We're talking about a middle-class suburban high school. Despite the play we're staging, the most violent anyone here gets is to stomp around in anger.'

The detective looked up from his notepad. 'Yet a crime, we are calling it a crime, did happen. An older gentleman died on *your* stage, in the middle of *your* production, after being poisoned.' He flipped back several pages. 'In addition, one of *your* cast members was somehow removed from the stage and left bound in a closet.'

The repetition of Ward's word emphasis prickled the back of Angela's neck.

'It was the prop room, but close enough. Am I under arrest?'

Ward looked at her and said nothing for a few beats. Finally, he sighed. 'The commissioner wants this case settled, and since you're the common denominator, fingers are pointing toward you.' He gave her a slight smile. 'But I'm not convinced...yet. For one thing, I see no motive. You're well liked. You have no relationship with the deceased except a professional one. You had nothing to gain and much to lose if you killed him.'

The prickles eased off enough for Angela to start churning the details she knew.

'Can you tell me what kind of poison killed Pete? How was he exposed to it?'

Ward shook his head. 'That's the odd thing. I feel a bit like I'm M. Poirot in this. The coroner identified the substance as hyoscine.'

The very poison the script said killed Sir Claud. 'That can't be.' She frowned in concentration. 'We had only a slurp of coffee in those cups, to add authenticity to the scene. Certainly nothing toxic or dangerous.' She had brewed the coffee herself in the teachers' lounge.

'Of course, you as the director would know that in the play the poison is administered via coffee, in a cup that's been tampered with by the villain.' He scribbled a note. 'And where are those cups now?'

Angela began to pace as she thought back to the previous

evening. 'All props are stored in our prop room. The cups would have been emptied and washed by the crew...' She stopped. 'Except that, because of what happened last night, and the fact that I sent everyone home early, the cups may still be on the stage.'

'Ah,' Ward said with a nod. 'Good. And the school is closed today? I will visit the stage area with a crime scene team and collect them.'

'I can meet you there to make sure you have all of them.' She had a fleeting moment of sadness. 'The superintendent cancelled tonight's performance, so we won't be needing any of the props. Take whatever you need for your investigation.'

Flipping over to a new page on his pad, Ward again poised his pen. 'Tell me about Pete Withers in this play. Why would you give the role to someone not a student?'

'He didn't have a role. This is, *was,* a student production. In any of our plays, all roles and all crew positions are open only to students. As the director, I make those selections based on auditions, student interest, and so forth. Pete's only responsibility was to clean up the stage areas after we were done.' A memory surfaced of Withers standing in the dim light at the back of the hall during rehearsals. At least, she had assumed it was Withers. 'He was seldom near the stage while we were, I think to stay out of our way.'

Ward seemed disappointed at that information, closed his notepad and stood. 'We won't need you at the school today, Ms. Trigg. The vice principal will let us in.' At Angela's doorway he paused. 'But stay close. I'm sure I'll have more questions.'

She waited until Ward was in his car to close her front door. The prickles she'd felt earlier remained. Someone was watching her.

With the night's performance cancelled, Angela spent the day going through her shelves of plays, rereading favourites, dipping into new ones, searching, as she always did, for something *different*. Something her classes would embrace, a drama that would showcase their strengths. Most of her students did not go on to a career in theatre. The odds of success were so daunting, who would? But taking on another's persona in front of an audience of 350 gave them a boost of confidence when they were about to step into the adult world.

For spring, she had selected Shakespeare: *Much Ado About Nothing*. As far as she could find, Robard High School had never tackled the Bard on stage.

And if she didn't jump ship for a new teaching gig, there was the following school year to map out. A new crop of seniors to carry the bulk of the dramatic load.

'Ginny,' she said. 'What do you think? For next year? Ibsen or Hellman?' Her first husband would have welcomed the question. Jim had been a teacher, too, but Economics instead of Drama. She liked the way his no-nonsense approach to life (supply chains, taxation) balanced with her freer spirit. When the drunk driver took him, she'd cast about for a salve to her grief, letting emotion override common sense. Ian McMaster was not her soulmate, skewing in the opposite direction. It was the big reason she relocated from St Louis to Kansas City, to put hundreds of miles between them.

With a sigh, Angela stacked the books she'd been perusing on her coffee table. Decisions on next year could wait. She needed to confirm with Nancy Jamison that she was ready for the cast party. Angela would pick up cakes and crisps from the grocery. Nancy, who taught English at Robard and was a huge theatre fan, was supplying the rest. The least she could do to help, she'd said.

The phone rang just as she reached for the receiver.

Detective Ward jumped right in, no pleasantries or small talk. 'The coffee cups contained no poison, but we found the hyoscine on your desk at the school. We now have reason to believe you are responsible for the death of Peter Withers. Report to the police station right away,' he said. 'Or, I can send an officer by to make your arrest.'

❁

Nancy met her at the station; Angela had phoned her before she left the house. Nancy's brother, Ed, a lawyer in Blue Springs, was on his way. Thirty minutes max.

'He's to say nothing until he gets here,' Nancy said.

Detective Ward was waiting for her as well. The charge, he said, was first-degree murder.

An officer led her to a holding cell, after she gave up her valuables into Nancy's care.

'This is ridiculous,' Nancy said. 'You are no more guilty of Pete's death than I am, and I wasn't even there last night.'

Angela could only nod; she was speechless. How did hyoscine end up on her desk? She'd never seen or used the stuff. She and Nancy shared the tiny office space, but they kept it locked. Only they and Pete Withers had a key.

Pierce would terminate her contract. Even if she were cleared of the crime, what would the arrest do to her CV? Who would hire her?

Nancy put her hand over her heart. 'Stay strong, Angie. We'll beat this. Ed's amazing.' She gave a wry smile. 'Now, let me get the cast party prepped. Wait until your students hear about this injustice.'

'Oh, no,' Angela managed to say. 'They can't know.'

'Of course they can. They must.' She was gone before Angela could continue her protest.

As promised, Ed Jamison arrived within the half hour. He was taller than Nancy and a bit wider, but just as personable. He went over the procedures she would be facing. A hearing in which she would plead not guilty; he would argue against bail, but she would likely need to pay to be released. He would represent her at trial.

'Trial?' She wiped her sweaty hands on her slacks.

'One step at a time, Angie,' he said. 'I made a few calls before I drove over. I think the police have a weak case and need to pin it on someone. I wouldn't worry.'

But you're not the one being held in a cell. She smiled, though. Nancy said he would give her a deep discount on his fee. Her teacher salary didn't allow her to tuck much away for a rainy day.

'Thanks, Ed. I appreciate your help. I'm mortified that they think *I* did it.'

After he left, she fought down the anxiety that threatened to overwhelm her. A comment from Ward bubbled up. *I feel a bit like I'm M. Poirot in this.* What would Agatha Christie's famous sleuth do in this situation? He would have left his mind open to any possible scenario. She pondered for a few moments. In this case, someone knew the plot of *Black Coffee* well enough to use the same substance that had poisoned the fictious character Sir Claud.

She'd done her own research before rehearsals began, learning that hyoscine was safely used medicinally in small doses; a large dose, especially in an older person with circulatory problems, could result in death.

She ticked off the apparent chain of events: Someone wanted Pete dead. They'd dragged his body onto the stage to make that point. But Pete wasn't supposed to be on stage, John was. Apparently the killer didn't want John dead; he'd been removed from action and stashed in the prop room. And the poison that killed Pete had ended up on her desk.

In the quiet of her cell, Angela pictured Poirot standing to one side, shaking his head at her. *The motive, think of the motive in this*, he murmured.

That was the key, wasn't it?

Two hours later, she'd gone before a judge, pleaded not guilty and been released on bail. Ed escorted her to her car and said he'd be in touch the following week to discuss next steps.

Back at her house, she listened to the many messages of support on her answering machine while Ginny meowed annoyance at her lack of attention. Parents and students alike had called. So had a local reporter, eager for a statement. Ed had cautioned her against speaking to the press.

'Just tell them, 'no comment' for now,' he'd counselled. 'A murder at a high school is big news.'

Principal Pierce had also left a message. He'd placed her on administrative leave; the district's lawyer had advised it. 'We're behind you 100%, Ms. Trigg.' But his tone left no doubt where he landed on the scale of judging her innocence or guilt. 'One other thing,' he continued. 'We can't find the custodian keys. They've gone missing since Withers died. Are you sure you don't have them?'

Although exhaustion ate at her, Angela pulled herself together for the cast party. The evening would provide a respite from her roiling thoughts, especially the image of Poirot waiting for her to solve the case.

'I'm going, Ginny.' She hugged the cat to calm herself. 'The kids need me.'

At Nancy's, anguish and anger swirled through the students. Where past cast parties had been relaxed and boisterous after a job well done, this one held pent-up energy that seemed like an inflated balloon about to burst.

'We'll find the murderer,' Tim said, his usual timidity gone, his physical stance mimicking what he used on stage for the famous sleuth.

'Right,' agreed Brenda. 'We are the *Black Coffee* cast, and we are here to rescue you.'

Angela dabbed at her eyes. 'I appreciate your passion, guys, but it's not your job to solve this puzzle.'

'We say it is.' Mark's gaze was so intense, Angela couldn't

hold it. He was destined for the police academy after graduation, following in his father's and grandfather's footsteps. On stage, he wasn't half bad; she could see him in undercover work, believably taking on a disguise, convincing the crooks he was on their side.

At Mark's insistence, the group sat down in Nancy's living room, the party itself effectively over as they began discussing the events of the previous night.

Both grateful and embarrassed, Angela answered their questions as they rehashed the play's first Act, looking for anomalies that might help determine how Pete Withers had ended up on stage and John bound in a closet.

'Did anyone notice anything odd backstage?' Mark again, taking the lead. 'Ms. Trigg was there until about five minutes before the start. Then she went to the lighting booth. How about Mr. Withers? Did any of you see him?'

And on they went. Yes, Withers was backstage, but wearing black so they hardly noticed him, even as he moved from one backstage area to another. The cast was busy primping their costumes. Gary made a last tour of the set, adjusting the furniture, conferring with crew members about the blackout sequence.

'That was all,' Gary said. 'Except for Mr. Withers trying to avoid us, nobody else was there.'

The group sat in silence for a few moments, and Angela once again felt her eyes dampen. These were good kids. They were trying so hard to help.

What am I missing?

John cleared his throat. 'Now that I'm thinking back, there *was* something.'

All eyes swivelled to their Sir Claud.

'Just before the lights went out, I heard a scuffle off stage left, behind me.'

'And then?' Mark leaned forward.

John shrugged. 'I don't know. Next thing I knew, I was in the prop room.'

'Wait.' Angela spoke up. 'During the blackout, I heard a dragging sound.'

'A scuffle and then dragging,' Mark repeated. 'How about you, Gary? Were you aware?'

Gary wouldn't meet Mark's gaze. 'Maybe I should have been, but no. Steve and I had gone to shut the rear auditorium door. Somebody left it open.'

'The rear door?' Angela said, puzzled. 'We never open that.'

Gary nodded. 'That's what I thought, too.' He paused. 'And another thing. Even before that, I could have sworn Mr. Withers was in two places at once backstage.'

'Another clue?' Mark said. 'Someone had to get John offstage with the lights out and stash him. Someone had to drag Mr. Withers onto the set. This had to happen in a matter of a minute or two, no more.'

Angela closed her eyes briefly, Mark's words triggering a connection. *Two.* 'Two people,' she said softly. 'There were two people involved.'

The group immediately began chattering, debating this new conclusion.

It was Brenda who finally asked the right question. 'Ms. Trigg, who would want to frame you with this? Everyone loves you.'

It was the question Angela had failed to ask herself. And once she did, the pieces fell into place. The mystery person at the back of the auditorium during rehearsals. The anonymous letter addressed to her. The feeling that someone was watching her. The missing keys.

Ian.

Her ex was bat-shit crazy if he had killed Pete Withers to get back at her. She shivered despite the warmth in the room. Ian and some lowlife friend he'd picked up. If it was true, she was in very real danger.

With her students staring at her, waiting for her response, she smoothed her expression. She did not want to scare them, but it was safest if they all headed back to the security of their homes.

'I have an idea,' Angela said and stood. 'But it's only a theory. I'm going to check it out. Thanks for a great time tonight.'

❦

Angela parked at the school. As head of the drama department, she had a single door key, useful for locking up after late-night rehearsals. Pierce hadn't demanded she turn it in after placing her on leave. The lot lights showed that hers was the lone vehicle. She hesitated. The prickles had returned in full force.

Letting herself in the door just off the rear of the auditorium stage, the same one Gary said had been left open earlier, she flipped on the lights, illuminating the backstage area and set, while the auditorium seats remained pooled in darkness. The coffee cups that played such an important part of the actual play were gone, off to the police lab. She paced the set, trying to puzzle out what had happened.

The click of a door offstage made her pause.

'Hello?' she called.

The only sound was the faint cycling of air from the HVAC system. Then the lights went out.

A moment later, hands gripped her neck in a stranglehold.

'You thought you could leave me behind.' The voice was a whisper in her ear, but recognisable. 'Never, bitch.'

'Ian,' she gasped, fighting against his strength, pushing herself to remember the props still on the set, anything she could use to defend herself. She could smell his sweat and feel his rage.

'And now that you've seen what I can do to punish you, I'm taking you back where you belong.' If the situation weren't so fraught, she would have laughed at the melodramatic lines.

'Why?' She tried to speak, but managed just a whisper. 'Why did you kill him?'

Ian relaxed his hold slightly and chuckled. 'I didn't mean to. Drake took out the kid, and I offered the old guy a nip of my flask, with the stuff in it. Meant for him to go to sleep. Then Drake and I dragged him on stage. Guess it was all too much for the geezer.'

Angela struggled, with Ian's hot, sour breath still in her ear. If she could only reach the one prop that could help her. Pretending to accede to Ian's demand, she allowed him to move her toward stage left. In the darkness, he couldn't see, but she knew the set intimately and reached out a hand to the table near Sir Claud's chair. The faux sculpture of a rearing horse was no more than ten inches high, but it was solid stone. She brought it down on Ian's head and neck with all the force she had.

He released her, stumbled back and fell to the floor, just as the lights flipped back on.

'Ms. Trigg.' Mark rushed onto the set, followed by Brenda, John, and Tim.

John and Tim tackled Ian before he could rise, and using duct tape, bound his hands and feet.

'The police are on their way,' Brenda said, helping Angela to one of the set chairs.

Angela felt her neck gingerly, knowing that tomorrow it would be black and blue. But she was alive. 'What are you doing here?' Her voice was more of a croak.

'It was Mark,' Brenda said. 'We saw a car follow you when you left. Mark decided we should also tail you; we were worried. And then when you ended up here, we figured you had a lead.' She paused to look at Ian on the floor. 'We heard what he said. You were right, it *was* two people.'

Tim slipped into his Poirot accent and held up a finger. 'The case is solved, Mme. Trigg.'

Angela managed a smile. 'Agatha would be so proud of all of you.'

Author Bio:

Dianna Sinovic is an author of mystery, speculative fiction, and horror, as well as a certified book coach and editor. Her short stories have been published in a number of anthologies, and her flash fiction appears monthly on the blog *A Slice of Orange*. Her novel, the paranormal thriller *Scream of the Silent Sun*, is a new release for 2025. She's a member of Sisters in Crime, the Horror Writers Association, and the National Association of Memoir Writers. Connect with her via her website, www.dianna-sinovic.com, or on Instagram, @dsinovic94.

Chapter Nine

DEAD ON MIDNIGHT

Sheena Macleod

When the clock strikes twelve on Hogmanay, 1926 arrives with a bang.

A Scottish Cosy Mystery.

When Dottie's mother, Lady Alice Hamilton-MacLean, drags her to her cousin's Scottish country estate on Hogmanay to see in 1926, she could never have imagined that the grand old house held so many secrets. As the clock strikes midnight, a gunshot is fired, and a guest is left dead. Everyone is under suspicion - from the laird's new wife-to-be to the butler who knows more than he's letting on.

Join Dottie and her friend, Bea, as they try to find out who fired that fatal shot.

Dottie pulled the goggles down from her leather motoring helmet as her friend, Bea, dropped the gears and roared the Austin 7 Chummy around a sharp bend.

'Ooh, don't you just love these country roads, Dottie? Beats the city any day.' The tyres of the four-seater automobile screeched as Bea straightened onto a long stretch and pressed her foot on the accelerator.

Lady Alice Hamilton-MacLean groaned in the back seat of the open-topped vehicle. 'Slow down, girls. At this rate, I'll be dead before midnight.' Dressed in more furs than an Arctic explorer, Dottie thought her mother looked like the large stuffed bear she'd seen in a museum in Edinburgh, and sounded like one, too. Squashed in beside her, Lady Alice's maid, Doris, slept the sleep of the just.

Thank goodness Bea had agreed to join her on this jaunt. Her mother had decided to drag her to Dottie's cousin's estate in the Highlands of Scotland on Hogmanay, for no other reason than to check out his new wife-to-be. Dottie sighed as she thought about the fun her friends would have tonight as they saw in 1926 at the 'Bluesy Bandit', the new jazz bar in Inverness. It promised to be a Hogmanay party to kick off the new year in style, and Dottie wouldn't be there.

She flapped a leather, gloved hand. 'Ooh, Mother, she knows what she's doing, don't you, Bea?'

Lady Alice harumphed. 'Trundling trucks around during the war, Dahling, does not qualify one as a driver. And as for this new-fangled automobile, there would be more comfort travelling astride a camel.' She nudged Doris with her elbow. 'How she can sleep through this, I don't know.'

Dottie straightened her knee blanket, just as the vehicle clunked over another dip in the road. Her mother did have a point, but travelling in an automobile was the bee's knees, and she adored it.

They approached a gamekeeper walking on the roadside, an open shotgun draped over his arm, and Bea squeezed the horn.

Beside him, a black Labrador Retriever raced around in circles, clearly disturbed by the honking *bhap, bhap, bhap* and the roar of the engine. The gamekeeper glowered after them as Bea sped past.

'Not far to go now,' Dottie announced, glancing at Bea through her goggles as a high ivy-covered wall with wrought iron gates appeared in the distance. Although the weather was chilly, the sun shone, making for a pleasant drive. They were staying two nights at Angus Robertson-Mackay's, the new Laird of Connachie's twenty-acre estate. At the thought, Dottie groaned and sank back in her seat. She pulled her fur stole tight around her, closed her eyes and filtered out her mother's incessant ramblings.

She must have dozed off for the next thing she was startled awake as Bea brought the automobile to a sudden halt beside a Rolls-Royce Twenty on the gravel driveway outside the largest estate house she'd ever seen. As she lurched forward in the passenger seat, Dottie placed her gloved hands on the polished wooden dashboard to steady herself. The building before her looked like a mix between a country manor and a turreted castle. Removing her goggles, she scanned the house, taking in the impressive building. *Maybe a weekend here wouldn't be so bad after all.*

'Trunks,' Mother roared to two liveried footmen who hurried down the sweeping front stairs to meet them, one tall of stature and the other broad built.

Startled awake by the noise, Doris sat up and wiped sleep from her eyes. 'Are we almost there yet?'

Hmm, or maybe not.

The tall footman opened the back door and bowed, while the other footman began unstrapping their luggage, ready to be taken up to their rooms. Lady Alice exited and strode towards the front entrance. Stepping out of the Chummy, Dottie rolled her eyes at Bea and followed her mother inside. With a grin, Bea tossed the automobile hand crank to the tall footman and marched after them, her long leather coat flapping behind her.

❦

Dottie and Bea were shown into a large twin bedroom on the second floor, while Lady Alice was allocated a room on the floor below, with a small adjoining bedroom for Doris. They'd been the first of Angus's Hogmanay guests to arrive, which didn't surprise Dottie, given Bea's speed on the road. After a quick freshen up, they hurried down the sweeping staircase and made for the drawing room, where they would be served drinks and nibbles. They would dress for dinner later, once Doris had finished unpacking their luggage.

When Dottie and Bea entered, Duncan rose from a chair beside a roaring log fire and tipped his whisky glass towards them. 'Ah, welcome to my home, Dottie, and thank you for joining us to see in the New Year. Who's your friend?'

'This is Bea. Surely you remember Beatrice, Dahling?' Lady Alice said as she strode into the room, pearls swinging. 'Your memory is getting to be as bad as your father's was. My brother was lucky to recall my name near the end. All these explosions during the war, likely.' She glanced around the well-furnished room. 'Hmm. You've not done too badly from his demise. Oh, well, I suppose I didn't do too badly myself.'

Duncan held out a hand and grinned. 'Beatrice Bendel-Thorpe? Major Bendel-Thorpe's daughter?'

Bea wiped her hands down her trousers, nodded and stuck out her hand. 'Jolly good to see you again, Duncan.'

He popped his whisky glass onto an occasional table. 'Let me introduce you all to my fiancé, Claire Penny.'

Claire stood, sending out a waft of Chanel No. 5 as she rose gracefully from the chair. She raised a cigarette holder to her lips and leaned towards Duncan, who lifted a lighter from the table and lit her cigarette. The large diamond engagement ring on her finger glittered as he held the flame towards her. Claire exhaled, leaving a trail of smoke furling around her and creating a slight aura of mystery. 'Ooh, Dahling,' she said to Bea. 'Is that a new fashion?'

Dottie looked at Bea, who shrugged.

'The trousers, Dahling? Are you one of these Bright New Things, all manly and able to fend for yourself?' Claire raised the back of her hand across her brow in a dramatic gesture, 'Nort for me, of course, but...'

Dottie growled. 'We've just journeyed from Inverness, these are our travelling clothes, Bea drove here.'

Claire Penny let out a puff of smoke and tapped the ash from her cigarette into an ashtray. 'Hmm, I see. Of course. I drive myself, and dashing good fun it is too.' She stubbed out her cigarette and draped an arm around Duncan's shoulders. 'And my gorgeous, smoochie pie here has just ordered us one of those new Rolls-Royce Phantoms. Haven't you, Dahling?' She pecked Duncan on the cheek. 'But enough of that. Who's for a martini? What?'

'Smoochie pie. Did you hear that?' Dottie asked once they were back in their room, changing for dinner.

'And questioning the way I dress. I wonder where she learned her manners?' Bea frowned and adjusted her slip before pulling on a low-necked gold dress. 'I'll show her what the 'new look' looks like. Pop the curling irons in the fire for my hair, Dottie,' Bea said, pointing a deep maroon fingernail at the top of a dressing table.

When Dottie clipped a pair of dangling diamond earrings on her ears, Bea's eyes widened. 'Ooh, these are the cat's whiskers. Where did you get them?'

Dottie checked them out in the mirror. 'Yes, they are rather nice. They were a Christmas present from Mother.'

'Your mother is a funny old bird, isn't she? I'm surprised she never remarried after your father died.'

'Hmm. Mother considered herself a bit of a suffragette. She once chained herself to the railings outside the polling station, but soon decided it didn't have the same appeal in reality as it did reading about it in the newspapers. And starving herself lasted until the next invite from her chums to go for afternoon tea at the Royal.'

Buckling on her Mary Jane shoes, Bea hooted with laughter.

Half an hour later, Dottie twirled in front of a full-length mirror set on a wooden stand. Dressed in a drop-waisted pale blue dress that fell just below her knees, blue t-bar shoes and a feather in her short hair, she gave a satisfied smile. She'd spent ages on her makeup, including perfecting the right amount of rouge on her cheeks. Smoky, mascaraed, kohl eyes stared back at her, but it was the ruby red lipstick she thought changed her look the most, making her lips appear rounder.

After patting her bobbed, finger-waved hair into place, she studied a postcard of the movie star Clara Bow. The 'It Girl' she most wanted to be like. Satisfied that she'd got 'The Look', Dottie grinned at Bea. 'Let's see what Claire Penny has to say about how we're dressed now. What?'

Arriving back in the drawing room, the butler handed Dottie and Bea a flute of Champagne each from his tray. As they sipped their drinks, Duncan escorted them around the room, pointing out the other house guests who had all now arrived.

Duncan tilted his head towards the fireplace. 'That gentleman over there is my old chum, Iain MacGregor. You'll be sitting beside Iain at dinner, so you can catch up with him then.' Looking dapper with his slicked-back hair and a spiffy black suit, in the fashionable style of Rudolph Valentino, a man in his early thirties, puffed on a cigarette and guffawed loudly at something

Claire Penny said. Wearing a beaded white, tasselled dress that fell to the knees of her perfect, slim frame, Claire looked the very picture of modern fashion as she pouted her dark red, cupid lips at Iain. Dottie caught Bea scowling and held back a giggle. *Well, we tried.*

Lady Alice sat at a card table playing Mahjong with three of the new arrivals. 'We won't disturb their game.' Duncan flapped a hand towards the table. 'That's Reverend Sinclair's wife, Rose.' He nodded towards a chair by the fire where the minister dozed. 'And Reverend Sinclair. The other couple at the table are neighbours, Lord and Lady Campbell. They were close friends of my father.'

Duncan made his way over to one of the settees, Dottie and Bea following close behind. 'These are my nearest neighbours, from the Highmoor Estate, Melissa and Hugh Rutherford. Unfortunately, their parents, Lord and Lady Rutherford, couldn't be here tonight.'

Hugh jumped up and stuck out a hand. 'A pleasure. I'm sure.'

'And all that jazz.' Melissa rose from the settee and grinned. 'Call me Mel.'

'I'll leave you to get acquainted. Dinner will be served in about one hour. And then it will be on to the Hogmanay celebrations.'

Hugh glanced over at the Mahjong players, then back at Dottie and Bea. 'Pity they weren't up for a few rounds of three-card brag. I'm feeling lucky tonight. Do either of you fancy a game, or three?'

Mel scowled. 'Give it a break, Hugh. We're here to have fun. I would have thought you'd learned your lesson after your last escapade.' She rolled her eyes at him. 'There's only so many times Daddy will bail you out.'

'My sister, unfortunately,' Hugh said and made his way over to watch the Mahjong players.

Dottie stared after him, a frown forming on her face as she

spotted Claire Penny sniggering behind her hand as she'd watched the disagreement between Hugh and Mel.

As Dottie and Bea sipped their drinks, the butler spoke to Duncan, who held up a hand and called for everyone's attention.

'Listen up, all,' Duncan said. 'Thank you for joining me at Moorside Hall this Hogmanay. Just as Father did, I've organised a New Year's Day ride out to the moor tomorrow before luncheon... for a bit of deer and bird spotting. The gamekeeper is in the gun room. Anyone who wants to join in, head over there now and give Brown your equestrian preferences if you have any and obtain the arrangements for where and when we will meet.'

Bea raised her eyebrow at Dottie. 'Should we?'

'Why not? We brought along our riding trousers and boots. Ooh, and we might see a Golden Eagle.'

'Ooh, yes. Let's do it. It sounds like the cat's pyjamas.'

They followed Duncan to the gunroom along with Iain, Hugh, Mel, Claire and Lord and Lady Campbell. Dottie's mother stayed behind with Rose and the minister. When she entered, the scent of gun oil, leather and old books filled Dottie's nostrils, and she glanced around. The large wood-panelled room looked quite divine. Like a museum, old books and artefacts filled every spare space. The pictures and paintings hanging on a wall, of past ride outs and family portraits, drew Dottie and Bea over.

'Ooh, look, Bea, there's my Uncle Fredrick, Duncan's father, with Mother.' Dottie pointed to a framed photograph. 'I wonder when this was taken? It looks quite recent.'

The butler bowed. 'Excuse me, ladies, if I may. This was taken two years ago, the year before Lady Alice's brother died.'

Dottie nodded and leaned in closer as another photograph caught her eye, of her mother, Uncle Fredrick and her father out on the moor. The gamekeeper and a lad of about sixteen stood behind them in the distance. She recognised the gamekeeper as the man she'd seen with the black Labrador as they'd passed them on the roadside earlier. 'Ooh, thank you. And look at this one. Mother looks so young. And there's Father with her.'

'Ahem, that one?' The butler glanced around. 'Duncan must have missed this. I don't think he realises it's still up there,' he said, taking the picture down from the wall. 'All the rest from the 1911 New Year ride were removed.'

Dottie glanced at him and shook her head. 'Sorry, why?'

'As a matter of courtesy. There was a dreadful accident that year. We'd all rather not be reminded of it. But I've said enough already. I'll let you look around and arrange with Brown about tomorrow's ride out. I'll put this picture with the others.'

After making their arrangements for the next day with the gamekeeper, Dottie and Bea hung around, looking into a tall glass cabinet containing shotguns and at the smaller pistols laid out in a glass display case, some of which had been brought back from the war.

Their attention was diverted when the butler announced that dinner would now be served in the dining room.

'We'd best get a wiggle on, Dottie.' Bea linked into her arm. 'I'm so glad you persuaded me to join you and Lady Alice. I'm having a whale of a time.'

Dottie smiled, for some unfathomable reason, she had started to enjoy herself too.

After a sumptuous five-course dinner, Dottie followed the others into the drawing room. The furniture had been pushed against the walls to allow for dancing, and Charles Harrison's recording of 'I'll Be With You In Appleblossom Time' played on the gramophone. Dottie hummed along to the popular tune as she stood beside the Victrola, searching through the 78s, while Bea chatted to Duncan.

The clock above the fireplace showed that it was already

after 10 pm, and excitement coursed through Dottie. *A new year for a new me*. She'd registered for an English degree at the University of Edinburgh and couldn't wait to get started on the first leg of her career as a journalist. It was a new time for women, and Bea couldn't be happier about it.

As the song came to an end, Dottie pulled the 78 of the 'Dixieland Jazz Band' from the cabinet and placed it onto the player. Iain MacGregor stepped forward and cranked the handle to power the turntable.

Hugh and Mel danced over and set to with the Charleston.

Dottie raised her brows at Iain, who shook his head. 'I don't know how.'

As Claire Penny made her way over to them, surrounded by a fug of smoke, Dottie gripped Iain's hand. 'What applesauce. Here, let me show you. To do the Charleston, it's toes in heels out.'

As the Champagne and cocktails flowed, and the evening wore on, creeping towards midnight, the Mahjong players discarded their game and joined the dancers.

At twenty minutes to midnight, Dottie and Bea raced up the sweeping staircase to their room and donned their cloche hats and warm winter coats. At ten minutes to, they hurried back down and joined the others on the veranda overlooking the lawn, where fireworks would be set off at the stroke of twelve.

When they arrived, the butler handed them a flute of Champagne from his tray to toast in the new year. Hugh reached out and helped himself to a glass, almost sending the tray flying. 'Not long to go now,' he said, his voice slurred as he staggered off.

Dottie leaned over the balustrade. The gamekeeper and the stable lad were preparing to set off the fireworks. She turned as a distant church bell rang out, and the revellers started the countdown to midnight.

'Ten, Nine,' Dottie joined in... 'And one,' she called, raising her glass as loud bangs filled the air and coloured sparks lit up the night sky. Bang followed bang, and mingled with the calls of 'Happy New Year' as the revellers moved around hugging, shaking hands or pecking cheeks.

When Dottie stepped forward to shake Hugh's hand, he slipped to the ground, blood seeping through his white shirt. Startled, she stepped back and glanced around, her body trembling. 'Oh, erm... help.'

Amidst the cacophony of noise, Bea hurried towards her. 'What's happened?'

Dottie swayed and shook her head. 'He just went down. Bea, can you have a look?' She gasped and held a hand to her mouth. 'I think he's been shot.' Bea had been in the ambulance reserves and knew a thing or two about gunshot wounds.

Bea knelt beside Hugh and felt for a pulse. She shook her head. 'Nothing. It does rather look like he's been shot.'

Duncan rubbed a hand through his hair. 'I'll phone the doctor's house and the police station.'

As the guests milled around the veranda, a pale-faced woman pushed her way through to the front, her long cream gloves smeared with red.

'Mother?' Dottie said, reaching out to steady her.

Mother clutched her strand of pearls and groaned. 'When I shook Hugh's hand, to wish him a Happy New Year, he was, well, he was a bit... staggery ... I... I just thought he'd been on the toot.'

As Dottie's gaze travelled around the wide-eyed guests, it soon became clear that Mother wasn't the only one with blood-stained clothing. 'Oh, baloney. Bea, look.'

The sleeve of Mel's fawn coat was dappled with red.

'Urgh,' Bea groaned.

Claire Penny squealed and rubbed at the fur collar of her white coat, trying to remove the bloody smears that had likely transferred as she, also, hugged Hugh, or she'd hugged someone who had.

'Hmm. It looks like Mother wasn't the only one to touch Hugh after he'd been shot. This will make it harder for the police to determine who did this.'

As the panic amongst the guests built, Duncan took control. 'Can everyone please go back inside?' he said, draping his arm around the visibly shaken Claire Penny. 'The police are on their way. They should be with us soon.'

'Looks like someone's bumped off Duncan's neighbour,' Dottie said to Bea as they made their way into the drawing room, linked one on each side of Lady Alice to steady her. They placed the distraught woman onto a settee beside the minister and his wife, who looked equally in shock. As they sat Lady Alice down, Doris hurried to her side.

'Darn. We've been on the toot, Dottie.' Bea lowered her voice. 'But, although I did feel a bit spiffy earlier, I'm quite clear-headed now.' She removed her coat and threw it onto the back of a chair at the Mahjong table. 'We need to keep everybody together until the bobbies get here, and we can work out what happened.'

'Could it have been an accident?' Dottie said, still shaken.

Dottie sat with Bea at the table the Mahjong players had vacated earlier. She pulled a blank piece of paper towards her and lifted a pencil. 'Okay, who else, apart from Mother, Mel and Claire Penny, has blood on their clothes?'

Bea raised her eyebrows. 'Ooh, good one, Dottie. Whoever fired the fatal shot will have blood on their hands. Write their names down. We can rule the rest out for now.'

After scanning the room, they finally agreed to add two more names to their list - Iain and Duncan's Father's friend, Lord Campbell, both of whom had traces of blood on their clothes. 'So that makes five suspects,' Dottie said, 'but seriously, Bea, Dhaling, I do think we should remove Mother's name. What?'

Bea looked over at Lady Alice, who was accepting a medicinal whisky from the butler, and gripped Dottie's arm. 'Hold up. Is that a blood splash on the butler's cuff? It's hard to tell as he's buttoned his jacket up tight. It wasn't like that before, was it?'

'Wait there.' Dottie rose from the chair. 'I'm not sure, but his jacket does look quite different. I'll fetch a drink from his tray and have a closer look.' The butler had been on the balcony handing out drinks before the fireworks started, but Dottie couldn't remember seeing him there after Hugh collapsed. As she sidled up beside him, Dottie noticed pale pink splashes on one of his cuffs, as if blood had been washed from it.

A burly sergeant arrived, escorted in by the gamekeeper, who remained with the others who waited to give their statements. The sergeant announced that a policeman was on the balcony awaiting the arrival of the doctor. An ambulance was also on its way. The sergeant glanced around. 'Aye, Aye. So what's been going on here? If Duncan doesn't mind, I'll take a statement from each of you in the small parlour. Starting with Duncan himself.'

Duncan nodded and showed the sergeant through.

Lord Campbell joined Dottie and Bea at the card table, while his wife comforted Mel. He wiped at the blood spatters on the front of his shirt. 'What a to do, eh? 1926 certainly came in with a bang. Poor Hugh, What?'

Dottie leaned on the table and cupped her chin in her hands. 'It seems the bangs from the fireworks masked the sound of the gun going off. Any one of us could have fired the fatal shot and then concealed the gun during the resulting confusion. Did you know Hugh?'

Lord Campbell frowned, causing his shaggy brows to join together. 'Darned right I did. He was the talk of the town. I don't know how his father put up with it. Quite the playboy he was, by all accounts. So, before you ask if he had any enemies who might have done this, I'd say he had plenty. There isn't a gambling house north of the border he doesn't owe money to. And, no, before you ask, he wasn't due me any, and I didn't kill him. Although many would excuse me if I had.'

Bea raised her eyebrows, urging him to continue. 'He was the cause of my son's death. Alistair was a couple of years older than Hugh. They travelled back together in the same train carriage when they returned home from the war. Hugh had picked up Spanish flu, and well, he passed it on to the others in the carriage, and then they brought it back here. Hugh survived. My son and many others around here didn't. Not exactly a murderable offence, but I've never liked the lad since. He's a wastrel, a rogue and a cad. You'll be lucky to find anyone here who will say any different. Now, if you'll excuse me, it looks like I'm next in line to speak to the sergeant. I'll be telling him much the same as I've told you. Then I'll be heading home to bed.'

'How sad, and so many with a similar story,' Bea said as they watched Lord Campbell leave the room with his wife. 'To have survived the war and then die after making their way home, it's a tragedy and no mistake. And Mel wasn't exactly singing her brother's praises when we spoke to her earlier. It looks like there's a lot more going on here than we first thought. What?'

'Let's split up and then meet back here.' Dottie looked around. 'We can speak to as many of the guests as we can. You start with Claire Penny, and I'll go and offer my condolences to Mel.'

As Dottie made her way back to the card table after talking to Mel, her mother flapped a hand, calling her over. 'Oh, what a to-do. I've never known the likes here before,' Lady Alice said.

'Well, not recently, anyway. It all rather reminds me of that awful accident at the 1911 New Year's Day ride out.'

Dottie recalled the photograph she'd seen earlier and the butler's words. 'I was going to ask you about a picture I saw of you and Father in the gunroom. The butler said it shouldn't have been out on display. What happened?'

Lady Alice sighed. 'You will remember me telling you about it, Doris?' she said to her maid.

Doris nodded and uttered shushing sounds. 'Don't distress yourself, Lady Alice. There's no point in dragging this all up again. Perhaps you should speak to the gamekeeper about it yourself, Dottie.'

Lady Alice held up a gloved hand, waving away Doris's concerns. 'There's no need for that. It happened a long time ago. There was an accident out on the moor that year. The gamekeeper's son was shot. Dead.'

Dottie's hands flew to her mouth. 'Ooh, Mother. What happened?'

'Hugh and the gamekeeper's son were about sixteen then. They were larking around on the moor when Hugh's shotgun went off, killing the lad. Hugh was cleared of any responsibility. It was classed as an accidental death. High jinks, the judge called it.'

With an idea forming in her mind, Dottie returned to the Mahjong table where Bea was jotting down all that she'd found out. 'Okay, you go first,' she said to Bea.

'There wasn't much to glean from talking to Claire Penny, no matter how much I grilled her about Hugh. She hadn't met Hugh or Mel before today. I did find out something interesting about her, though.'

'Come on, don't keep me in suspense. Spill the beans.'

Bea grinned. 'Claire Penny was a cabaret dancer. That's how

Hugh met her. Most of her rude behaviour today has been an act. Underneath it all is a rather vulnerable woman who was scared we'd think of her as a gold digger. We had quite the chat, and she decided to come clean. I must say, she isn't all that bad. Duncan could do a lot worse. What about you, what did you find?'

'Well, according to Mel, Angus was meant to have travelled home from the war in isolation in a separate rail carriage along with the others who had flu symptoms, but he refused to do so. And he didn't let on about it to the others in his carriage, either. His symptoms were relatively mild. But it was what Mother told me that piqued my interest the most.'

'Come on then, let the cat out of the bag. What did Lady Alice have to say?'

After she'd given her mother's account of the 1911 accident, and Bea had jotted everything down, Dottie said, 'So, what do we have?'

Bea scanned through their notes. 'It seems many people around here had reason to dislike Hugh, and some would have a definite motive for murder. He was a bit of a playboy, to say the least. His irresponsibility and high jinks over the years have caused much loss and pain to others, and he doesn't seem to have been held to account for any of it.'

Dottie nodded. 'His father constantly bailed him out of gambling debts, and his behaviour must have brought shame to his family, including Mel.'

'Although bringing Spanish flu home wasn't intentional, many around here died because Hugh had refused to isolate himself.' Bea frowned. 'Although he claims otherwise, this certainly provides Lord Campbell with a strong motive.'

'And then there's the accidental shooting of the gamekeeper's son at the 1911 New Year's Day ride out to the moor,' Dottie added. 'We need to speak to the police.'

After dilly-dallying, the police sergeant finally agreed to hear Dottie and Bea out. Duncan escorted them through to the small parlour. When they reached the open door, Dottie was surprised to see the butler, gripped by the arm, and ready to be led away to the police station for further questioning, while he loudly protested his innocence.

'Oh, I say. Hold on there, chaps,' Dottie said. 'I think there are a few things you need to hear.'

After Dottie and Bea had given their account of all they had found out, the gamekeeper confessed to shooting Hugh in retaliation for him firing a gun at his son all these years ago. Although Hugh had been a young lad at the time, the gamekeeper felt he had never shown any remorse for his actions and had never been held to account for his reckless behaviour since then. Blinded by a need for justice for his son, the gamekeeper utilised the noise of the fireworks to shoot Hugh as he stood on the balcony.

After the police escorted the gamekeeper away, and Mel had left for home, accompanied by her father, who had come straight from the police station to collect her, the butler announced that New Year's dinner was ready to be served.

Dottie was seated beside Claire Penny, who remained friendly throughout the sumptuous meal. As they chatted together, without a nasty barb uttered between them, Dottie could tell that Claire was as devoted to Duncan as he was to her.

After dinner, she joined Bea and Lady Alice on a settee in the drawing room, where the butler supplied them with after-dinner cocktails. '1926 has proved to be a blinder of a year, so far. What?' Dottie raised her class to Bea and Lady Alice. 'Chin chin.'

The following morning, Dottie fastened the strap of her leather motoring cap as Bea pressed her foot on the accelerator and roared the Chummy along a straight stretch of road towards home. 'If we get a wiggle on, Bea, we should make it in time to go to the 'Bluesy Bandit' tonight.'

Lady Alice harrumphed in the back seat. 'What? Visit a Jazz bar? Oh, no, Dahlings, I think I will give that a miss. How anyone can class that noise as music, I don't know. I'd rather listen to barn owls screeching. You can count me out, girls. I have to say, though, Claire Penny wasn't half as bad as I first thought. Duncan's wife-to-be is rather snazzy. I liked her style.'

Dottie turned around in her seat. 'Really, Mother? You'll be telling us next that you're going to become one of the Bright New Things.'

Squashed in the back seat beside Lady Alice, Doris placed a hand over her mouth and stifled a giggle.

Catching Doris's eye before she turned to face the front, Dottie grinned, causing peals of laughter from the maid. Soon her mother and Bea joined in. Their hoots audible above the roar of the engine.

When they passed two men in peaked caps and tweed jackets making their way into a country pub, Bea honked the horn. *Bhap, bhap, bhap.*

'A Happy New Year,' Dottie called to them from the passenger seat and pulled down her goggles. 1926 beckoned, and she couldn't wait to embrace it.

Author Bio:

Sheena Macleod is an award-winning crime fiction and short story writer who lives in Scotland. She has had several short mysteries published and is the author of two historical fiction novels and one historical non-fiction book written to celebrate the 50th anniversary of women gaining the right to vote in the UK. Sheena blogs at *allaboutbooks. blog at WordPress.com*.

Chapter Ten

HOW TO WIN A LADY

Meg Woodward

Will Forbys (Villi Vorbus in German) is a Danziger Scot in the 1370s who is also a rich young Hansa merchant. He has also gained a reputation as an Enquirer after Truth. When a business trip coincides with a tournament in which the prize for the major competition is, to his disgust, a beautiful, gifted but illegitimate noble lady, rivalry gets out of hand and deaths occur. Will is summoned to find the killer(s). The story is based on truth and points a way into the novels about Will's enquiries.

'That's the prize.'

Will Forbys blinked at the Magdeburg Mayor's words. Before them a veiled girl held a large dish laden with sweetmeats. The platter was well enough polished and tooled but it was pewter, not even silver far less gold. Why were the contestants around him so eager to compete for such a trinket in the tournee planned for the following day? Then he realised that it would hold a fortune in coins. He reached for a honeyed walnut and the girl bobbed and floated away.

'And this gentleman is Hans Talhoffer. He supervises the Goslar contingent of knights.'

Talhoffer had followed Will into the city guildhall. Both were aberrations in the kaleidoscopic Hanseatic melee, tall, hatless and soberly dressed. Will's cream-coloured hair contrasted sharply with his brick-red, wind-scoured features, while Talhoffer's dark curls formed a cap sprinkled with silver at the temples. Like Will he was clean-shaven apart from impressive sideburns. It was these which eventually jogged Will's memory. He had seen this man before, in Austria, a dirty, dishevelled rogue who had just been apprehended after a street skirmish in which a Hungarian soldier had died. Then, bright clothes and fancy boots had declared him a man about town, and amused defiance had danced in his dark eyes. Now, these eyes danced again when Talhoffer registered Will's sudden recognition, after polite conversation on trade deals.

Large gatherings of challengers and supporters attending tournees were ideal cover for doing business. In the broad meadows by the River Elbe, local traders were already setting up booths and stalls. Big tents at one end would house groups of knights from different cities overnight, keeping youthful carousing apart from more sedate patrician gatherings indoors. In the middle, the large empty space was being marked out with sawdust and ropes for the swordplay and tilts to come. As groups arrived, marching in livery to the city gate, each enacted a traditional confrontation before being invited into town.

At Vespers in the cathedral, everyone watched as the competitors gathered around the tomb of Otto the Great. Will remembered that Otto had married the granddaughter of England's Alfred the Great, then wondered why his strange mind retained such useless information. After a short Mass the Bishop, mindful of the risks candidates would face the next day, held communion for the fighters. The three servers in white robes swung incense thuribles with vigour, leaving Will choking in the hateful fumes.

'How will they organise such a large competition?' Will asked as he and Hans Talhoffer headed for the guildhall again.

Hans flashed a quick smile. 'Look at the trees.' Hung from the lower branches were numerous shields. 'These belong to the visitors. Tomorrow begins when a Magdeburg fighter taps a shield. The owner will engage him in an agreed form of combat.'

'And if they can't agree?'

'Each will name his preferred weapon and they'll toss for it. All very fair. Survivors will challenge whom they please in turn until there are just two left and a final grand competition finishes things. That involves three bouts, one with lances, one with swords and one the weapon of choice of the fighter with fewer wins during the day. The prize will be there too, of course.' The dark eyes no longer smiled. 'She has no say in the matter.'

This time the rogue did not laugh as shocked comprehension hit Will.

The first incident occurred early in the evening. Will, as a senior merchant although probably the youngest, was feasting in the guildhall when rumours filtered in about a stramash between Brunswick and Hildesheim men. Minutes later came the news that the Hildesheim champion had been injured, rendering him unlikely to take part in any challenge. The offended Brunswick men denied any part of that. It was no way to win an honourable fight; and since it had happened in the dark it proved impossible to gather evidence against anybody.

Next a case of flux was reported, this time affecting a Paul Beneke. 'Mine,' muttered Hans, again seated beside Will. 'My best.' When Hans asked for permission to investigate, Will went with him.

'Trots and spew,' Hans sighed. The lad was undoubtedly ill. Inevitably someone muttered poison, which made Hans immediately order all the Goslar challengers to stick together and remain in their tent for the rest of the night. Will doubted if they would obey; this was a rare opportunity for young gadabouts to have fun away from home. Hans invited Will to investigate the sickness, since part of Will's trading involved apothecary goods, but he found no specific reason to suspect anything other than, perhaps, a bad fish. Since everybody had eaten the same food there was nothing to make a case with. Two untoward incidents were not unusual in competitive circumstances. Rivalry and dirty tricks were bedfellows. But Will did not forget them.

Back inside the guildhall, to Hans's irritation Will did what he usually did, remained silent and apparently half asleep. But Will's ears were open and his was brain working furiously, so both of them heard a nearby whispered debate. The sons of three local councillors, allowed to join the banquet because of their high birth, were discussing how they would treat the 'prize' if one of them won her. After sharing her, they would make money by hiring her out to wealthy merchants, even debating how high a fee they dare ask. Even more distasteful was that the girl, now unveiled and sitting at the top table beside the mayor, might have been within earshot. It was almost unheard of for women to attend a Hanseatic feast and her presence provoked unsettled muttering. Will looked at her more closely – and stopped breathing for a good minute. No wonder they all lusted after her. She could have been an angel, with her delicate beauty and air of serenity, except, he noted, that her fingers clutched her beaker very tightly. His disgust at the planned competition leeched into rage. After several minutes of worried admiration Will realised that there was another woman present, almost out of sight by the bright drapery on the back wall. That one seemed to be made of plump buns of various sizes baked together, head, body, limbs. Even the nose was round, and her mouth was pouting in intense anxiety. Plainly she did not like what she was hearing.

'I remember you from Austria,' Hans murmured, interrupting his thoughts. 'A boy scared out of his wits.'

'I was eleven,' snapped Will, reliving the terror of that unexpected brawl. 'And I'd just seen my first death.'

'A boy with devil's eyes.'

Will sighed. Hans could not miss the phenomenon right then. As his emotions intensified, Will's pupils grew enormous leaving a thin but blazing blue outer ring. There was nothing Will could do about it. He could never lie to his mother as a child any more than he could conceal strong feelings of any kind even now. All he could do was stare at his boots until he had control of himself.

'A boy,' Hans added softly, 'who went to the authorities next day to say that he had seen who really did the killing. Saved my life that did. So are you going to save the girl? Enter the lists?'

'I'm no knight.'

'Yea, yea, just Villi Vorbus.' It was the Germanised version of Will's name. 'Head of the richest trading house in Danzig. But son of a Scottish knight, aren't you? That would count. And,' Hans chortled, 'an Enquirer after Truth no less. Folk here must know that. If there's any more trouble, no doubt they'll ask you to investigate.'

'So I'll have no time to fight. I'm grossly out of practice anyway, not like all these young bloods. I came here on business.'

'And the girl goes to her fate?' They both looked at her. Calm and courteous, she was maintaining a conversation which certainly interested the men around her, while the bun lady watched her every move with love and fear and, Will thought, fury.

'Who is she?'

'The Mayor's niece, Freya. Illegitimate unfortunately. When her mother died a few weeks after her birth, her uncle took her in and raised her. Now comes payment, it seems. That,' he scowled, 'makes Rupert her cousin. Yes, Rupert von Rostend, the entitled Magdeburg champion over there. The one with copper hair.'

'And her servant by the arras? I imagine she'll try to protect her mistress?'

'Ah, Dame Alesha. Might not get far,' Hans growled. 'Had to intervene an hour ago to stop those three louts taunting her. Nasty with it they were. Trouble is that Freya's father, reputed father, was executed for treason, again reputed. His ship went down taking a year's profits. Most of the goods belonged to the then town councillors, and this Mayor was one who voted against him.'

Will knew all about ships going down, a recognised trading risk. 'And the owner had not put a protective levy in place, hm?'

'Plenty folk don't insure cargo. It's not compulsory.'

'But if something goes wrong, the cargo shareholders want revenge,' Will murmured, noticing the bun woman slip away when the girl rose and walked towards a harp by the fire. Her voice was as beautiful as her face and even Will, a musical dud, could tell that she was a skilled musician. Hans was enthralled, leaving Will to observe and think. Unusually, Freya was given total silence as she sang, and Will again sensed embarrassment. Of her being offered as a trophy? From her servant's reaction and the girl's own tension Will assumed this was being forced on her. There was nothing wrong with a lady performing as heroine of the tournee, a token honour, but to force any female to be given over in person to a winner was another matter. Then again, if the girl were unhappy in her present life perhaps she was willing and Rupert's behaviour in the past hour might suggest misery.

'She's a courtesan already,' snarled Hans, unnerving Will. 'Had to survive somehow. Has all the attributes, educated in a lot more than the basics, and she's well regarded.' Hans glanced at Will. 'I do wonder if her earnings go to her uncle. My guess is that she hopes to become a wife tomorrow.' Will wriggled. 'And not to one of those louts. Some say she's even a bit of a scholar like you. You need a wife, don't you?'

It was fury which made Will turn his devil's eyes on Hans, dismay that even this stranger knew of his late grandfather's demand. A condition of his remaining head of the Danzig trading house was that Will marry a German-born lady before he reached the age of thirty. 'I'll choose my own wife, thank you. You can join the listings. You're the Goslar fight master, aren't you?' Again, Hans just laughed.

The evening was drawing to a close when a servant entered to say that a number of other prospective fighters had been stricken with the same malady as the Goslar champion, including Rupert's two fellows. This time, the Mayor did ask Will to investigate. Hans went too, intrigued to observe his methods.

Will visited Rupert first. 'Can you please tell me what you all ate? Was there anything which you did not share in?'

'Are you accusing me of compromising my friends?' the man flared.

'Not at all. But perhaps someone else did.' Rupert simmered down and listed everything they had eaten, which Will presumed had come from the same pot as the rest of the company shared.

'Do you know if food eaten by the visitors outside came from the same kitchen as yours?'

'Ah, no. The groups prepare their own.'

'Then if this is a miasma, an infection breathed from one to another, have you or your friends met with any of the other victims of this flux?' It turned out that they had, except for a small contingent from Quedlinburg which had only just arrived. They had been served with food left over from the guildhall, and one of them was now sick. That sent Will to the guildhall kitchens to check on the ingredients used.

'Everything came from local markets,' the head cook insisted. 'We always use folk we know.' The man was worried, anxious to free his staff and himself from blame.

'Well, something is making people ill,' muttered Will. He did not mention that up till now all the victims were fighter candidates. 'May I ask you to talk to the cooks of the other food eaten by sick visitors? See if you can establish if there is any one ingredient which is common to all? It would help me greatly.' Courtesy usually encourages help and this time it did. The cook returned an hour later with just one snippet of news. Before his return, though, several other contestants, from both Magdeburg and elsewhere, had succumbed to the mysterious sickness. The listings for the coming tournee were shrinking rapidly.

While the cook was about his searches, Will managed to meet with the Lady Freya through a brazen approach by Hans. This time she was seated in an alcove in the antechamber with her maid who was most unwilling to allow their approach.

'My lady, forgive me,' Hans blundered in, 'we've been asked to check your health.'

'Her health.' This was Dame Alesha. 'How dare you...'

'And yours, madam,' Will interrupted rapidly, his cheeks aflame. 'We have all eaten the same food as some of the sick contestants. I wanted to ensure that neither of you have been affected.'

Freya laid a hand on Dame Alesha's arm to halt another explosion. 'We are well, sir. Do you know how many are ill?'

'Thirteen at the last count. All contestants, but none, I think likely to die of their afflictions.'

'But put out of action?' The servant's query was sharp.

'Probably.' Will looked more closely at the bun lady. 'You don't like this contest?'

'Do you?' she snapped back. 'An insult, especially on top of what has gone before. It's not right.'

'What went before, may I ask?' Again, the lady touched Dame Alesha's arm but the servant had the wind in her sails, sensing support from these men before her in a situation she felt to be dire.

'That uncle and his family. Treated her like rubbish all her life instead of the lady she really is. Forced her into...' she adjusted her words. '...suffering. Couldn't even use her proper name.'

Will blinked. 'And what is that?'

After a long pause, the lady said it with quiet sadness. 'Thyrea.'

Will searched his memory. 'Thyrea? As in the Greek dominion?'

His reward was a glorious smile. 'Indeed. You are the first one ever to know that. It was my father's wish.'

'Was your father Greek?' Will's question was careful. It could explain his death, an unprotected stranger easy to blame for misfortune.

'Prince and all,' butted in Dame Alesha. 'I was nurse to him before I was to Thyrea, poor little orphan. I'm all she has to protect her now.'

'Hush, *madonna*,' Thyrea murmured. 'We must look forward. We cannot change the past.'

'Forward? When that devil is in charge of your future? I'm telling you, I'm all you've got, for nobody else is doing anything to stop the rot.' That last barb made both men look at the bun lady and wonder if she was doing something herself.

'Mushrooms,' said the cook. 'That's the only ingredient which everybody ate. Not Rupert though. Can't abide them. Always picks them out. But everybody else had them as well, so why aren't all of you sick?'

Why indeed? That sent Will checking the source of the mushrooms, or sources, for mushrooms had been included in all the cooking pots. September was their high season. The individual cooks from the guildhall and the five separate camp kitchens had all bought their own ingredients in the Magdeburg market. But chasing that clue would have to wait till morning because everyone else was already in bed. The Hansa rule demanded that all members retire two hours after Compline. The local monastery bell had tolled over the city roofs ages ago and would ring again for Lauds and wake them all again at dawn.

By morning another sixteen candidates were sick, but still nobody else. The Mayor and Council were panicking. For every bout of fighting in which a candidate failed to take part they would lose a double fee, but they were far more afraid that they might be held responsible for the illnesses. Small wars had been fought over less. An hour later another eight were struck down. And Will had discovered that mushrooms on sale in the market were provided by many different gatherers. One name mentioned was indeed Dame Alesha. One sympathetic stallholder added that it was a way in which she made ends meet, for the Mayor did not give her a salary for attending Freya. Thyrea.

'Thyrea, such a beautiful name for such a beautiful lady,' sighed Hans over breakfast. Then he grinned at Will. 'I shall return it to her. Loudly. The least we can do, hm? But hasn't Dame Alesha been busy? How did she get round all those cooking pots in such a short time and still show her face in the hall?'

Will grimaced. 'She didn't.'

'Not alone, no. But can't you feel the displeasure here? The air is thick with it, so there'd be plenty who would help.'

'To do what? Add bad mushrooms to all the pots from which everybody sups, yet ensure that only today's knights become sick?'

Hans frowned, then brightened. 'So she had a helper in each camp. To put something into the right bowls.'

'How could the Magdeburg servers tell which was a fighter and which a supporter among the visitors?'

'Asked, of course.'

'Then we shall ask too.' It turned out that each contingent cooked and served its own food. Disappointed, Hans headed off to help the lady Thyrea and her nurse prepare stomach-soothing medications for the sufferers, insisting on repeating the girl's proper name every five minutes while flirting and laughing every time she blushed. A glowering Dame Alesha hovered throughout. When the distant monastery bell for Terce rang out Will left them to attend the performance of a new play, a Grail written by a poet he knew slightly. The stage would later be used by the city patricians to watch the competitions. More fighters were becoming ill, but several of the earliest sufferers were recovering, to Will's surprise. Perhaps the day would be saved after all. The play was middling poor in Will's opinion but was well attended by candidates, non-fighters and citizens who all applauded the basic message, that fighting while searching for the Holy Cup which caught the Blood of the Lord was an admirable profession.

Afterwards, the Bishop summoned Will and delivered a shock. Two of the Quedlinburg men had died of the sickness. After careful questioning, Will learned that the late contingent had been given a private communion as soon as they arrived, before being quartered and then fed from the guildhall kitchens. Under the Bishop's supervision, Will examined the victims' bodies, not the first he had done by any means, but there was nothing on the torsos or skin to indicate anything that might have triggered the sickness. No punctures, no bites, no unusual powder or stain, no injuries at all.

'I'm sorry, your Grace. I suggest that they died because the vomiting and flux together were so severe that there was not enough water inside them to keep them alive. Even when they drank, it came straight back up again. Their companions also say that there was blood in the vomit.'

'So, poison is possible?'

'Hm.' It was not what the Bishop wanted to hear. This was no longer a disruptive prank to disable opponents. Nor did the Bishop like Will's idea of how the ingredient was administered.

'And what poison?'

'There are several possibilities. Bad mushrooms yes, soaked and squeezed. Rotten shellfish, or fish of any kind. But I wonder if it could have been poison because these men had blood in their vomit. I suspect in their stools as well. And they died too quickly for normal sickness.'

'What, then?'

'Arsenic perhaps?'

The Bishop pondered. 'Several council members are rich through mining. The stuff is easy to obtain. Please, Herr Vorbus, say nothing of this publicly for the moment. We shall bring the two dead men into the vestry where it is cool. I shall arrange for two coffins to be delivered. But I think you must warn the Mayor to alert the constables. This news could cause a riot.'

At Sext there was another brief service, again with wafts of incense, and Will frowned at one of the servers as his copper curls glinted in a slant of light entering from one of the high cathedral windows. Back in the meadows, life had erupted into a frenzy in the midday heat. A large party of patricians and dignitaries had arrived in the field from the castle, including at least as many women as men. These ousted the burgesses and townsfolk who had been shrewd enough to come early to ensure the best places from which to exhibit their gaudy gowns. Disgruntled at their removal, the townsfolk in turn had displaced the lower classes, servants and folk with little clout and less time to spare. However, even the poorest groups driven to the very margins were festooned like their betters with packages of food and drink to while away the long sultry afternoon as they watched the jousting and fencing. There would be no archery that day. In case anybody came empty-handed, stalls and booths were bursting with temptations of all descriptions, food, drink, trinkets and fancies, cheap jewellery and ribbons, toys and games, anything which might catch the eye of people with coins in their pouches. The noise made Will's head spin.

A canopy was now erected over the stage. High above the throng sat the von Rostend family and their noted guests, with Thyrea right in the middle. Her golden dress glinted and glowed, exhibiting her worth in both monetary and social terms. Her hair flowed loosely around her shoulders suggesting virginity, although many in the crowd may have known that message was false. Nevertheless, she looked young and sweet, unbearably beautiful and innocent, and apparently calm and happy enough to be there. However afraid she might be, however shamed she might feel, she played her part superbly as the heroine of the day.

News of a spate of sickness had little effect on the rising excitement. Perhaps fear was allayed because Paul Beneke, the first victim and Goslar champion appeared, raising a loud cheer. In light armour, his wan face hidden behind a mesh visor, he opened proceedings when one of Rupert's co-conspirators tapped his shield hanging on the nearest tree. Paul chose to use rapiers, accepted because his opponent had also barely recovered but was determined to give his best performance. Between them they gave a fair demonstration of clever manoeuvres, enough to provide excitement for those not experienced enough to tell they were struggling. After some minutes the sword master in charge intervened, declared a draw and sent each of them to choose another shield from among the bright escutcheons on display on the trees. Paul's new opponent was another Goslar man who chose to use the lightweight epee as his weapon, hoping to spare Paul. Eventually he ceded the bout, knowing that Paul was their best candidate and trusting that he would continue to recover and bring eventual glory to their city. The other newcomer was a Brunswick man who chose daggers and went on to knock the weary Magdeburg knight out of the running.

At this point a trumpet blared and one candidate from each city came forward to tap a shield. In no time a number of fights were under way in different areas of the field. The weapons varied, heavy and light swords, curved falchions, long and short daggers, stilettos, quarterstaffs, even flails which proved highly entertaining to watch but which produced impressive swearing from the participants. As each candidate knocked out another he could choose to select a new opponent immediately or wait to recover - which incurred noisy catcalling. It became clear that new victims were succumbing to the strange malady while others were recovering at varying rates and entering the lists as they felt able. On the fringes, betting booths were doing phenomenal business, and the sun grew ever hotter. Will doubted if the canopy was helping Thyrea and her companions much. Most looked hot and bothered in spite of a slight breeze, but somehow, she remained cool and collected, and remarkably still.

The Mayor sent a boy to fetch Will. 'Well? Is this sickness because of something people have eaten? My son mentions mushrooms. It would explain why he's not ill.' Below their feet Rupert was in the midst of a fierce longsword bout with a giant from Quedlinburg who was getting the worst of it. Rupert's skill was undeniable.

'But all of us noncombatants have escaped. I don't think mushrooms are to blame. Sir, the Bishop has asked for discretion, but he wants me to tell you that two sick men have died. He thinks that you should be prepared to call out the guards...'

'Why? People die of sickness all the time.'

'Not like this,' Will insisted quietly. 'Since it is only the fighters who have been affected, it must be through something all of them ate or drank – or perhaps touched – but not the rest of us.'

'Such as?' The Mayor looked bewildered.

Will hesitated before answering. 'Bread and water? Last night?' The act of communion the previous evening had involved only and all of the fighters, except Rupert who had been busy as a server. The Mayor was not stupid. His face froze and the ruddiness of his cheeks faded to grey as he struggled to his feet. The unexpected movement brought him to the attention of his companions, including Thyrea. Her eyes met Will's, saw the huge black pupils, then swiftly looked away as she swallowed hard trying to regain her calm demeanour.

The Mayor glanced around as if seeking escape, looked down to where his son was finishing off his opponent, saw Dame Alesha staring at him from the back of the podium in horror and exclaimed, 'So she put bad mushrooms into the holy bread. The conniving old witch. I should have...'

'No, not the bread. I heard that sometimes she has a hand in preparing the wafers, but not this time. And the priest tells me that the same batch was offered to all of us at this morning's mass and nobody became sick. Tainted water would be much easier to pour away in secret and the chalice refilled.'

'With unblessed water?'

'Does the cathedral not stock reserves of blessed water in case of spills?'

'It would still have been her,' the Mayor insisted. 'She's Greek. You must know how Greeks are renowned for their skills at poisoning...'

'No.' Will despised the man's lack of morality. 'Just because she is Greek, she doesn't attend Catholic worship.' The only other candidate was Rupert, serving at the altar, as they both knew.

Rupert had just defeated his opponent and was considering whether to take a rest or tap another unclaimed shield. A glance at the trees showed very few left hanging from the branches.

Where had the afternoon gone? Rupert had done well enough to heed the rule for the final two challengers, that the candidate with fewer wins would choose the weapon for the last bout. He glanced towards the platform expecting congratulations from his father, then quailed at seeing his horror. Then he shook on seeing Will's devils' eyes blazing at him. Realising he had been unmasked he sped off to prepare his horse for the tilt.

Within half an hour his opponent for the final triple combat was known, Paul Beneke after all. Their swordplay was scintillating, but Paul's illness was catching up with him. When it came to the tilt, Paul had difficulty controlling his horse and Will feared for him, especially when Rupert smirked in an astonishing show of bravado. Will wished Hans were around to stop this joust but he was nowhere to be seen.

What happened next shocked everyone. The first tilt was a dead man's pass, and the second a perfunctory shoulder brush. For the third and last, each rider determined to gallop with points ahead. There was a loud clash and Paul lost his seat, flying backwards to hit the ground with a thump which shook the stadium. Everybody could see that his head was not how it should have been positioned on his shoulders, and the field grew silent. Into the stillness Will distinctly heard Dame Alesha moan, 'No. It's the wrong one.'

Will later readjusted his reading of that cry when Paul's stableman brought him two pieces of broken girth strap. The centre was torn apart, but the edges of the break bore straight cuts from a sharp blade. Could old Alesha have done that? Or did Rupert's cockiness hint at prior knowledge of the damage?

That was when Hans appeared at last. 'I stand in Paul Beneke's shoes,' he challenged loudly.

Clad in lightweight chainmail he marched to the trees and fished out a half hidden, battered black shield. Rupert began to shake. This man, everyone realised, had won nothing that day. He would have the choice of weapon, and that shield looked as if it had been through wars, and successfully since it was still here.

'I choose waisted hooking shields,' Hans declared, his eyes cold. He beckoned two squires forward with a huge matching pair. A gasp swept through the crowd. Shield fighting was the most dangerous form of combat. Very few men tried it and only ever in single combat, never on the battlefield. These weapons were spiked top and bottom, and cruel curves at each corner were sharpened into lethal pointed blades. If he could use these, Hans Talhoffer was a highly skilled fight master. Or he knew the value of intimidation. Rupert had never even touched one of these far less tried to use one. Knowing when to concede, he dropped on one knee.

Hans looked up at the Mayor whose stiff nod acknowledged him as champion of the day. The cheering swelled, but Hans had not finished. Casting his shield aside, he marched towards the stage and he, too, dropped on one knee, opening his arms wide. The gesture made the applause waver as curiosity took hold.

'My Lady Thyrea,' Hans bellowed. 'Will you marry me? I vow before all these people that I shall be faithful and loyal to you. I shall protect and respect you and keep you safe...' He hesitated long enough to glare first at the Mayor then at Rupert. '...for the rest of my life.'

Bewilderment made Thyrea remain silent for so long that Will thought she was going to refuse. Then she smiled her glorious smile, rose, stepped down from the dais and walked towards her suitor. The crowd erupted. Hans's face was a picture. Only then did Will realise the fight master was besotted with her. 'And Dame Alesha will come too, of course,' Hans added, turning towards his whooping Goslar supporters.

'But, your Grace, you cannot control how large a sip a worshipper would take,' Will had told the Bishop earlier. 'Most people just moisten their lips, but the Quedlinburg group arrived hot and thirsty. No doubt our two victims took a good mouthful.'

'Enough to kill them,' the Bishop murmured. 'That makes it murder.' From that Will realised that the killer would not be reprieved.

❁

Later, when the visiting parties were gone, Will faced Rupert. 'You should know that two men died of the poisoned holy water. The Bishop is... displeased.' Rupert grew as pale as his father. Then Will held out the broken girth strap, which he had mentioned to nobody so far.

'I didn't do that.' Rupert objected. 'Anyway, we chose the horses by lot.'

Will did not expect that. So, had Dame Alesha cut it? Or had her words just reflected her fear that Rupert had won her lady after all? The only other candidate was a man with dancing dark eyes who had just won himself a bride, and who had carried her far away by then.

Author Bio:

Meg Woodward has written all her life but not professionally. Publishing, teaching and heritage guiding has been her career during which she published many articles and short stories, nonfiction reports and publicity material before turning to novels in retirement. Two Hansa novels are published, two more coming soon and a fifth half written, all with the same enquirer as the hero, all available on Amazon.

Chapter Eleven

DEATH IN DOUNBY

Barbara Stevenson

A Stone Age Whodunnit

Life in Stone Age Orkney can be hard, but moreso when there is trouble between the men from different villages who are working to build a new Stone Circle. The matter gets out of hand when a body is found in unnatural circumstances. Marna must use her skills at detecting to find out the truth before more violence ensues.

There hadn't been a good murder on the island for ages.

There was nothing for Marna to investigate, not even a missing comb or a lost duckling. She was meant to be studying plants and new dyeing methods, and she was on the verge of producing a dark blue dye from black nightshade, but it wouldn't flower until another full moon had passed, and anyhow, the workshop she used had been damaged by recent storms and she was waiting for it to be repaired. This meant she had no excuse for not helping her mother.

She conceded that grinding bere into flour was necessary if you wanted to make bread, but she didn't understand why it had to be such hard work and, frankly, boring. All it involved was pouring the grain into the lower quern stone and rotating the upper stone to smash open the seed heads; it was a job for the boys, with strength in their arms and no thoughts in their head to distract them from the task. Marna had lots of thoughts in her head. Since early spring, life at the Ness had been hectic. As a centre for the potters who were developing more efficient techniques and trading with visitors to the island, the Ness was always busy, but now the priests were preparing for the summer solstice celebrations, which meant gathering oil for the lamps and dyeing cloth for their special garments. On top of that, work had restarted on the new stone circle at Brodgar.

There was a stone circle near Barnhouse, which they could see from the Ness. It had been built a long time before anyone living was born. A new stone circle, with five times as many stones, had been planned before Patro, her stepfather, had become High Priest, but he was anxious that the new circle should be bigger and better than any of the other circles he had visited on his travels outside of Orkney. He had recently been to Avebury and since then he hadn't stopped talking about the stones there.

The size, the weight, the colour, the carving. Anyone would have thought the stones danced around themselves.

Subsequently, he had arranged parties to quarry stones from

the coastal cliffs and drag them several miles using rope made from willow bark and nettles. Seaweed was used to aid the movement on rougher ground - the slimier the better. The younger boys enjoyed gathering the kelp, playing sliding games when they weren't being watched.

Marna wasn't really interested in the building work, but she was keen on seeing the bands of young men from the surrounding villages who had arrived at the Ness. Some were skilled stone carvers, but many were there to do the hard labour, pulling ropes and digging the holes for the stones to be hoisted into. They came from all across the island and naturally they had plenty of stories to tell. Instead of being stuck in her house on a sunny morning, grinding bere, Marna wanted to be out on the moor, chatting to the workers, helping where she could and generally being part of the bustle and excitement.

As Marna was moaning to herself, her mother entered the house, carrying a pot of whale oil. There was a lid on the pot, but nothing could hide the stench.

'Haven't you finished that yet?' her mother asked. 'I need the flour to get started on the bannocks. The folk from Dounby are here to work on their stone, and you know what appetites the men from that village have.'

'I've been at it since I got up. There should be enough ground by now,' Marna said, more in hope than belief. She hadn't put a great deal of effort into the task.

Her mother peered over to inspect her work, but the pot of oil she held got in the way. 'Here, take this,' she said, shoving it towards Marna.

Marna rose from where she had been kneeling over the quern stones and took the pot. It was heavier than she thought, and she needed both hands. Her mother tutted as she staggered under the weight.

'Put it on the dresser before you drop it. You know how important whale oil is for the lanterns, and not so easy to obtain these days,' her mother chided.

Marna did as she was told. She had to move aside one of the smaller pots already on the stone shelf to make room. Once the whale oil was safely stored, she lifted the lid from the smaller pot and looked inside. It was empty. An idea came to her.

'We are out of burdock,' she said, demonstrating the empty pot to her mother. 'You'll need burdock roots to flavour the bannocks.'

'And for the dandelion ale,' her mother agreed.

'I'll go and gather some. I'll fetch more meadowsweet while I'm out as well.'

'There's no need, I can ask...'

Marna didn't wait for her mother to finish. Ignoring her protests, she grabbed a reed basket and left the house. Her family lived inside the Ness, because of her stepfather's position, but most of the workers lived outside the walls. There were dormitories in the Ness for visitors, but most of the buildings were for work or ceremony.

It was a short walk up the hill to the site where work was taking place on the stone circle. There were only two stones in place. The first one had been erected by the men of the Ness, among them Marna's brother, Thork. It had been put in place the previous autumn, before the days were too short and the wind too bitter for outdoor work, but that didn't stop Thork continuing to boast about his part in its erection. Marna had watched them working. Thork had a loud voice and he was good at shouting instructions, but most of the hard work was done by others. She expected her brother to be at the site now, giving his advice to the men from Dounby. Dounby wasn't far away, just at the top of the loch of Harray, so the village could afford to send a strong team of workers. It was unlikely the men would need, or appreciate, opinions from Thork about their work. Marna suspected she would be required to prevent the inevitable squabbles from developing into serious fights.

It wasn't long before she heard her brother's bellowing voice. It wasn't the only one raised. A quarrel had broken out, much as

Marna had feared. It wasn't easy striding across the bushy heather, but she began to pick up speed. She could see the men. There was a stand-off between Thork and two of his friends, Drake and Conno, and a red-headed lad from Dounby, who was backed up by two of his own supporters. They looked equally matched, and both sides were eager to prove their strength. The red-headed lad had his fists clenched and there was a twisted look on his face.

'What's up, boys?' Marna called cheerfully as she approached them.

With hair growing richly on his chin, and already a father himself, she knew Thork hated being called a boy, and guessed the men from Dounby would object too. They might direct their anger against her, rather than one another.

'Stay out of this, Marna,' Thork ordered. He tightened his grip on the wooden staff he was carrying. It wasn't actually a weapon. It was decorated with carvings and, as the step-son of the High Priest, he carried it to pretend he had authority.

'Mum sent me. She wants to know when you men will want to eat. She is organising the folks in the Ness to prepare a feast. It is being laid out in the main gathering hall.'

The two friends of the red-headed lad nodded their approval. One of them licked his lips. Their leader stared at Marna with unnaturally wide eyes. It was more as if he were looking through her at something in the distance. After a moment, he raised an arm, as if shielding his face from her.

'Go back to your cooking, girl. Tell your mother we'll be along when our business is finished here.' He waved her away.

'Don't address my sister like that,' Thork answered, pushing out his chest and moving a step closer. Marna could tell the red-headed lad was eager to lash out at him. His friends seemed afraid to stop him.

'Patro said he might come up and see what progress is being made before it gets dark,' she said, hoping her lie was convincing.

The threat of the High Priest turning up worked better than the promise of dinner. Patro had a reputation for being strict and although he was no longer in his prime, nobody wanted to be seen slacking or quarrelling in his presence. The two friends of the red-headed lad quickly moved to return to their work.

The red-head hesitated. 'This isn't over between us,' he spat at Thork. Thork stood his ground and the lad turned and followed after his friends.

Drake and Conno jeered, but Thork made a face, telling them to stop.

'What was that about?' Marna asked.

'Flanen, the red-head, had the cheek to say our stone was squint and didn't align properly with the sun.' Thork grunted. 'What would he know?'

'Aye. Did you see his lips as he spoke? They were like a girl's,' Drake put in. 'All plump and reddened.' He bunched his own lips with his fingers to emphasise the point.

'He is the best stone worker in Dounby,' Conno argued.

'That doesn't say much,' Thork snorted.

'Patro thinks highly of him,' Conno answered. 'I heard him say he was going to invite Flanen to stay on at the Ness, even after the Dounby stone is raised.'

Thork frowned. 'Over my dead body. Or his.'

Thork looked towards the man he had called Flanen. He shook his head, then turned away to walk back to the Ness. He raised his arm, signalling Drake and Conno to follow him.

Marna would have liked to go with him. She knew he would be reporting to Patro, and she was curious to hear what was said, but she had told her mother she was collecting burdock and meadowsweet. She couldn't go back empty-handed. There was plenty of meadowsweet to pick at the side of the loch, but she would have to go farther to find burdock. Uprooting the plants was messy work, which took time.

The task took longer than Marna had allowed for, not helped by falling into the loch while reaching for a healthy bunch of meadowsweet. As well as getting soaked, she lost the plants she had already gathered and had to rescue her basket from a belligerent duck. The sun dried her tunic as she wove new reeds into the basket, to cover the hole from the duck's bill.

Although it was the season for burdock, she found it impossible to find any. No doubt other villagers had got to the best plants before her. Her path took her further from the Ness, along the banks of Harray loch, towards Dounby. It had been before noon when she set out, but now the sun was dropping lower in the sky and she knew she should turn back. As the High Priest's wife, her mother prided herself on being the perfect hostess, but she would need her help, given the number of workers there were to cater for. There were other women in the Ness who could cook and serve food, but her absence would be noted. Besides, it was too late now to add any burdock she found to the bread dough, or flavour the ale with fresh meadowsweet. Her mother would have found what she needed elsewhere. Marna hated admitting defeat. Perhaps, if she tried the small copse of willow trees she could see in the distance, there might be burdock there.

The area was shaded, which made it hard to see past the first tree, but there was something odd about the way the willow branches were swaying from the tree behind. There was no breeze, so they shouldn't be dancing. She moved closer. There was something stuck in the tree. Marna suspected it might be a young deer. She hurried to help it, but as she got closer her heart jumped and she dropped her basket.

She had been right, there was something trapped. A bird's nest of tangled red hair. The head, thankfully, was still attached, but hung at such an angle that Marna doubted it would remain so for much longer. The rest of the body was still warm. Marna hadn't intended touching it to find out, but as she neared she tripped on an unearthed root and flung out her arms to stop herself falling. She let out a gasp and jumped back as quickly as she could.

Once she had regained her composure, she noticed there was no blood, apart from a small clot that had dribbled from the mouth. On closer inspection Marna saw the problem. A rope was around the man's neck, half hidden by his locks of hair. This was no accident; someone had deliberately killed Flanen, for she recognised it was him. Marna's mind flashed back to the incident with her brother and his friends. Thork had a hot temper, but she had seen him return to the Ness. He wasn't the sort to hold a grudge for long. He wouldn't have waited and followed Flanen when he was alone. She wasn't so sure about his friends. Conno was alright, but she didn't like Drake. He was a loudmouth, who spoke before he thought what harm his words might do. He also had the strength to take on Flanen.

She soon recovered from the initial horror of finding the body. It wasn't the first dead person she had seen, although it was the first with a rope around his neck. Her mind began to ask questions, trying to figure out what might have happened.

What was Flanen doing here anyway? He should have been at the Ness.

The small wood was a little over a hundred good strides from Dounby, so perhaps he was returning home.

Why would he do that, when he knew a feast was being laid on at the Ness?

He was a leader, he wouldn't have left his men and gone home alone, unless there was a really important reason.

Perhaps he had arranged to meet someone.

This seemed a reasonable possibility. Marna had done some sleuthing before, unearthing a killer at Maeshowe and revealing who was behind the strange deaths in Eynhallow. As she thought of these previous murders, it occurred to her that, like then, she might be in danger herself. Especially if she remained where she was. The body was warm, so the killer wasn't far away.

'Marna, there you are. We've been searching for you for ages.' It was her brother's voice. She turned to see him and his two friends march towards her. They stopped abruptly when they saw Flanen's body trapped in the tree. Conno's face turned pale and he looked like he was about to bring up his dinner.

'It's Flanen,' Marna said, unnecessarily. 'He's dead.'

'How? Who did it?' Drake demanded.

'How should I know?' Marna retorted. 'I found him here not long before you arrived.'

'We'll have to cut him down,' Thork said. He reached for his flint knife and stepped towards the tree.

'Careful,' Marna advised. 'I haven't inspected the site yet. There may be clues which will tell us what happened and who did this.' She stared pointedly at Drake.

Thork sighed. He was used to his sister's unnatural compulsion to investigate every death on the islands. Man or beast. Natural or otherwise.

'We can all see what killed him,' Drake said. 'He's got a rope around his neck. It doesn't look like one of ours. It's made of burdock fibre and we all know where that grows. This rope belonged to a Dounby man.'

'Or woman,' Marna said.

Drake scoffed. 'No woman could get the better of Flanen, or have the strength to strangle him.'

'What if he wasn't strangled?' Marna said. She didn't like being contradicted, and her instincts told her there was something wrong with the scene. 'There's a rope around his neck, yes, but he could have been dead when it was placed there.'

Drake rolled his eyes.

'There are no signs of bruising around the neck,' Marna explained.

'There's no blood either,' Thork said. 'He couldn't have been stabbed or attacked with an axe.'

'There may be blood on his back,' Marna said. Having objected to the body being moved, she was now curious to find out.

Thork nodded to his friends and the three men removed

Flanen's body. They laid it face down on the ground as carefully as they could.

'Still no wounds,' Drake said.

'There are some scratches to his face and arms,' Conno admitted.

'Those probably came from the tree branches,' Drake argued.

'It's just willow, the wood is soft.' Conno didn't like being corrected. 'Maybe he put up a fight.'

'That wouldn't surprise me,' Thork agreed.

Marna thought for a moment. 'Flanen was acting strangely when you argued with him earlier.'

'No more than usual,' Thork said. 'Flanen likes to pick fights.'

'This seemed different.'

'His vision must have been causing him problems,' Conno said. 'He was convinced our stone was crooked.'

'He was just mouthing off,' Drake said.

'Maybe not,' Marna said. She rubbed a finger to her chin. 'He could have been poisoned.'

Thork sighed. Drake laughed.

'I'm serious. I know about plants. See how pale his skin is.'

'He's dead,' Drake argued. 'You can't expect his skin to be glowing with health.'

'But did you not notice how wide his eyes looked earlier?' Marna persisted.

'That may well be, but he didn't put the rope around his neck and tangle himself in the bush,' Thork objected.

'Someone could have given him a potion to weaken him,' Conno mused.

Drake scoffed, but Thork nodded. 'That's a good point.'

Conno blushed, pleased to be given praise from Thork.

'Flanen's knife is missing,' Marna noted. 'He had a knife in his belt, I remember, because I thought he might use it against you.'

'So, he lost his knife. We don't have time to search for it

now,' Thork said. 'We'll have to take the body back to the Ness before it gets dark.'

'You can't carry him all that way,' Marna protested.

'No, but we came by boat across the loch,' Thork answered.

'We can't take him back. The Dounby men will think we killed him,' Drake said. 'Or at least they'll try to blame us, especially if it was one of them who did it. There could be trouble.'

'Which is why we need to find out what really happened,' Marna answered. She had already walked across to an area of flattened heather and was poking it with her foot. Thork looked at his friends and shrugged. They reluctantly joined Marna in her search for the knife. Thork found it, among a bunch of berries.

'There is a blood stain on the stone blade,' he announced, as if it had been his idea to search for the knife. He touched the blood with his finger. 'It's still red.'

'Which means he may have marked his killer,' Marna said. 'We just have to find someone with a knife cut.'

'You can't accuse everyone with a cut somewhere on their body of being a killer,' Drake said. 'I cut my hand on my axe when I was chopping wood two days ago. I'm sure others have had similar accidents.'

Drake demonstrated the cut. It wasn't deep, but the edges were fresh and it looked more recent than Drake claimed. Marna sympathised, but she decided to ask Thork, when they were alone, whether Drake and Conno had been with him the whole time, after they left Flanen.

'Let's get him in the boat,' Thork said. 'We are late for dinner as it is.'

'How can you think of eating?' Conno asked.

Marna guessed it was his first dead body. He wasn't keen to handle it. The body was awkward to manipulate, but between them they half-carried, half-dragged it to the edge of the loch, where the boat was waiting.

'There won't be room for all of us and Flanen,' Drake said.

'I'll walk back. I'm not that hungry, I'll get some supper later. Besides, I'm not keen on dining with the Dounby folk after this.'

Flanen's body was sprawled across Thork's small boat. There was hardly space for the rowers and Marna feared her addition would run the risk of it capsizing. Drake's argument made sense, but Marna sensed he had another reason for lingering behind. *Perhaps he meant to look for something he had lost, or re-arrange the scene to throw the blame on one of the Dounby lads.*

She couldn't think of a reason to object, so kept quiet.

Conno, Thork and Marna got into the boat and arranged themselves around the body, which kept drooping onto them. Conno and Thork took the oars. It was heavy work and the journey was slow and uneven. Marna tried to stop herself from touching the body when the boat rolled. It had started to smell, and she held her sleeve against her nose. Conno and Thork didn't have that option while they rowed. Marna could see them screwing up their noses.

'What did you do after you returned to the Ness?' she asked them as casually as she could. 'Did you speak with Patro?'

'Thork did,' Conno answered. 'Your mother asked Drake and me to get more wood for the fires.'

'There's a stack in the store room,' Marna said. 'Fetching it wouldn't have taken very long.'

'We met some of the boys who were tending the cattle. One of the calves had fallen in a muddy ditch. They needed our help to get it out.'

There was no mud on Conno's tunic. Marna allowed that he could have changed it before dinner.

'You don't have to answer my sister's stupid questions,' Thork broke in. His voice was angry.

'No, but if I don't ask them, the chief of the Dounby folk will,' Marna argued.

'You believe you can work out what happened by asking questions?' Conno asked. There was a hint of admiration in his voice.

'Not just by questioning, but also by observation,' Marna answered. 'In fact, I've got an idea what might have happened. I will need to speak to Flanen's two friends, the ones who were with him at noon. I also want to see their arms. I suspect one or both of them will have cuts or bruises. I don't suppose you saw them, when you were out with the cattle?'

Conno shook his head. 'We weren't near the site of the circle.'

'I don't think they were either,' Marna answered.

They continued the journey in silence. Marna was busy thinking and the lads were straining under the weight of the body. Finally, they spotted the smoke rising from the buildings of the Ness and rowed with increased vigour to the bank. A small party was waiting for them, including Patro and the two friends of the dead man. They spied Flanen's body in the boat and rushed into the water to meet them. Their efforts to drag their friend out of the boat and away from the rowers resulted in the boat listing. Thork made a swipe at them with an oar to prevent the boat capsizing. He hit the first man, knocking him under the water.

'Hold.' Patro's voice was commanding.

The Dounby men let go of Flanen. They helped their friend to surface as Thork and Conno directed the boat to the shore. Thork jumped out and pulled the boat up onto the sand. Immediately everyone present could tell that Flanen was dead. Their faces turned various hues, from sickly green to angry red.

'Murderer.' One of the dead man's friends pointed the finger of an outstretched arm at Thork. His arm was bare from the elbow. Marna had got out of the boat and could see the edge of a slash poking out from the hem of his rolled-up sleeve. She nudged Thork.

'How did you get that cut?' Thork demanded bluntly. Marna saw the eyes of her stepfather, Patro, roll in exasperation.

'On the stone we were chiselling,' the man answered. 'There were others who saw me do it. You are trying to deflect attention from your own guilt. We heard you quarrel with Flanen. We heard him say it wasn't over. Now look what has happened.'

His words were fierce, but there was hesitation in his voice. Marna sensed he was trying to convince the others of his innocence, rather than Thork's guilt.

'We found Flanen's knife covered with blood,' Conno spoke up.

'Aye.' Thork's eyes burned as an idea occurred to him. Marna groaned. Thork's ideas were never good ones. 'Let us test whose blood it is,' Thork continued. 'We should gather in the centre of the ancient Stones of Stenness, the circle built by our ancestors to meet with their gods. If we beseech them, when the sun dies and the moon is reborn, the soul of Flanen will rise up and demand vengeance against his assailant.'

Patro gave an audible sigh. He was the High Priest of the Ness, but Marna was aware that he didn't believe the old tales of spirits of the dead rising on demand. However, it was clear the Dounby men did, because she could see them shaking.

'There will be no need for such a ceremony,' Patro said. 'We can discuss this matter indoors, in private.'

'No. The crowd gathered have a right to hear.' Thork stood his ground.

Patro raised his eyebrows. He did not like being contradicted. He raised his staff and was about to respond when Marna interrupted.

'So they shall,' she declared. She was tired of the posturing of the men. She had arranged everything in her mind, and was convinced she knew what had happened. A little more actual evidence to show the folk would have helped though.'

'How can you know who killed Flanen?' the man with the scar asked in a mocking voice.

Marna was used to strangers questioning her abilities, but she was tired and hungry and answered haughtily, 'The facts are plain for everyone to see.'

The man scowled and waved away her remarks with his hand.

She looked towards Patro. Her stepfather was aware of her powers of deduction. She had proved them to him on several occasions in the past. At first, he too had been scathing, but he had come to trust her.

'We shall hear what Marna has to say,' Patro said.

His voice carried authority and the crowd quietened.

'Be brief,' Patro said in a low voice to her. 'We are waiting to dine.'

Marna thought that getting to the truth of Flanen's death was more important than supper, but she nodded. Taking up a position on a rock where most people could see her, she began. 'When I saw Flanen this morning, he was indeed arguing with my brother Thork, but his agitation seemed too extravagant to be caused by a mere battle of words over a trivial matter.'

Thork coughed, unhappy that the insult to his stone should be regarded as minor, but Marna ignored him.

'Flanen's eyes were wild, and he shielded them when he spoke. I didn't understand this at the time. I thought, perhaps, he didn't want to look at me. Perhaps my hair was unkempt or covered in dust from the flour I was grinding, but now I realise I was standing with the sun on my back. To look at me, he had to squint his eyes to the sunlight. From his reaction, I'm guessing that made them smart. Then there was the accusation against my brother, that the stone he helped raise was at an angle. This was clearly false. Anybody could see the stone was standing as straight as...' Marna hesitated. She had started a comparison but couldn't think what to compare the stone to. '...As the guard stone itself,' she said, referring to the single stone that showed the setting sun the way to the entrance of Maeshowe tomb at the winter solstice.

Patro sighed again, this time loudly, exhorting her to get on with the account.

'When I found Flanen, against the tree, he had a rope around his neck, aye, but there was no bruising to indicate he had been strangled by it. The rope alone did not kill Flanen, although struggling against it would have hastened his death. As Conno said, we found his knife nearby with fresh blood on it. What was more telling, though, was that we found the knife near a bunch of berries.'

Normally Marna would have paused to allow her listeners to work out what she meant, but even from a distance she felt the heat of Patro's breath on her and hurried on. 'Drake had made a joke of Flanen's lips being red, like a girl using rock lichen to attract a boy. Except Flanen's lips weren't plumped up, as he pretended. They were red from eating berries. The berries that grew near Dounby, which Flanen would have seen on his way here, were those of the deadly nightshade. My mother taught everyone in our village never to eat these berries, but they are tempting to those who do not know of their poison.'

'So Flanen was poisoned?' Thork said.

'Yes, but not by any man or woman, by his own hand.'

The crowd began to murmur.

'I've never known a case of poisoning where the victim is found with a rope around his neck,' Thork said.

Marna had an idea about that, but she hesitated to share it without more proof. Fortunately, Flanen's friend, the one with the scar, spoke up.

'The girl speaks truly. We had been given warnings by the healers in Dounby about the power of these berries, but Flanen laughed at us when we told him. He was hungry and didn't believe a few berries could harm him as he was fit and strong. He didn't just eat a few though. He guzzled handfuls, enough to stain his lips as she said. By the time we arrived at the Ness we could tell his vision was impaired, although he denied it. He began acting strangely and lashing out at everyone. We feared for his safety, as well as our own. After the quarrel with Thork, I persuaded him to come home with me. We got near Dounby, but he began to have mad fits, as if possessed by swarming bees. I didn't know what to do. I feared if I left him and went for help in the village he would do himself harm. I had a rope, which we had been using on the site and I tried to contain him with it. I tossed it round his shoulder. He drew his knife and managed to loosen the rope, but somehow it became entangled round his neck. In a rage he staggered into the tree and then he just collapsed. I knew he was dead.'

'And you just left him there?' Marna asked.

'There was little else I could do. I couldn't carry him myself, and I feared going on to Dounby, lest I be accused of his death. I panicked and decided to return to the Ness, hoping nobody would have seen me leave.'

'You should have told me everything, on your return,' Patro said.

'Aye sir and I would have, if we had a chance to speak alone.'

Patro nodded, accepting the man's word. He raised his staff, the head of which was carved and painted with a magnificent sea eagle. It struck awe into everyone present, including Marna.

'Flanen's body shall be laid out in the Ness tonight. Afterwards it will be attended to with every rite demanded by his family in Dounby. Tonight, we shall remember his life as we eat and toast his departed spirit. We pride ourselves here on our dandelion and burdock root ale.

'Aah.' Marna couldn't help letting out a small gasp. With all the goings on, she had forgotten the burdock.

Author Bio:

Barbara Stevenson writes historical and fantasy novels, often combining the two genres. She also writes Stone Age Whodunits set in Orkney, with Marna as the sleuth, under the pseudonym of B K Bryce.

Chapter Twelve

CAVE MOUTH CRIME

Loretta Mulholland

During the Great War, men from all over this land laid down their tools and ploughs, leaving for far away fields to fulfil their patriotic duty. On the Atlantic Archipelago, the people of the tough but idyllic Slate Islands were no exception. As the spectre of fate hovered cruelly above the continent, the women and children who were left behind held their communities together, despite the fear that at any given time word from the mainland could mean another of their community had fallen.

What did Ellen see? Was the stranger who'd come to teach the children up to no good?

Can Isa, the wise mother of the isles, unravel the strange goings on that are emerging?

A Scottish Island Mystery

That day she heard the scream, Ellen was hanging out the washing. It came from the hillside. Looking up, she saw a figure dart into the mouth of the cave. She dropped her pegs, hitched up her skirt and ran towards the noise. As the wind tugged at her rusty hair, she scrambled up the brae. The screaming had stopped, but when she looked down, she saw ripples in the quarry loch. Floating on the surface was a dark, body-like shape. It was her turn to scream, but before she could make a sound, everything went black, and she fell to the ground.

Earlier in the same day, Aunty Isa strolled down to the jetty to collect provisions for herself and some boxes for the store that she ran. She was remembering a time, not that long ago, when Lachie's sons would help her carry the groceries up the hill and into the clachan. Since the war had come, the slate quarry and machinery stood unused like sculpted metal figures in a barren landscape. The island, the smallest of the Scottish Atlantic Slate Islands, fell silent on that last day of its working life, when most of the men volunteered.

'It hadnae been doin well afore thi war anyway,' Isa muttered into the wind. 'Was goin doon after yon Welsh slate quarries started up.' She shuddered at the memory of the island emptying of men, crossing the sea, remembering the women and children's tears and her own dread of the letters and telegrams that might follow. She had no one left to mourn, but everyone else she knew did.

The breeze heightened, bringing her back to the present. The wee ferry chugged louder as it came nearer to land. Aunty Isa watched as Lachie steered it expertly into the choppy water that lapped at the sides of the jetty. Only a little while ago, his two lads would have been on that boat with him. Isa let out a chuckle as she remembered the days when they would bring their bicycle, taking turns or giving each other backies as one rode and the other carried tins of ham, bottles of milk and water, sacks of flour and oats, and on good days, maybe some fresh fish and butter.

But with conscription the lads had been taken away and their father left to worry. As Lachie stopped the engine and flung a rope towards the bollard, Isa noticed how his shoulders drooped and he coughed hoarsely. 'Yon man's a shadow o himself,' she thought. 'Livin every day in dread.'

As she approached the boat, Lachie assembled a few cardboard boxes for his oldest and most faithful customer. Wind whipped at his bunnet and rain splattered into his skin as he greeted her, 'Mornin Aunty Isa. A bit wild thi day, eh?'

The boat bobbed in the waves that slashed into the stone-built pier and scattered a couple of shags from the black shoreline. Isa still smiled when he called her 'aunty', as everyone on the island did in recognition of her age, kindness and wisdom. 'Yer no wrong there,' she answered, and her old friend glanced up and gave her a wink.

As they made their way back to the clachan together, Isa's spirits rose. Clouds lifted, the wind died, and the sun shone. Meadow buttercups and bell heather scattered the brae that led to the row of labourers' cottages.

Isa saw a bunch of women sitting outside, as they so often did, around eleven each morning after they'd sent the children to school, done the dishes and washing, swept doorsteps, and gathered wildflowers to place in a jar and brighten the windows in the clachan's one and only street. Here they were, chatting on chairs, pulling weeds from the path, and exchanging news and gossip, before resuming the day's work. Baskets containing colourful balls of wool, knitting needles and half-finished work were strewn by their sides.

'Look at that,' Aunty Isa said to Lachie, as the wet grass squelched beneath their feet. 'Nae wonder their knittin is the pride o the West Coast, eh Lachie?'

'Aye hen,' he agreed. 'They must've knitted enough socks,

scarves and blankets for every soldier in Flanders by now.' He smiled as Isa led him into the store and they went into the back to shove the kettle on.

'At least we've no suffered too much from the war yet,' Isa said, as she watched steam rise from the kettle moments before it whistled.

'That's true,' Lachie replied. 'It was terrible to lose Johnnie and Joe, though. Right hard fir their wives an the wee ones.'

'Aye, an Jamie Armstrong tae. His mither took that right bad,' Isa replied, nodding as the boiling water swirled the tea leaves around the pot.

'Well, ye were a great comfort tae thi lot o them,' Lachie answered.

Hearing his voice tremble, Isa shifted the subject.

With conscription, everyone's fears about the seriousness of the war heightened, but the women hid their worries through hard domestic graft and the near-constant clacking of steel knitting pins.

The families left liked to swim and bathe in the little loch, created by the quarry flooding two winters ago. It lay at the foot of a hillside where a large cave dominated the skyline. Though the population had peaked at 150 during the height of slate production at the turn of the century, only a dozen women remained, with twenty children and a few singles, creating an eerie kind of emptiness. The schoolteacher had gone off to fight at the front too, and when a stranger had arrived on the island in the spring of that year, lessons resumed. The women were relieved.

Some were lucky enough to get letters from their menfolk. Aunty Isa never got any but she had comforted those who did when the news was not good and no one felt lucky.

The women kept knitting, the children kept learning, the

seabirds kept cawing, and the quarry kept quiet. Clocks ticked on mantelpieces while chalk scraped the board.

Aunty Isa noticed some changes after the new schoolteacher had arrived. The children had become quiet. More reserved than before, Isa thought. One morning, as the women sat outside in the sunshine, knitting together, Ellen told them of a worry she had.

'My Tommy's comin back from school wi red hands nearly every day. Ah don't know whit's goin on,' she complained, pulling tighter at her wool. 'I asked him whit wis the matter but he wouldnae tell me. I asked wee Violet tae, but she jist looked at me wi yon wide eyes and shook her heid till her pony tail came loose.'

The school bell tolled every day at nine o'clock sharp. Bessie from No. 11 had this task, after she'd lit the fire in the schoolmaster's house, prepared a breakfast of hot bread and porridge and set the kettle on the stove. He was a 'crabbit auld git' she'd told the others and 'ay moanin aboot thi weans'. But Lachie had delivered a pile of new books on English and Geography and a parcel of jotters and pencils, so Auld Grumpy Drawers was managing to get money from the Board, at least.

It was break time at school but no bell rang. Some children squirmed in their seats and others whispered across the room as Auld Grumpy Drawers scratched sums in yellow chalk on the board. Violet, the youngest in the school, shouted out and covered her ears at the screeching of used chalk scraping the black surface, and the master turned around, nostrils flaring, moustache dripping with sweat. He lifted a dandruff dusted shoulder, raised his arm well above his head and looked for a moment, as though he was about to throw the stub straight at the girl's face, before dropping his arm again, frowning in self-disgust.

Too late though, the poor wee lass was terrified and cried even louder. Tommy sat on the opposite bench. He stood up in fury and launched his new jotter and pencil straight at Auld Grumpy Drawers, and a riot broke out. The children piled out into the yard chased by their teacher, but everyone stopped when they saw Ellen. Her curls were matted with blood. Someone had wrapped a shawl around her, her neighbours flapped about in panic, shouting orders to each other about kettles and towels.

Tommy barged through the small crowd straight into his mother's arms. Ellen lifted a hand from beneath the shawl and placed it on his head. When he looked up, he saw her lips quiver, as she turned her face away to wipe her tears on the shawl. She had no idea what had happened to her or how she had got back to the clachan. Violet and the other children came towards her till all the islanders surrounded her - except the schoolmaster who headed back into the building unnoticed by everyone, apart from Aunty Isa. She observed him wipe his brow, but he did so with what looked like a lady's handkerchief, with wild yellow roses embroidered round the edges.

Wondering about his reaction, and the hankie, Aunty Isa took more notice of what was going on in the schoolhouse after that. She started chatting regularly to Bessie too, who seemed glad of the attention and soon the girl was visiting her new friend on the odd night, bringing along gingerbread or sultana cake that she'd baked.

At first, she thought the old woman was just after some company but one evening as the sun sank low and reflected in ribbons of orange against the blue waves. Aunty Isa asked her a question, 'Whit does thi auld git dae in thi evenings when school's oot an his tea is done? Naebody sees much o him, dae they lass?'

Bessie slurped at tea the colour of tablet then placed the cup back upon its saucer. The painted primroses matched those that had opened in the springtime on the hillside behind them. The young girl screwed her eyes against the sun.

'Y'know Aunty. Ah've nivver thought aboot that fir a minnit. No a single second,' she said, turning to smile at the kindly old face that questioned her. 'Bit Ah think wi ought tae find oot, dae you no?'

The two women, one seventeen, one seventy, clinked their teacups together, before placing them on their saucers. Bessie handed Aunty Isa another slice of gingerbread from the plate between the crockery. Isa felt butter melt and spices tingle in her mouth as the sun dipped below the horizon. All was still on the island, yet the old lady thought she sensed movement in the gloaming, though she saw nothing.

For two months the pair monitored the goings on of Auld Grumpy Drawers but came up with nothing untoward. Lachie kept bringing, the children kept playing, the schoolmaster kept muttering; but letters from the menfolk began dwindling. The women knew only that most were in France.

One morning while the washing drifted on a gentle breeze on the single rope they all shared, Aunty Isa heard shouting and banging coming from the door of No.6. Lisa MacFarlane, mother of four, a stout woman, forever looking for more food for her brood, screeched at Bessie, 'It could ainly have been you. Yer thi first yin doon thi pier in thi morns, ay girnin at Lachie fir an extra pint o milk or a few mair tatties. Ah know yer sort,' she added, snatching at the nearest object to throw at the girl.

'Awa n boil yer heid,' Bessie replied, dodging a flying hair-brush, 'Ah never touched yer

stinkin fish..'

Bessie ran behind swaying shirts and skirts and started off towards the quarry, while Aunty Isa shuffled across the path towards Lisa, thinking to calm her and find out what all the stooshie was about.

Some women stayed in their cottages to avoid any more trouble that morning and the street was eerily quiet. But Ellen had noticed the young teaching assistant run off. She gave her ten minutes to calm down before starting after her.

Bessie floated in the cool water and stared at the sky. She lay barely moving, rotating her hands like miniature paddles to keep herself afloat in the almost black water. Her skirt and blouse ballooned around her, and she enjoyed the sensation of lightness easing the anger out of her. She closed her eyes as the sun grew higher and let her mood soften, as nature soothed the frown on her brow, and bright patches flickered behind her eyelids. She opened her eyes slowly, as though in a dream. Then she saw it. A figure standing far above, at the mouth of the cave.

She sprang up, splashing wildly, gulping in mouthfuls of water and spluttering dollops out again. She shook her head and began to swim to the shore, shouting between strokes,

'Hey you.'

She reached shallow water and found her feet, bending to wring out her clothes. When she looked up again, the figure had gone.

'Bessie, Bessie, are ye awright?'

She turned and saw Ellen running towards her.

'Did ye see that, Ellen? Did ye see someone up yonder by thi cave?'

'Bessie - yer shiverin ...'

'Did ye, Ellen? Listen tae me.'

She was bawling at her friend now, as Ellen tried to grip her shoulders and steady her nerves.

'Yer soaked, lass. Come away an never mind yon crabbit wee bag doon thi street. Lisa's ay greetin aboot somethin since hir man has stopped writin.'

Ellen was edging Bessie away from the direction of the cave now, coaxing her back to the clachan, but Bessie kept turning round. Her eyes darted across the landscape, from the abandoned rails that led to the pier, to the old engine house. Nothing moved bar the oyster catchers and lesser black backed gulls who soared towards the cave mouth, swooping and gliding as they pleased.

'If ainly you could talk,' Bessie whispered to the birds, while Ellen marched her homeward and spoke about getting her changed into dry clothes, as though no woman had ever plunged into the quarry fully clothed before.

As soon as the two came into sight of the clachan, Bessie saw Aunty Isa hobbling towards her, arms waving furiously.

'Ah'll take hir tae mine, Ellen,' she ordered. 'Ah'll look after her and see she's fine afore she goes hame.' And before Ellen could refuse, the young girl was snatched from her arms and bundled into Aunty Isa's But'n'Ben.

Bessie squinted low in front of the walnut dressing table mirror to get a decent view of herself in the old-fashioned tartan frock that Aunty Isa had lent her while her own garments dangled over a wooden clothes horse to the side of the house.

'Here ye are hen,' said the old lady, handing Bessie a cup of warm cocoa and a bannock and jam. 'Noo, tell me a aboot yon cave sightin an Ah'll lit ye know what I found oot while ye were awa fir yer swim.'

Bessie relayed what she'd seen but added that she thought Ellen was ignoring her.

'She kept turnin ma heid awa as though she wis tryin tae stop me lookin up at thi cave. When Ah said Ah'd seen someone, she kept shooshin me and tellin me Ah'd had an awfy fright.'

'Ah'll bet she did,' said Aunty Isa, 'an fir guid reason. Ah think they've got somebidy hidin up there an they dinnae want you, me or onyone else tae find oot about it.'

Bessie choked a little on her bannock.

'Hidin? Who? How?'

Isa peered at her young friend with mischief in her grey-green eyes.

'Ah've no figured that oot yet bit Lisa says she thinks Lachie knows mair than he's lettin on. She widnae lit go o yon vanishin fishes story. Ah convinced hir it couldnae hae been you cos ye were at thi schoolhoose this morn. Ah seen ye maself collecting coals fir thi fire fir breakfast and it wis thi schoolmaister himself who went doon tae thi pier tae get thi messages.'

'Thanks Aunty,' said Bessie.

'Yir welcome, hen,' she replied. 'Ah seen yis baith wi ma ain eyes an Ah telt hir so,' she said, blowing on her cocoa and sipping gently.

'So, if it wisnae me that stole Lisa's fish an ainly Auld Grumpy Drawers that wis doon at thi jetty thi morn ... wait - naw - dae ye mean ...?'

Bessie looked across at her wise old companion who smacked her lips as she downed the last of her cocoa.

'Precisely lass. Auld Grumpy Drawers himself.'

'Bit how?'

'Weel hen, that's fir us to find oot, isn't it?'

Three days later, the two women lurked at the corner of the storehouse until all the oil lamps in the clachan were turned low or had fizzled out altogether. It was still light outside, even at ten at night, but inside the cottages it was dark and dank as a late afternoon in winter. They chose this dreich evening deliberately, reasoning that most would stay indoors during the summer drizzle and that any funny business would be better done when the clachan and quarry were most likely to be deserted. There was no wind, but the mizzle sank into their clothes like invisible ice claws in that way that only west coast rain can. Bessie pulled her Paisley shawl closer into her chest, but Aunty Isa's beady eyes were fixed on the building at the opposite end of the street. Then she saw it.

A figure – Auld Grumpy Drawers himself - leaving the schoolhouse. Instead of walking towards them though, he darted to the back of the building and headed up the brae behind. Isa tugged the fringe of Bessie's shawl,

'Look lass,' she whispered. 'Auld Grumpy Drawers is heidin up thi hill ... '

Bessie pushed down on her frail friend's shoulders to get a closer look. She just managed to catch sight of a shadow before it disappeared over the hill.

'Quick,' she shouted, 'We need tae git efter him.'

'Wait fir me,' Aunty Isa said, tying her bonnet closer under her chin as she moved, vaguely thinking it might protect her if she were about to be clobbered over the crown. But Bessie was charging ahead and grasping at grass clumps and bell heather to steady herself as she leapt up the hillside.

'Bessie.' Aunty hissed, trying to whisper, though her agitation was getting the better of her. But as she struggled, she felt a tingle creep across her body again, as though something - or someone - was watching her. She turned round quickly but saw nothing. She turned to face forwards again but Bessie had moved out of range.

The girl reached the summit and caught sight of the school-master again. She could see he carried a bundle under his overcoat, flaps fluttering as he fled, revealing - what? A gun? Bessie's heart beat faster and she stopped still. She heard groans and pants behind her and guessed at Aunty's wrath, before she heard the old woman rasp, 'Ah wis right scared then. Could ye no have waited oan me?'

'Shhhhhhhh,' said Bessie. 'He's got a gun.'

'Whit? Yer kiddin lass. Whit's thi schoolmaister doin wi a gun?'

'Ah'm tellin ye Aunty. He had a gun. Ah saw it. It's no just a bag o fishes he's carryin.'

They stood at the peak looking for their prey but there was no sign of life. All was silent bar the sea, waves lapping at the dark shoreline, slates glinting black as coal in the moonlight, as the last moments of daytime disappeared. They had lost sight of him.

'C'mon lass, let's go hame,' Aunty said. 'It's too dark tae be goin intae yon cave thi night.'

Beyond the hillock, the cave mouth yawned, and a thin sliver of light beamed from within. The schoolmaster reached into his pocket, pulled out a torch, and signalled in reply.

Next morning Bessie was late for work. She rang the bell first thing, but the children had already gathered, and Auld Grumpy Drawers emerged from the school door, muttering as usual, but his tummy was grumbling louder than his voice. He glowered at Bessie and told her to get the fire lit and put the kettle on. He looked in an even worse mood than usual.

Aunty Isa was up early, as was her habit, sweeping the floor and fetching bottles from the store. She needed fresh water and was heading down to the pier when Lisa joined her, carrying bottles for water and a large basket for butter, flour, oats and sugar.

'How're ye feelin thi day hen?' asked Isa.

'A guid Aunty, thanks tae yer kind words thi ither day. Ah feel so daft noo…screechin at Bessie. Bit Ah'd still like to know whit happened tae ma fish yon day.'

'Ach never mind…Lachie might have some mair thi day.'

'Hope so,' replied Lisa. 'Ah wis thinkin tattie scones fir thi night's tea bit fish cakes wid go doon a treat,' she said, and the two women made their way down to the shore, chatting happily like days gone by as they approached the jetty.

The red of the boat's hull reflected in the sea and contrasted with the blue-green hues of the water in a shimmering glow of blood-like strips. It felt like a perfect day was unfolding, until the women drew closer and caught sight of Lachie's ashen face. Then they noticed the bundle of newspapers and the word *Somme* splattered all over the headlines. Lachie held a sealed envelope in his hands and was shaking it in Lisa's direction.

'Came for you this mornin, hen,' he said softly.

Lisa knew she was a widow before she even touched the flimsy paper. She fell to the ground, basket and bottles rolling into the Atlantic. Aunty Isa drew her close and wept with her as Lachie retrieved her things and poured them each a glass of fresh water. Isa held the tumbler to Lisa's mouth, but she could not swallow.

The boat lay moored for longer than usual that day, as Isa supported Lisa and Lachie carried their supplies back to the clachan. Everyone came out of their homes one by one, as though a form of telepathy had delivered the tragic news. Another one of their own. Gone.

The clachan women came together to support the family, looking after the children, caring for Lisa, saving their tears and fears for the privacy of their own dwellings. Even the school-master helped, volunteering to take the children for extra hours - homework classes he called it - simply to give the women time to mourn. For mourn they did, collectively, till time passed and survival mode kicked in, replacing the grief, at least temporarily.

Days went by and Aunty Isa, Lachie, Bessie and Auld Grumpy Drawers stepped up to keep the store and school running while the women organised themselves. Lisa and Ellen travelled to Glasgow to retrieve John MacFarlane's remains and attend to the funeral arrangements while island life ticked over as it had always done.

Aunty Isa was slightly baffled in the days leading up to the burial. The ceremony was being held in the church on the mainland. There were fewer people on the island, yet Lachie was bringing more supplies than before. The changes dawned on her gradually. More cheese. Milk. Even - Isa was sure - fish. But when the day's collections were over and the few remaining inhabitants had gone home, there were still goods left over. And the boat stayed put.

Aunty Isa left it until the eve of the service before investigating. The children were away too by then. She wouldn't attend, she said, but would have everything ready for them when they came back – fresh sandwiches, baked scones, a few drams. She would need Lachie's help, she added, and he agreed.

When Lachie arrived on the island early that morning, Aunty Isa was waiting for him. She knew he was up to no good and suspected he would arrive much earlier than their agreed time of 10 o'clock, so she'd headed down to the shore before dawn. She watched him from behind the sole remaining rusty crane that stood on the jetty. He tied up the boat, went into the cabin, and emerged with a bundle in his arms. Looking over his shoulder, glancing all around, he put his fingers in his mouth and let out a low whistle. From out of nowhere, it seemed to Isa, the schoolmaster appeared. 'He must have taken the back road to the pier,' she thought. 'Over the hill behind the school.'

Neither of the men saw her, as Auld Grumpy Drawers stepped into the boat and hauled out another sack of something. He hopped off the vessel with youthful agility and the two men fell into step with each other, heading for the cave mouth. Neither one looked back.

Isa followed slightly later. There was little cover on the island, but it was not quite light, and she could see their destination clearly. She moved stealthily all the same, desperately trying to think of an excuse for her presence should they come out of the cave unexpectedly. She passed the quarry, with its still waters undisturbed by the few sleepy seabirds on the slate shore but she needn't have bothered with stealth. The men remained inside while a solitary winged creature called from above, drowning out any rustles that her movements might have made. When Isa reached the cave, she heard voices. Not just of the two men she knew but another, younger male, she was certain.

She gasped aloud, then heard footsteps coming towards her. Lachie appeared from the cave like a spirit from within.

'Isa.' he exclaimed. 'Naw. Ye cannie be here, wummin.'

Before she knew it, the schoolmaster was right behind him, pointing a pistol at Isa's face.

'Put yon doon, ye stupit git.' she shouted at him. 'Yer nivver goin to use it on an auld wummin like me.'

'An auld wummin wi a big nose and an even bigger mooth nae doot,' he replied. 'Hauns up.'

'Whit?' said Lachie. 'Dinnae be so daft man. Yon's Aunty Isa yer talkin to. Shoot hir an ye'll have to shoot thi whole island.'

Isa covered her mouth, then her hands dropped, 'Lachlan McLuckie, yer speakin sense there awright. Everybidy knows we're thi only ones left here thi day. Whit would ye say if Ah wis ti be found murdered in yon cave?'

'Naebidy would find ye ...' Auld Grumpy Drawers began.

'Ach haud yer wheesht Angus,' Lachie interrupted, 'Ye know fine yer never goin to kill hir. Or anybody else.'

Angus lowered the weapon. His face softened, his cheeks flushed.

'Thi man has a hairt,' Isa thought to herself. Then she heard another voice,

'Da, are ye okay oot there?'

Angus glared and tutted at Isa before turning his back and heading to the cave's interior. A kittiwake called out above as Isa and Lachie faced each other.

'Whit on Earth, Lachie? Whit on Earth?'

But as she spoke, she saw tears form in her old friend's eyes. 'Whit could Ah dae, Aunty?' Lachie replied. 'He asked me tae hide his laddie. He's nearly nineteen. Birthday in two weeks. His brither wis yin o thi first to sign up in Glesga at the start o thi war. Killed in Ypres at a stroke.'

Lachie wiped his eyes before continuing, 'Wee Donnie wanted to sign up tae. Angus telt him naw bit he wis still determined. Started screamin and shoutin at me in protest thi day Ah brought him here.' Lachie shifted loose slate at his feet before continuing, 'Then he found oot that his big brither got killed and noo he's right scared cos he'll be called up oan his birthday or marked a coward if he objects. He's no strong, and he's a that Angus has left, after thi lads' mither passed awa jist afore thi war.'

Isa tasted salty tears trickling down her face; Lachie's sons were still out there and Angus had no one except Donnie. Her throat went dry when she remembered the embroidered hankie the schoolmaster had held to his brow the day that Ellen was injured. She felt guilt at her suspicious mind now that she was imagining the man's awful loneliness. She turned back to her friend then, 'Bit ye nearly killed one o oor lassies Lachie.'

'Naw, naw. Ah couldnae have hurt Ellen. Bit when she saw me yon day – after thinkin she'd seen a deid body floatin in the quarry, she heard me comin an got an awfy fright. Ah think she fainted then bumped hir heid aff thi ground.'

Lachie removed his bunnet and wiped the sweat from his forehead before going on, 'Ah looked after her afore takin her back tae thi clachan. Stopped thi worst o thi bleedin. Ah felt terrible so Ah did and Ah telt Angus this couldnae go on. 'One day wi might really hurt somebidy,' Ah said. So, we telt Ellen and she kept oor secret, thinkin o her man, Ah suppose. Mibbe even hir wee Tommy an aw, if the war drags on fir years.'

As Lachie spoke, Angus came back to the entrance, his arm over the shoulders of a tall lad, thin, frail, and frightened looking. Isa's stomach lurched. 'Aw son,' she said softly, 'Ye need a good meal inside ye. An a proper rest. Us wummin will keep ye safe. Ellen will help me convince the rest. Yer tae young to be in that muckle war.'

Donnie eyed the odd old stranger as though he wasn't sure if he wanted to leave the cave. Sensing his reservations, Isa added, 'An' ye'll have a pal in Bessie tae – ye'll like hir, Ah'm certain o that. Yer ane age son. Weel, nearly,' she said, giving him a little wink.

Donnie's face lit up, 'Ah might have seen hir aready, he said shyly, 'doon in thi loch.'

The four of them made their way back to the clachan, full of questions for each other.

'Who's yon auld wummin anyway, Da?'

'She's yer Aunty Isa son. Ellen's aunty tae. And Bessie's. She'll help ye settle awright.'

'Ah surely will, said Isa, 'Dae ye like fish?'

'Naw,' said the lad. 'Hate thi stuff. Thi bones choke me.'

Lachie laughed but Aunty Isa was perplexed, 'Who stole Lisa's fish then?'

'Ah,' said Angus. 'That would be me tae ... a wee treat fir Poppy,' he said, crimson-faced again. 'Ah didnae mean to tho. Jist seen them an' thought o ma wee kitty. Ah gave Lisa's weans extra pencils and a playpiece yon day tae make up for it. She disnae know that tho.'

'Poppy?' said Donnie. 'She's here tae?

'Aye,' said Angus, 'and she's nearly as hard tae hide as you. Lachie telt me nae pets are allowed on thi island – laird's orders. Too many other mouths tae feed he says. There's never been any animals oan this place. No even a coo. That's thi reason Ah didnae tell you.' He coughed a little, before adding, 'Ellen's weans help me look after hir - bit dinnae tell thir Mammy,' he laughed, holding a finger to his lips.

'So that's how Tommy's hauns wir so rid fir a whiley.' Isa said.

'Aye,' said Angus. 'He wis allergic to hir at first. Ah've sorted that by keepin hir ootside noo – weel, in thi auld henhoose roon thi back o the school. Sometimes she strays a bit, tho nivver far.'

Isa had a wee giggle to herself as she remembered that feeling of being watched. 'Ye've a lot o secrets lads,' she ventured, 'bit we'll a help ye keep them hidden here.'

'Aye,' replied Angus, 'Bit whit aboot yon floatin body in thi quarry that Ellen saw minths ago, eh Lachie?'

'Oh that,' said Lachie, 'Ach that wis jist an auld army kit bag and a pair o cracked boots Ah decided tae dump. Thir wis a huntin rifle innit tae. Dinnae want ye gettin ony whacky ideas, Auld Grumpy Drawers,' he said, snorting as they entered Isa's cottage and began to discuss how they would break the news about Donnie and explain Ellen's mysterious floating body to the rest of the islanders.

'Ah think yer best no tae tell yon story,' said Aunty Isa, pulling out a frying pan to make some eggs for Donnie. 'Nae-body knows anythin aboot a body in thi loch – best to keep it yon way,' she said, before telling the lad to get a saucer from the cupboard and 'take some milk doon thi street for thi wee kitty.'

Author Bio:

Loretta Mulholland is studying for a PhD in English at the University of Dundee. She has presented her research at the National Library of Scotland as part of the centenary celebrations and has been published in anthologies by *Scottish Pen, The Saltire Society* and *Speculative Books*. She was Fiction Editor for Dundee University Review of the Arts (DURA) online magazine from 2019-2024, has had short stories and flash fiction published in *Northwords Now* and *Thi Wurd* and has written reviews for D C Thomson and www.intocreative.co.uk .

Chapter Thirteen

BREAK A LEG

Lisa Harkrader

On the set of *Heiress Ahoy*, stunt double June Holloway's job is simple: take the risks so the stars look good. If all goes well, she may even end up with the speaking part she's dreamed of. But when a string of accidents threaten the idyllic Santa Catalina film set and long-submerged secrets bob to the surface, June must unmask the villain before the next mishap turns deadly – and her career runs aground.

———

Hot Off the Lot
by Chick Landry

———

*SANTA CATALINA ISLAND, August 1, 1936 – Land ho, darlings.
Yours truly has dropped anchor in Catalina, where Hollywood's hoisting
its sails on* Heiress Ahoy, *sequel to the seafaring caper* Anchors Ahoy.
*You remember that one – the picture that could've been a Titanic-sized
disaster but instead turned an extra named Beau Marlowe into America's favourite hero and tossed a financial lifeline to director Max Kingsley. With Marlowe's last couple pictures barely keeping the box office
afloat, the studio's praying this one doesn't sink. Will Avalon Bay save
him, or will he run aground? Keep your lifebelts handy.*

———

'Scene four, take thirteen.'

As the slate clapped, a gull screeched, and a sudden breeze
gusted across the yacht's deck, fluttering my veil. I rubbed my
palms and peered at Max Kingsley, perched in his director's chair
on the Navy subchaser moored a few yards away.

He pinched the bridge of his nose – a habit he'd picked up on
take seven – before lifting the brass megaphone. 'And . . . action.'

I sprinted, silk skirts bunched in one hand, bouquet in the
other, bridal veil streaming like a pennant. My satin pump hit
the chalked X. I leapt, caught the thick mooring rope, and
vaulted over the rail. The bright tang of sea air filled my nose,
the wedding gown ballooning around me as I swung over the gap
between yacht and subchaser.

Fifteen feet below, the brilliant turquoise of Avalon Bay
sparkled in the sun, warm and inviting, just like the postcards.

But from this height, if I slipped, that water would be as
inviting as concrete.

At the peak of my swing, I cut a look at the subchaser and a glint snagged my eye. My chalk-marked X on the deck was shiny. Wet. A spill? Ocean spray?

Didn't matter. I couldn't plant a landing on a slick spot. Not if I liked my bones in one piece.

I released the rope as rehearsed, twisting in midair to clear the wet patch. My shoes hit dry deck with a solid thud, knees bending instinctively to absorb the shock. I tucked and rolled – diagonally over one shoulder to keep from breaking my neck – clipping my elbow against the lifeboat as I somersaulted past.

I rolled to a stop behind it, hitting my mark dead on.

Ella James, our very young leading lady, crouched there, wearing an identical white gown, holding an identical bouquet. She shot me an uncertain look. I gave her a nod.

And prayed she got it right this time. Deliver five words in the right order. Without dropping the flowers, without getting wrapped in the veil, without letting out a giggle so high-pitched it made the sound man curse.

She nodded back, but as she stood, Beau Marlowe burst into the frame. He stopped short, his eyes darting toward the lifeboat, then the dangling rope, then back again.

I tensed. What was he *doing*? He was supposed to simply stroll up, all swagger and charm, and smile. The way he'd rehearsed. The way he'd done it twelve times before.

The way Max Kingsley wanted.

He froze, then caught Ella's eye. Swagger and charm snapped into place. He flashed his most dazzling matinee-idol smile, dimpled chin angled toward the camera.

Ella, on cue, held out the bouquet. 'Permission to come aboard, sailor?'

I held my breath. A hush fell over the set. Max Kingsley narrowed his eyes.

'Cut. Print it,' he said at last.

The crew erupted. Grips dragged sandbags. Lou Rossi cranked film. Script supervisor Sylvia Carmichael jotted notes in sharp staccato across her clipboard. Ella sagged with relief.

Max Kingsley climbed down, arms wide. 'Ella. Fabulous.'

Oh, sure. I rubbed my elbow. *Ella* was fabulous.

'The star gets the glory,' a voice murmured. 'The stunt double gets the bruise.'

I looked up. A guy with tousled, sun-bleached hair towered over me, hand outstretched. I took it, and he hauled me to my feet.

'Thanks.' I shook out my rumpled skirt. 'I'm—'

'June Holloway.' He shot me a crooked smile. 'The girl who makes falling look easy. I've heard about you.' He tucked his hands into his trouser pockets in an awkwardly charming way.

'And you're Archie,' I said.

I'd heard about him, too. Archie Clark. Once a rising star. Now Beau Marlowe's assistant and sometime stand-in.

'Guilty.' He smiled again, but his eyes flicked toward Beau, now being fussed over by wardrobe and makeup.

'Need to get back to him?' I asked.

'Nah.' Archie shook his head, amused. 'He's where he likes to be: centre of attention. He's fine. Although for a minute there I had my doubts.' He shook his head, the sea breeze ruffling his hair. 'The way he came barrelling in on that last shot, I thought for sure I'd be running interference with Max.'

'Tell me about it,' I said. 'Ella finally nails it, and suddenly Beau goes rogue.'

'His instincts were good. If a girl in a wedding gown drops from the sky, most guys *would* burst in, more startled than suave.' Archie shrugged. 'Max must've decided he liked it. Otherwise, you'd still be swinging on that rope.'

I laughed, but my gaze drifted to the rope – and my landing mark.

'Funny you should mention that.'

I gathered the veil and strode across the deck, the ship gently rocking beneath my feet. I stopped at the chalked X, where the gritty, deck-grey planking still glistened.

Archie hovered at my shoulder. 'What is it?'

I handed him my bouquet, then crouched and dipped a finger into the puddle. Not seawater. This was slicker. Heavier. I rubbed my fingertips.

'Oil,' I said, straightening.

Archie frowned. 'We should tell Max.'

'No.'

My voice was sharper than I'd intended. Archie stepped back.

'Sorry,' I said. 'It's just, Mr. Kingsley promised me a speaking part if this picture goes smooth.' I glanced at our director, his head bent close to Sylvia's as she tapped a lacquered red nail against her clipboard. 'I can't let anything go wrong. Not like—'

I stopped, horrified at what I'd almost said.

A flash of pain flickered across Archie's face.

'I didn't. . . I mean—' I swallowed.

'Not like last time?' He gave me a sad smile. 'It's okay. I've made my peace with it. And you deserve your name in the credits.'

I smiled. 'Thanks. But you're right. I do need to take care of this.'

I glanced across the set. Lou Rossi was polishing his camera with a rag, like an overprotective father wiping a baby's nose. I headed his way, Archie close behind.

'Hey, Lou,' I said. 'I cheated the landing on that last take. Did it frame okay?'

Lou glanced up, squinting against the sun. His gaze flicked to the bouquet in Archie's hand, and he raised an eyebrow.

Archie raised an eyebrow back and hugged the flowers to his chest like a wounded bride, completely deadpan. I laughed. He really did have the timing of a comedic leading man. Shame he didn't get to use it anymore.

Lou lifted his cap and mopped the back of his arm across his brow. 'Looked clean through the finder. I wondered about the sudden change.' He settled the cap back on his head. 'I figured you had a reason.'

'I wanted to ask you about that. There's oil on the deck. Could the equipment be leaking?'

'Oil?' Lou frowned. 'What kind of oil?'

I led the way back to the offending puddle.

Lou bent, dabbed at it, then sniffed.

'Camera oil.' His eyes narrowed. 'But that much wouldn't drip from any of our gear. That's been spilled.'

He balled the rag and scrubbed hard at the deck until the slick wasn't more than a dark stain on the gray paint.

I studied it, then glanced around. Not a camera within yards of this spot. 'How would camera oil get spilled here?'

'Good question.' Lou straightened. 'Watch yourself, kid.'

Lou squinted through the camera. 'Try it again. From the hatch to the rope.'

Archie crossed the deck, matching Beau's trademark saunter. Lou called for a light adjustment.

'Once more,' he said.

Archie crossed again.

'Got it. Good,' said Lou.

Archie joined me at the bow, elbows propped on the rail. As water lapped against the hull behind us, we watched the principals take their places. Beau found his mark. Sylvia checked the position of a life preserver against her script notes. Ella lingered at the prop table, trailing her fingers over the jumble of ropes and signal flags.

She'd traded her silk gown for a navy uniform: blue shirt, bell-bottom dungarees, white Dixie cup sailor cap. This was the scene where the charming seaman disguises the runaway-stowaway bride as a sailor. I lounged against the rail in my own uniform, a carbon copy of Ella's. I'd need it for a chase scene later. For now, I was an onlooker.

'Does it feel strange being on this side of the camera?' said Archie.

I thought about this. 'Not strange exactly. More like. . . adrift. I'd rather part of the action.'

'Wouldn't we all?' A voice rolled over my shoulder.

I turned. A man strolled up, linen jacket unbuttoned, Panama hat cocked back on his head. I studied him. He looked familiar.

'What about you?' He tipped his head toward Archie. 'Is it strange being back –' He held a hand wide. '– here?'

'Chick Landry.' Archie let out a chuckle. 'Why am I not surprised?'

Chick Landry. Of course. I gave myself a mental head slap. Hollywood's favourite gossip hound.

I narrowed my eyes.

The guy who'd made a name for himself on the back of Archie's broken bones.

Five years ago, Archie had landed the lead in *Anchors Ahoy*. I didn't work that picture. I was still doing trick dives into the dunk tank at the county fair back home. But I devoured Hollywood rags, and I knew the story. The studio brass had been so sure of their up-and-coming star that Archie was able to wrangle a bit part for his struggling pal Beau.

Then it all went sideways.

I remembered exactly what Chick Landry had written.

Catalina Island nearly swallowed a rising star, but never fear, Hollywood's found a new hero. While filming the nautical romp Anchors Ahoy, *a special effect backfired, and fresh-faced leading man Archie Clark froze in the face of danger. When the smoke cleared, he'd taken a nosedive overboard. Who should plunge in to save him but an unknown extra named Beau Marlowe. With the panache of Valentino and the fearlessness of Errol Flynn, Beau pulled Archie from the drink. Now Tinseltown is aflutter. Word is, Beau Marlowe's star is rising faster than a speedboat on Avalon Bay, and the unexpected buzz may just keep this heavily insured film's ledger sheets afloat.*

'You have some nerve.' I jerked my chin at Chick Landry. My Dixie cup slid cockeyed. I shoved it back into place. 'Archie came out of that film with a shattered leg and a blank memory. You came out with a national column. Archie lost his breakout role to Beau, and you. . .you—'

'Easy, sailor.' Archie touched my elbow. 'Chick's not the bad guy. He did me a real favour.'

'*Favour?*' I gawked at him.

He nodded. 'Rumours began swirling I screwed up the stunt. That that's why I froze.'

I stared at him. 'That's ridiculous. It was a faulty flash pot.'

'But if the rumours had stuck, I'd never have gotten another job. Not in Hollywood. Not even as Beau's assistant. Chick made sure the story was about bad equipment and studio shortcuts, not me.'

'It was some of my best work.' Chick held up his hands as if framing the words on a marquee. '*Hollywood's new hero might be Beau Marlowe, but let's not forget the botched rigging that put him in the spotlight – and Archie Clark flat on his back. Remember, darlings, solid gear costs less than broken bones in the long run.*' He dropped his hands. 'What can I say? I'm a sweetheart.'

Archie laughed, then his expression dimmed. 'I felt bad for Jimmy, though.'

'Jimmy?' I said.

Archie nodded. 'Prop master. James Ellery.'

'The studio fired him after the accident.' Chick lowered his voice. 'He claimed he had nothing to do with it, but they had to pin it on somebody to get the insurance payout.'

Archie shook his head. 'Jimmy was always so careful. Really proud of his work. Even brought his little girl around so she could see how it all worked. What was her name? April? Opal?'

Chick cleared his throat. 'Speaking of accidents.' He pulled a notebook from his pocket. 'Rumour has it this picture's had its own close call. Care to comment?'

I almost choked. 'What?'

I cut a look toward the set, where Max Kingsley stood beneath the boom mic, arms crossed, narrowed gaze drilling us.

Crud. The last thing I needed was the director thinking I was leaking secrets to a gossip hound. I closed my eyes, and opened them at the sound of heels clicking across the deck.

Sylvia Carmichael stopped before us, clipboard hugged to her chest. I felt like a schoolgirl caught passing notes.

'Sylvia. My favourite watchdog.' Chick touched a finger to the brim of his hat. 'Always a pleasure.'

Sylvia smiled in spite of herself. 'Pleasure to see you, too, Chick. But not here. You know how Max feels about reporters.'

'I've been apprised.' Chick let out a dramatic sigh. 'But he's missing the boat. Most directors, we have an arrangement. It's mutually beneficial. Symbiotic, even.'

Archie's mouth twitched. 'Like fungus on a tree trunk?'

Chick shot him a withering look. 'Like a bee on flowers. They give me honey. I keep the public's appetite pollinated.'

'Well, buzz somewhere else, little bee,' said Sylvia. 'I know you won't actually leave. Just stay out of Max's sight. It'd make my job a lot easier.'

'Which is what I live for, Miss Carmichael.' Chick bowed his head in mock courtliness.

Sylvia swatted him with her clipboard, then turned and clicked away.

'Quiet on the set.'

Conversation halted. The crew scattered to their posts. The actors found their marks, Ella behind a wooden barrel that wobbled when she took her place, Beau sliding in at the last second, flushed and winded.

Sylvia checked her notes, instructed wardrobe to tilt Beau's cap to a jauntier angle, then glanced at her clipboard again.

'Ella,' she said.

Ella didn't answer. Didn't even turn her head.

'Ella.' Sharper this time.

Ella blinked. 'Oh. Sorry.'

Sylvia sighed. 'When Beau gives you the rope, hold it in your left hand. Got it?'

Ella nodded.

Chick raised an eyebrow. 'Poor girl,' he whispered. 'Even puppies respond to their own names.'

He caught Sylvia watching him and sidled off behind the one of the life rafts, out of sight.

'Take one.' The clapboard snapped.

Ella strode across the deck, trying for a sailor's swagger.

But her pacing was off. She hit her mark two beats early and stood, hands twitching, until Beau caught up.

'Hey, swabbie,' she said. 'Wait for me. I'm not as—'

'Cut.' Max pinched the bridge of his nose. 'Ella. Sweetheart. You can't tell Beau to wait if you get there first. From the top.'

On the second take, Ella managed the timing, but when she saluted, her elbow clipped Beau's chin. He rubbed his jaw as the crew groaned.

Makeup touched up Beau's chin. Max rubbed his eyes. Ella found her mark again.

I shook my head.

'Why her?' I whispered to Archie. 'Of all the starlets in Hollywood, why cast one who's barely had a bit part in a role this big? It almost seems cruel.'

Archie tucked his hands in his pockets. 'Lots of scuttlebutt on that one.' He kept his voice low. 'Beau thinks Max wants to sleep with her. But that's where Beau's mind always goes. If you believe Chick's column, Max owes her family a favour.'

I frowned. 'Why?'

He shrugged. 'Who knows? Me, I think she's just got that *look*, you know? She seems familiar. I keep thinking I've met her somewhere, and maybe that's the point. She's got one of those faces that makes audiences think they know her. Maybe that's what Max is going for, that instant bond.'

We watched as Ella jammed a shim under the barrel, then gave it a nudge. I had to give her credit. The wobble was gone.

'Quiet on the set. Again.' The assistant director clapped the slate.

Ella started across the deck, her swagger not bad this time. And her timing was bang on.

'Hey, swabbie,' she said, in character. 'Wait for. . . *ah*.'

She pitched forward, arms flailing, Dixie cup sailing across the set.

Beau stared for a moment, eyes wide, before lunging forward, arms out to save his leading lady.

But Ella had already saved herself, catching a mooring rope before she could face-plant on the deck. A grip darted in, but Beau elbowed him aside, wrapping a protective arm around her.

Ella pushed it off. 'What is *that*?' She stared at a cable snaking across the deck.

Beau gave it a sideways glance. 'That's what tripped you? Poor darling. Good thing I was here to—'

'Cut,' Max thundered. 'Clear this deck. I don't want anyone breaking their neck.' He looked at Ella. 'You okay?'

She nodded.

'Good.' Max turned to the crew. 'That's a wrap. We'll pick it up tomorrow.'

I crossed my arms.

'Tell me I'm not crazy,' I said. 'That cable wasn't there before.'

Archie shook his head. 'You're not crazy.'

As he spoke, the overhead rig gave a soft groan. I looked up sharply. Archie's gaze followed. We locked eyes, then traced the line of the cable as it wound through light stands and tripods.

I opened my mouth, but before I could say anything, the cable snapped taut, yanking a stand half a foot across the deck. The boom mic wobbled. One of the big overhead arc lamps, mounted high on a scaffold above the set, listed dangerously, joints creaking.

Beau stared up at it. 'That's not supposed to—' He froze, speechless.

I lunged forward, but Archie was quicker. He sprinted up the scaffold ladder and caught the lamp's pole in both hands before it could pitch forward onto the set – where Max, Ella, and Beau stood.

Crew shouted. Grips rushed to steady the equipment. The gaffer eased the lamp from Archie's grip.

Archie bent forward, hands on his knees, and blew out a breath.

❦

'You didn't freeze,' I said.

Archie drew back to meet my eye. 'I . . . what?' He lifted our hands and turned me beneath his arm, catching the rhythm of the music.

The room glittered around us, cast and crew filling the dance floor now that dinner was done. Waiters whisked away plates while the orchestra swung into their number. We were on solid land now, in the circular ballroom at the top of Catalina Casino, the round pavilion that jutted into Avalon Bay.

'Twelve stories of style and sophistication,' Max had called it, 'but not a roulette wheel in sight.'

He wasn't wrong. My eyes swept the vast room. A sleek wooden dance floor gleamed underfoot. A dome soared above, lit by Tiffany-style chandeliers. Tall French doors ringed the space, framing night sky and lights from the boats rocking gently on the water below.

The Casino wasn't for gambling. It was for showing off. And tonight, Max was showing off in style.

Archie turned me through the whirl of satin skirts. Lou and Sylvia swung past, Lou surprisingly light on his feet, Sylvia laughing, her shoulders unknotted for once. Lou caught my eye and dipped his head I greeting. Sylvia waggled her fingers at us over his shoulder.

I waved back, waiting till they were out of earshot, then tilted my head toward Archie.

'When you caught that arc lamp,' I said. 'You saw disaster coming, and you charged *toward* it. You didn't freeze.'

Someone had, but it wasn't Archie. But I didn't say that part.

'In fact.' I poked him lightly on the arm. 'You were kind of heroic.'

He snorted. 'Yeah, that's me. With my bum leg and hotshot assistant's job. The big hero.'

'You *were* a hero,' I said. 'And it's got me thinking.'

He cocked an eyebrow. 'Should I be worried?'

'You should be happy. Because if you didn't freeze today, who's to say you froze then?'

His step faltered, rhythm breaking for a beat before he recovered.

'Then?' he said.

Across the floor, Beau swept Ella into a grand, showy dip, his grin dazzling while she scrambled valiantly to keep her footing. At the table behind them, Max sat by himself, no longer the grand host now that no one was watching. He swirled his glass, looking worn down. Not, I noted, like a man planning to hand a stunt double her big break.

But this wasn't about me. Not right now.

I looked at Archie. 'During the first movie,' I said softly. 'The accident.'

'Look, June, I know you're trying to help, but—'

'Hear me out.' I gently squeezed his shoulder through his tuxedo jacket. 'It was instinct today, right? The way you saw danger and raced to stop it? Well, you don't plan instinct. You can't turn it off and on. It just. . . is. And your instinct was to charge forward, to save Ella and Max.' I paused. 'And Beau. I doubt that's changed since *Anchors Ahoy*.'

The song wound down in a shimmer of cymbals. Couples wandered back to their tables. Archie and I slipped through the French doors onto the promenade that circled the ballroom.

As we strolled around the gentle curve of the pavilion, a breeze stirred the warm night air. Music and laughter drifted out from the windows as we passed, mingled with the hush of surf below. In the distance a buoy bell clanged.

'So,' said Archie. 'Two accidents in one day.'

'Yeah.' I shook my hair in the breeze. 'So much for my determination to make everything go smooth.'

Archie nodded. 'And I've had enough disasters to last a lifetime, believe me.'

We strolled for a moment in silence.

'Sooo,' I said slowly. 'Is someone very careless? Or did they plan it?'

Archie looked up sharply. 'You think somebody did it on purpose?'

I shrugged. 'I think it's possible. Don't you?'

We stopped at the balustrade, leaning against the smooth stone to gaze out across the ocean.

'Yeah,' said Archie. 'I've been thinking the same thing. But here's where I stumble: why? What does anyone have to gain?'

I thought about this. 'And if they're targeting somebody, who? I got the brunt of the first one, Ella the second. And Beau and Max were both standing under that light.'

Archie frowned out at the water. 'Maybe it's not about a person. Maybe it's sabotage. Someone trying to wreck the whole picture. But again, who gains?'

'Chick?' I suggested. 'Maybe he needs something to write about. He *was* lurking around all day.'

Archie laughed. 'Chick's never had any shortage of things to write about. Although. . .' He chewed his lip. 'Maybe he's chasing the same thrill he got last time.'

'Trying to recreate it?' I said.

'Nah.' He shook his head. 'Chick likes drama, but if the shoot stopped, so would his copy. So who else? Somebody on the crew with a grudge?'

I turned this over. 'Lou could easily spill camera oil. But I honestly can't imagine him doing anything deliberate.'

'Or Sylvia,' said Archie. 'She lives to protect Max and the production.'

'Who does that leave?' I said. 'Beau? Max? Ella? They were nearly flattened.'

'And none of them would risk it. Beau needs this picture after two duds. Ella's trying to prove herself. Max is fighting to keep the production on track, especially after—'

I caught his glance.

'After last time?' I kept my voice soft. 'What actually happened back then?'

Archie's silence stretched, his gaze fixed somewhere past the horizon. He pushed off the balustrade and started walking. I fell into step beside him.

'I don't remember much,' he said. 'Max had planned this big special effect. Flash pot to mimic the bang and smoke of the ship's gun. He was sure it would make the picture. But the whole thing went pear-shaped. Too much blast. Smoke everywhere. I do have a vague memory of that. Or maybe it's just the fog in my brain.'

He twisted out a laugh. I gently bumped his shoulder.

'The rest is what they told me when I woke up. A piece of scenery started to fall, and I just. . . froze. Beau tried to pull me clear, and we both got slammed through the railing. Hit the water. Beau hauled me to a life preserver until the crew could fish us out. Next thing I knew, I was in a hospital bed with my leg busted.'

He rubbed absently at his leg.

After a moment he said, 'But since we've been back here, little things keep nudging at me. Bits and pieces.'

'Like what?'

He blew out a breath. 'Just before filming started. I remember seeing somebody crouched down. Near the flash pot maybe? And before I heard the bang, I remember thinking, *It's too much*.'

'Too much? Too much what?'

'I'm. . . not sure. I just—' He shook his head. 'Doesn't matter. Not until I can piece it together.'

Something flickered. A quick movement on the curve of the promenade, past one of the French doors that marched evenly around the bend. I stopped.

'What is it?' Archie asked.

I moved along the curve, keeping my steps light so my heels wouldn't click against the tiles.

But when I rounded it, the stretch of promenade lay empty. If someone had been there, they'd had already slipped back inside.

Only a scent lingered. Cologne. Spicy, musky, and sharp.

The next morning, Ella and I sat side by side below deck. The ship's mess was now a dressing room, and makeup girls were applying identical makeup to the two of us.

Sylvia swept into the room. 'New call sheet. Max reshuffled the scenes. He wants to get the shipboard shots wrapped.'

My girl was swiping mascara onto my lashes, so when Sylvia tucked a paper in my hand, I felt rather than saw it.

As she swept back out, I kept my gaze straight ahead, careful not to move and get a mascara wand stabbed into my eyeball.

Beside me, Ella breathed out a soft, 'No.'

I flicked my gaze sideways. Even under a layer of pancake, her face had gone pale.

'Ella?' I said.

She didn't answer.

'Ella,' I said again.

She looked up, eyes wide.

'Are you okay?' I said.

'I don't think I can—' She looked at the paper in her hand. And swallowed. 'But I have to.'

I stared at her. She looked so young, so haunted.

And suddenly I knew who she was.

On deck, I found Archie leaned against a barrel, staring at a sheet of paper.

He looked up as I approached.

'We have a problem,' we both said at the same time.

'The new scene?' He brandished the paper, a call sheet like mine.

'No.' I pulled mine from the pocket of my dungarees, 'I haven't had a chance to read it yet. I meant Ella.' I lowered my voice. 'She's the prop master's daughter.'

He blinked in confusion.

'April. Opal. Whatever you called her. Her father's the one who got fired.'

Archie blinked again. 'James Ellery . . . Ella James. *That's* why she looks familiar.'

I nodded. 'She switched her dad's name for her screen name. It's why she didn't answer to Ella. It's also how she knew to shim the wobble out of that barrel.'

Archie glanced down at the barrel, then jerked back from it, like it might explode.

He looked up. 'That's what Chick meant. Max owed her family a favour.'

'Maybe it's why she's here,' I whispered. 'Revenge.'

Archie motioned toward the sheet in my hand. 'You should read that.'

I scanned the page.

Scene 47: Forward Deck
Cast: Beau Marlowe, Ella James
Props: Mooring rope, life preserver, binoculars
Special Effects: Flash pot
Action: Characters cross deck as forward gun fires
Stunts: June Holloway, double for Miss James
Blocking: Archie Clark, stand-in for Mr. Marlowe

I met Archie's eye. 'It's the gun scene from last time.'

He nodded grimly. 'We're about to shoot it again.'

'From the top,' Max called.

Archie jogged back to the mark – Beau's mark when real shooting began.

Sylvia glanced at his position, then jotted it down. Beau hovered close, clearly itching to show Archie how it was done. Chick lurked behind the life raft, Ella by the prop table. I edged close to keep an eye on her. Lou bent to his camera.

Max paced.

Directors normally left pre-checks to assistants, but Max wanted every detail just so.

He stopped. Snapped his fingers. His gaze flicked to me. 'June. Take Ella's mark.'

'At the gun mount?' I frowned. 'But she doesn't enter till later.'

'Who's directing this?'

I shut my mouth and found Ella's mark, a step from the forward gun. And from the flash pot at its base, primed for filming.

At Max's signal, Archie sauntered toward the gun.

Beau followed like a shadow. 'Wait.' He stopped Archie from stepping over a hatch cover. 'You're not supposed to cross there. It's not secured.'

'Stop.' Max waved Beau back. 'Out of frame till we start shooting.'

As they reset, my mind whirled. *You're not supposed to.* Yesterday, when the arc lamp started to fall, Beau had blurted, *That's not supposed to. . .*

I looked up. Beau had stepped back, but still hovered. He wanted this picture to work. No, after two flops, he *needed* it to work.

Suddenly it clicked. Not Chick chasing earlier glory. Beau. He'd staged small accidents to play the hero again, to stir up buzz. But the second one had gone too far. He'd nearly crushed himself, Ella, and Max.

And now he was trying to keep it from happening again.

Relief loosened the knot in my chest. I tried to catch Archie's eye, to signal that everything was okay, we were all safe. But blocking had already begun.

As Archie crossed, Ella edged closer, frowning at the flash pot at the gun's base.

Archie's eyes locked onto it. His face drained. 'It's too much.'

My eyes snapped to the pot. Too much. Too much powder. And the charge was about to go.

I lunged, shoving Ella behind the prop table. The flash pot exploded, fire and smoke tearing across the forward rail. Beau froze, eyes wide. Archie hurled him sideways. They slammed to the deck as the blast seared the air.

I staggered toward them. Max caught me by the shoulders.

'You okay?' He peered into my face.

I coughed, nodded, and caught a whiff through the acrid smoke. Spicy. Musky. Sharp.

I jerked back. 'It was you.' My voice rasped.

Chick stumbled out from behind the raft, hacking. Sylvia caught his elbow and held him upright.

She stared at Max. '*What* was you?' she choked out.

'June's had a terrible shock.' Max reached again.

I stepped away. 'Five years ago, the picture was in the red. You set that blast for the insurance money.'

Ella's hands flew to her mouth. 'It wasn't my father. I knew there had to be proof.'

'Today you tried it again,' I said. 'Not for money. For silence. Archie was too close to remembering.'

Max's face hardened. 'That's a lie. You can't prove any of it.'

'Oh, I don't know,' said Lou. 'Might be on the reel. After June spotted oil, I wanted to make sure the rig was running smooth.'

Max paled. 'You've been filming?'

Lou nodded. 'Since I got here this morning. If you tampered with the flash pot, it's in here.' He patted his camera.

Archie limped up behind me, steadying Beau.

Beau let out a shaky laugh. 'Looks like Archie saved my bacon. Again.'

Beneath his sooty face, Archie shot me a crooked smile. 'I think the stunt double saved us all.'

Hot Off the Lot
by Chick Landry

SANTA CATALINA ISLAND, August 4, 1936. The winds have shifted, darlings. Director Max Kingsley has stepped off the bridge to spend quality time with the Los Angeles County Sheriff's Department. Into the breach steps Sylvia Carmichael, clipboard queen turned captain of the ship. She's decided Heiress Ahoy *plays better as a buddy picture. Who's her pick for leading man No. 2? None other than Archie Clark, who turned a near disaster into a rescue worthy of Douglas Fairbanks. And it seems this wasn't the first time. In the twistiest of Hollywood plot twists, it turns out Archie was the true hero of* Anchors Ahoy *five years ago, pulling buddy Beau Marlowe to safety, rather than the other way around. Who saw* that *one coming? Meanwhile, stunt wonder June Holloway is trading pratfalls for fanfare with a featured part of her own. Keep your spyglasses polished, kittens. This voyage is just getting interesting.*

––––––––

Author Bio:

When Lisa Harkrader was in third grade, she wanted to be a writer, an artist, and a spy. Today, she's a writer and illustrator who has published forty-five books for children, has received the William Allen White Children's Book Award and four Kansas Notable Book awards, and has been on children's choice award lists in eight states. And she still wants to be a spy.

Chapter Fourteen

THE DISAPPEARANCE OF MISS ELIZA HAWKINS

Penny Hutson

Eliza Hawkins has vanished without a trace, but only her friend and former student, Rachel Woods, suspects foul play. When she cannot even stir the local Constable in their small Victorian village to investigate, she picks up the trail herself. But when Rachel's mother also disappears, Rachel knows there is something more sinister going on.

If she doesn't find help quickly, she may never see her mother or Miss Hawkins alive again. She reaches out to the handsome, young William, but is he really interested in solving this case, or does he have another agenda? The answer will surprise you.

Eliza Hawkins was missing, but no alarm bells rang in the village square. No men with hunting dogs searched for her in the high hills of the nearby Hampshire Downs or the surrounding moorlands, and no official record was made. Everyone, including the local authorities, which consisted of one constable and his part-time assistant, believed her to be on holiday with family in Scotland or doing whatever it was that unmarried women, who lived alone, did during the school's summer session.

No one dared speculate what that might be. The English were too polite for such things. It's not that the people of Dunbridge did not gossip, but they were not the vicious sort. There were no grudges against the schoolteacher, perhaps because they barely knew her, but most likely because the children liked her. So, surmising about the woman's private affairs would have been rude.

In truth, no one suspected anything was wrong, except for her former student, Rachel Woods. Although she'd been away at the teacher training college in London this past year and hadn't seen Miss Hawkins since Christmas, the two had kept up a vigorous correspondence. Not once had her teacher mentioned the possibility of a visit home. In fact, in all the years Rachel had known her, the woman had never done so before. She also avoided questions about her family and life in Scotland and appeared so uncomfortable speaking of it that Rachel had long stopped inquiring.

Naturally, over the years, rumours had circulated concerning the schoolteacher's past, but none bigger or more widely believed than her being deserted at the altar at the already too-old age of twenty-eight or thirty. That she left her hometown of Dundee, Scotland somewhere between 1870 and 1872 before coming to Dunbridge was probably true, having heard it from Miss Hawkins herself. That she came to this small village in England to escape from and perhaps heal a broken heart was pure conjecture. Many believed she chose Dunbridge for its name, which sounded much like her birthplace. This was also rumour but not a nasty one, so the townspeople had no problem spreading it.

Now, more than 20 years later, the woman had disappeared. And Rachel intended to find her.

As one of the few persons and perhaps the only student to have spent time with the woman outside the classroom, Rachel had visited her home many times during and after grammar school. She loved her teacher and the lively discussions they had about a wide array of topics, including the meaning of true love. Had anyone known that young Rachel sought such advice, they would likely have informed her of the uselessness of asking someone who had not themself any practical or real-life experiences in such matters. If the locals had known Miss Hawkins as Rachel did, they would have carried quite a different opinion of the woman who kept to herself much of the time over the past twenty years.

Rachel woke up early the next morning determined to do something to find Miss Hawkins. Maybe she had returned and was at home making breakfast at this very moment. Had Rachel overreacted, as everyone else seemed to think? She grabbed a leftover scone, kissed her mother on the cheek, and headed toward the door.

'Where are you off to at this hour?' Her mother called after her.

'To Miss Hawkins' place.'

She strolled the wooded path lined with giant dogwoods, Scots pines, and sweet chestnuts. Birds chirped as leaves rustled in the cool breeze. Even in the summer, early mornings in Dunbridge remained cool and dry. She bit into the day-old scone, regretting she'd not waited for a cup of tea to wash it down.

When she arrived at the house, the door creaked partly open as she knocked on it. Her first clue something was amiss. Although no one locked their doors during the day, almost everyone secured them in some way at night or if they planned to be away for a while. Burglars were not so much the concern, as a strong gust of wind or creature wandering about which might knock open a door or window and allow damaging rain-water or animal inside.

'Miss Hawkins?' Rachel pulled the door open a few inches and leaned closer. 'Hello? Anyone home?'

After a moment, she swung the door fully open. The familiar scent of lavender soap, burnt wood, and drying herbs assaulted her the instant she stepped inside. At first glance, nothing appeared out of place in the small kitchen and sitting room. The teacher's dust-covered travel trunk sat in the corner where it had been for years. A plate with bits of breadcrumbs lay on the wooden table that still wobbled just enough to spill a glass of wine if its owner wasn't paying close attention. Miss Hawkins intended to have it fixed, but for one reason or another, never got around to it. A pot filled with water hung above the cold hearth. Rachel half expected the woman to saunter in at any moment.

One thing was certain. This was not the home of someone on holiday. Fear poked the back of Rachel's throat. She swallowed as she crept toward the only other room in the house – the bedroom.

'Miss Hawkins? It's Rachel.' With trembling fingers, she pushed in the half-open door and gasped.

The bed was empty save for a mass of tangled blankets and pillows. An oil lamp lay on its side in the floor surrounded by shattered bits of glass. Sunlight pierced through the uncovered windowpane where the curtain rod had been knocked askew.

Something twisted in Rachel's stomach, and she ran.

An hour later, Rachel stormed out of the courthouse doors. A horse and wagon bolting down the cobblestoned street nearly slammed into her.

The Constable's words still rang in her head. 'I can't run to the home of every person whose bedroom's a mess, my dear girl.'

He patted her on the head as if she were a child. 'Go on home now. I'm sure she'll turn up when she's ready.'

Miss Hawkins was in trouble, and not even the Constable would lift a finger to help. Perhaps a call to Scotland Yard would light a fire under the old geezer. More likely they'd give her a similar patronizing answer.

Rachel would investigate on her own.

She visited Mary Carver first. The woman's ability to obtain information, normally unavailable to others, remained unparalleled in their small village. If anyone knew what happened to Miss Hawkins, it would be Mary. She was prone to exaggeration, but anything Mary could tell her was more than what Rachel currently possessed.

When she arrived at Mary's cottage, the woman clutched her fists to her chest and grinned widely, as if she'd been waiting all day for someone to ask that very question. Mary leapt into the long ago suspected secret relationship with Victor Sallow. Rachel did not believe any of the rumours then or now, but since the man's wife died last year, new rumours had sprouted about clandestine midnight visits between the two. Rachel didn't believe any of them either.

'Those stories are so old, Mary. And no one really believes them,' Rachel lied. 'Don't you have anything better?'

'Just 'cos they been knockin' around a bit, don't mean they ain't true.' Mary huffed. 'She's been seen lollygagging up that way just last week.'

'Who told you that?'

'It's all over bleedin' town, and no one's set an eye on 'em since.'

Well, that was something Rachel didn't know, if it was even true, but she couldn't just walk out to Victor Sallow's place and ask about Miss Hawkins, or could she? Did she imagine the woman would be there sitting in the parlour having tea with the man? More likely he'd be insulted at the suggestion of impropriety.

She would speak with others in town, first. Surprisingly, Mary had been somewhat correct. Many had heard that same story, but no one she spoke to had seen the incident themselves.

Tired, frustrated, and worried about her friend, Rachel trudged home to help her mother prepare the evening meal. At dinner, she discovered her mother had spoken to Miss Hawkins at the fish market last week. She had been polite but seemed distracted and in a hurry. When her mother asked if everything was alright, the schoolteacher insisted she was fine.

No one had seen or heard from her in more than a week. It was time to visit Victor Sallow. Rachel planned to go the next day, but rain poured down all day, making the rocky climb to his hillside farmhouse impossible. She filled her day with chores and reading. On the day after, William stopped by unannounced and uninvited to ask Rachel to accompany him to a dinner and dance at the Rothchild's estate. Mother felt obligated to ask him for tea, and he happily agreed. By the time he left, it was too dark to travel. Rachel wished her father were still alive. He would have taken her to Victor Sallow's place in the buggy that afternoon, and William would have never dared to show up unannounced, much less stay past tea.

It wasn't that she didn't like William. She just wasn't ready to claim him as a permanent beau quite yet; and if she did go with him to such a formal event, no other young man in town would dare ask her to anything else.

So, she avoided giving him an answer. And since William was a gentleman, he did not pressure her further. Truthfully, she was more concerned about Miss Hawkins than her own dating affairs. That could wait, but if Miss Hawkins was in trouble, that could not.

Her hesitation may cause William to ask another girl. She couldn't expect such a well-situated and handsome young man to wait for her forever, but she pushed those thoughts aside. She must focus on finding Miss Hawkins.

The next day Rachel reached the summit leading to Victor Sallow's farmhouse as the sun was still rising in the sky. Beads of perspiration clung to the back of her neck and around her waist. As she rounded the curve in the road, her heart sank.

The doors of Mr. Sallow's house and barn were closed, and the windows were shuttered. Was he on holiday? Rachel sighed but continued. Perhaps Mrs. Dougherty had some news of Miss Hawkins. Housekeepers often knew things their employers did not.

When she reached the front door, she knocked. 'Hello.' Rachel shouted. 'Mr. Sallow. It's Rachel Woods.' She paused and knocked again. 'Mr. Sallow? Mrs. Dougherty? Anyone home?' Had they all gone on holiday?

Taking a deep breath, she swung around and nearly collided into a tall man standing close behind her. 'Oh.' Rachel stepped back. 'Mr. Sallow. I didn't hear you coming.'

The man didn't move. A sour grin formed on his face. Strands of silvery grey marked his dark hair at the temples and forehead, giving him the mature but confident appearance of man who was used to being in charge. 'Miss Rachel. What brings you out this way?'

'Actually, I was looking for Miss Hawkins.' A slight tremor betrayed her attempt at being casual.

'And you thought she would be here?' His lips twisted into a grimace.

'No,' she said louder than intended. 'Of course not.' Heat swam up her neck, and she lowered her voice. 'I, um, well . . . maybe. I don't know.' Rachel forgot everything she planned to say.

'Well, as you can see, she's not here.' Clearly annoyed, he swung his arm out indicating the area around them.

'I just thought you might know where she'd gone.'

'Miss Hawkins is not in the habit of disclosing her personal affairs to me, so I'm afraid I can't help you.' He whipped around and marched toward the barn.

'Oh,' Rachel said to his back. 'I forgot to ask.'

The man stopped, turning only his head to the side. She could see his profile and long aquiline nose, noticing for the first time the lack of any facial hair. Hadn't he sideburns before?

'What about?'

'I didn't see Mrs. Dougherty. Is she on holiday?'

Without turning any further, he said, 'What need do you have with my housekeeper?'

'I thought she might know something of Miss Hawkins' whereabouts.'

'I can assure you she's had no contact with her either.' The reply spilled out much too quickly. 'Good day, Miss Woods.' And with that he strode off, making it clear the conversation was over.

Rachel arrived home to an empty house. No dinner boiled in the pot. No bread baked in the oven. By the time the sun lowered itself to the tree line, she headed out to the nearest neighbor's and then into the marketplace, but no one had seen her mother today. Desperate, she went to William's. He mounted his horse and begged Rachel to stay with his mother and father while he gathered a search party of men.

As the sun dipped below the horizon, he returned alone. The barking of blood hounds faded as the night sky darkened. Her mother had vanished. What clues had she missed? Was there a connection to Miss Hawkins' disappearance? William took Rachel home. Maybe her mother was there with a perfectly reasonable explanation, but she wasn't. When Rachel resisted going back to his house, William lit a fire in the cold hearth. He understood why she needed to stay there.

By morning it was clear something terrible had happened. Rachel sought William's advice, and he walked with her to the courthouse. At William's insistence, the Constable wrote out an official report of her mother's disappearance, but he didn't appear to take the matter very seriously.

'Are you sure she isn't somewhere sleeping it off?' The Constable yawned and scratched his head.

How dare he speak of her mother as if she was the town drunk. She never imbibed more than a glass or two of sherry. Rachel stormed out of the building. Tears streamed down her face.

The search party resumed that afternoon despite a thick layer of fog. Some brought torches, others their hunting dogs and rifles. William directed everyone to fan out. One group searched house by house in the town, questioning its occupants, the others searched the nearby woods and hills.

Dunbridge had a railway station, so the possibility arose that she may have taken a train to London or one of the many stops along the way, but Rachel knew her mother would never leave town without telling her.

By dusk neither her mother nor Miss Hawkins had been found. Everyone headed home for the night, except for Rachel. Too exhausted to resist William's mother, Rachel stayed at their house. As one of the most affluent families in Dunbridge, the Asher residence had no shortage of spare bedrooms.

Several nights passed with no new evidence or clues. Slumped in a chair by the fireplace in the Asher's parlor, Rachel feared neither woman would be found alive. She jumped when someone knocked rapidly on the door.

Young Tommy Lock, a boy from the village who often ran errands for the Ashers, swung open one of the double doors and sprinted into the room. He spoke in an urgent tone. 'Miss Rachel, come quick. Master William says they've found something.'

She tossed on her cloak and ran with Tommy all the way to the courthouse.

When they arrived, William, his father, the Constable and a two other men Rachel didn't recognize stood around the single jail cell. Lloyd Collins, the blacksmith's apprentice, sat on a bench inside it. A sweat-stained greasy shirt clung to his thin frame. He ran his fingers through his reddish hair and grimaced. 'I'm so sorry, Miss Rachel.' The man dropped his face onto his hands and sobbed like a baby.

Rachel stepped closer to the cell. Her body trembled. 'Lloyd, what have you done?'

The man lifted his head. His soot-stained face was smudged with tears. 'I had no choice. She was going to tell me Missus everything. I didn't think she'd hurt them.'

Lurching forward and grabbing the iron bars of the cell, Rachel shouted. 'Who? Tell me what's happened.'

William gently pulled her back. 'Jack,' he tilted his head toward one of the men Rachel didn't know, 'overheard Lloyd in the pub last night claiming to know something about your mother's disappearance.'

Rachel sucked in her breath. 'Where is she?'

'We're heading out there now,' said William. 'Thought you'd want to go.'

'Of course I do. She's alright, isn't she?' Her gaze flipped from William to the apprentice.

The man in the cell lowered his head.

'We won't know till we get there.' William put an arm around Rachel and led her out of the courthouse. The Constable and the others followed.

'Whoa, boy.' The man driving the buggy pulled hard on the horses' reins. 'We need to go on foot from here. It's not far, but the path is too narrow for the buggy.' William jumped down and lifted Rachel out of the seat.

As the party neared a small cottage at the end of the trail, Rachel ran and shouted. 'Mother? Where are you?'

William caught up to her and pulled her to a stop. 'Let the Constable handle this.'

'After you,' said the Constable. He gestured for William to go first. 'I'm an old man.' He shrugged and smiled sheepishly.

Rolling his eyes, William released Rachel. 'Stay here.' He stepped onto the rickety wooden porch and banged his fist on the front door several times. 'Come out now. We've the Constable with us, and you're surrounded.' He waved for the other men to go around back. When no one answered, William eased the door open a foot or so.

A muffled voice emanated from within. William threw the door wide open and barreled inside. Rachel rushed onto the porch behind him.

The Constable shouted. 'Wait.'

Rachel ignored him and stepped into the darkened house. Although she couldn't make out the words, she clearly heard voices. 'I think they're in the root cellar.' Rachel said.

She and William headed out the back door, meeting the other men sprinting around the side of the house. 'The cellar.' William pointed. One of the men pulled up on both handles of the slanted nearly horizontal doors, but a padlock held them in place.

A woman's voice cried out. 'Down here.'

'Mother.' Rachel stepped forward.

The Constable threw his hand out in front of her. 'Let the men get her out.'

Rachel crossed her arms in frustration but nodded.

William snatched a shovel leaning against the house and struck the lock several times with the shovel's metal handle. The lock fell to the ground. Jack lifted one of the doors into its vertical position, and William lifted the other. William descended into the dark stairwell, pausing between each step. After a few agonizing moments, Rachel's mother climbed out of the cellar squinting in the sunlight and holding an arm in front of her eyes.

Rachel threw her arms around the woman. 'Mother, I can't believe we found you. Are you alright? What happened? How did you get here?'

'Give her a moment, girl.' The Constable placed a hand on her shoulder. 'There will be plenty of time for explanations.'

Rachel smiled. 'Yes. Let's go home.' She linked arms with her mother.

However, the woman refused to move. 'Where is Miss Hawkins?'

'We haven't found her yet.' Being so relieved to find her mother safe and unharmed, Rachel had forgotten Miss Hawkins was missing, too.

Her mother frowned and pivoted toward the house. 'What do mean? She was here.'

'There, there.' The Constable patted her back. He peered at Rachel and lowered his voice. 'Being confined in such a way can cause hallucinations and confusion.'

'No.' She pushed her daughter's arm away. 'There.' She pointed. 'Look.'

Rachel and the Constable spun around but saw only Jack

peering down the steps. Rachel's shoulders dropped. Then, the top of William's head emerged inch by inch out of the cellar. He struggled with something in his arms. The men rushing to his side blocked Rachel's view. They helped William lay his burden on the grass.

Rachel dashed over and stumbled to her knees. 'Miss Hawkins.' She clasped the woman's hand.

Her former teacher and friend looked up and smiled weakly. 'Hello Rachel.'

Rachel sat between her mother and Miss Hawkins in the Asher's large but comfortable parlor. A young serving girl offered biscuits and pastries from a silver tray. Mrs. Asher declined. Rachel picked a treacle tart and placed it on the delicate blue China plate in her lap. Mr. Asher poured William and the Constable a glass of brandy from a clear glass decanter.

'What I don't understand is why she did it?' Rachel scrutinized William, as if he held all the answers.

Instead, the Constable replied. 'It's quite elementary, my dear.' He chuckled at his reference to the popular new detective stories currently in publication in The Strand Magazine.

Mrs. Asher smiled politely. Rachel raised her eyebrows in surprise, and the others appeared confused.

Unfazed, the Constable continued. 'Unfortunately, it was after the death of Mrs. Dougherty's father that her mother discovered how much he owed the moneylenders.' He sniffed. 'To spare her mother the debtor's prison, she thought to pinch a few pieces of Mrs. Sallow's jewellery and sell them.'

'And since his wife has passed,' said William. 'Mr. Sallow wouldn't likely notice them missing.'

'Correct.' The Constable spoke as if he had solved the crime instead of William and Jack.

'So, if I hadn't asked where she'd gotten that lovely new piece of jewellery, she'd likely have gotten away with it.' Miss Hawkins' teacup clinked softly as she set it onto the saucer.

'Right again.' The Constable raised his index finger in the air.

'And,' said Rachel. 'She wouldn't have needed Lloyd's help in abducting you.'

The Constable snorted. 'It were easy after she put a sleeping potion in their teas.'

'But why abduct my mother?'

'Well . . .' the Constable raised his finger again.

William cut him off. 'Miss Hawkins made the mistake of telling your mother about it the last time they spoke.'

'At the market?' Rachel peered at her mother.

'That's right,' her mother said. 'I didn't realise the significance of it at the time.'

Rachel looked at William. 'But how did Mrs. Dougherty know Miss Hawkins spoke to my mother about it?'

'I told her.' Miss Hawkins shifted uncomfortably. 'I thought maybe she'd let me go, if she believed I wasn't the only one who knew what she'd done. I never thought . . .' She closed her eyes and shook her head.

Rachel reached over and squeezed her friend's hand. 'You couldn't possibly have known she would take mother, too.'

'Don't blame yourself, dear.' Rachel's mother touched the teacher's shoulder. 'You were distressed.'

Still holding Miss Hawkins' hand, Rachel regarded the others in the room. 'But if she planned to sell the jewellery, why wear it?'

'Good question,' said the Constable. 'Vanity? Perhaps it was a sort of advertising the goods for sale?'

Rachel shuddered. 'I hate to think what she ultimately planned to do with both of you, if we hadn't found you.'

'There's many stories of people locked up for years,' the Constable said.

'How awful.' Mrs. Asher frowned. 'How on Earth did she get that man to help her?'

William placed an arm around his mother. 'Simple answer. Blackmail.'

'Indeed.' The Constable cleared his throat. 'Forgive me for saying, madam, but the man had a penchant for the ladies.'

'So, that's what he didn't want Mrs. Dougherty to tell his wife?' said Rachel.

'Exactly,' said the Constable. 'The good news is that she is headed to London for a trial and will likely spend a long time in Newgate Prison.'

The Constable deposited his empty glass on the edge of a polished teakwood table. A frowning manservant swept it up as the Constable ambled toward the door. 'Ladies.' He bowed to the women, then swivelled to face the men. 'Gentlemen. I believe my work is done here.'

'There is one more thing I must know.' William stood, his hands clasped behind him.

'Oh?' His mother straightened, as if preparing for the worst.

He stepped to the center of the room. 'I must know if the beautiful young Rachel Woods will marry me or not.' He sank to one knee in front of Rachel and held out the most beautiful ring she had ever seen.

The women gasped. Rachel's mouth fell open, and she stared at William. The room fell silent, and its occupants froze, as if suddenly encased in stone.

Rachel broke the spell by saying, 'I will.'

Author Bio:

Penny Hutson began her writing career as a newspaper reporter at the tender young age of seventeen. She studied creative writing at Old Dominion University in Virginia, USA, and became an English teacher and later school librarian. Now retired, she lives with her husband in Virginia Beach, VA and spends her days writing, quilting, traveling, and hanging out with her grandson in southern California.

She has published two non-fiction pieces on writing in *Dreams, Doubts, & Determination: Encouragement for the Faith-Based Writer* and one short story in *Coastal Crimes 2: Death Takes a Vacation*. Visit her on the mystery writers' blog "Sand in our Shorts."

It seems to be perceived wisdom that you cannot bring out a cozy mystery without there being recipes. Given this is a historical book, there aren't many recipes we can use these days. Jugged hare etc. has rather gone out of favour. However, in Cadavers and Conspiracies my young detectives sit down to a plate of pickled vegetables and I thought that might be one we could still use today. You are certainly getting value added in this book.

Pickled Vegetables

These can be vegetables you grow yourself, from the supermarket or even from your local community garden. It can save them going off and prevents food waste, something we are always considering in this modern world. I am sure they were thinking the same in my historical world where fridges were unheard of and times were hard.

Vegetables

Peppers

Chillies

Cucumber

Carrots

Green Beans

Courgette

Asparagus

Onions

Pickling Juice

Vinegar - I use white vinegar or white wine vinegar both for colour (it doesn't dull the vibrant colour of the vegetables) and because I am coeliac.

Water - dilutes the vinegar and makes it less strident

Sugar

Salt

Spices

Garlic

You can add herbs and spices to taste. Try playing with different flavours.

Method

Put all the pickling ingredients in a saucepan and bring to the boil

Chop your veggies to a size you prefer and pop in mason jars. You can try mixing vegetables or have one vegetable in one jar.

Once the liquid is boiled pour it carefully into the jars until the vegetables are covered.

Leave on the countertop to cool.

Once cooled pop them in the fridge.

When to use

You can use after about 24 hours. However, like many things the longer you leave them the better they taste.

If you want a true authentic victorian meal, try the vegetables with cold mutton. Yes, you can still buy mutton in the UK, straight from the farms. I can't really speak for other countries but I am sure you may be able to buy it from farms.

ACKNOWLEDGMENTS

My thanks go to the staff of Surgeons Hall Museum in Edinburgh, who answered all my questions with patience and at length.

Thank you to the Sisters in Crime Members who attend the Sunrisers, Ponders, Early Birds and Brunchers write ins each day. You keep me at my computer and writing.

Thank you to my Sisters in Crime siblings in the Once Upon a Crime Chapter. You spur me on, keep me writing and bring a lot of laughter to my writing life. Especial thanks go to Linda Mather, Biba Pearce and Jayne Garner for arranging our writing retreat each year. This retreat gives me so much inspiration.

ALSO BY WENDY H. JONES

A Right Cozy Crime Series

A Right Cozy Christmas Crime

A Right Cozy Culinary Crime

Coming April 2026

A Right Cozy Library Crime

Cozy Crime Series

Cozy Christmas Crimes

Coming November 2025

A Right Cozy Crafty Crime